SNOWBOUND

"You have to get control," Marilyn told herself as she tried to slow her breathing, distracting herself with the matter at hand. She felt a shiver go up her back under her coat and blanket, a damp shiver; fearful perspiration and a pounding heart. She suddenly felt as though she might not be alone. Before she could resist the urge, Marilyn swung her head fast to the left, and then to the right. Around her was white. Everything. When the wind picked up and carried with it a load of snow, there was nothing she could see through the dense, thick curtain of white.

Resolutely, she dragged herself to where she knew the road to be and stumbled up it on legs that refused to run, through snow that was too deep for it anyway. She rushed, and looked behind her, and had the oddest feeling that she was running out of time. . . .

Dell Books by Susie Moloney

A Dry Spell
Bastion Falls

Susie Moloney

BASTION FALLS

A DELL BOOK

Published by Dell Publishing
a division of
Random House, Inc.
1540 Broadway
New York, New York 10036

The trademark Dell® is registered in the U.S. Patent and Trademark Office.

ISBN: 0-440-22344-X

Reprinted by arrangement with Key Porter Books Limited

Printed in the United States of America

Design by Kathryn Parise

Published simultaneously in Canada

February 1999

10 9 8 7 6 5 4 3 2 1

OPM

Everything, always, for Mick.

1

There are no falls in Bastion Falls. There are, however, two large rivers that run fast through the town and the surrounding land. One is duly named the Henderson River after a founding father; the other is more curiously named Toman Creek. The story is that early residents could see Toman Creek for only short distances as it wound its way around groves of pine trees and hilly banks, and they decided it was a creek; it remained so, maps notwithstanding. It was named Toman because at its narrowest point, it was said only a two-man canoe could get through without banking itself. Toman Creek is so like Bastion. The community decides for itself what is what, whether supported by facts or not, the rest of the world be damned.

It is beautiful country, and although all over the world places with their own share of beauty claim the title, the people around Bastion are quite sure that it is God's country. Most of it is solid rock, rolling up to jagged peaks. When it is dark, and the moon shines off

the rock peeking out through the snow, parts of it are
often said to belong to the other side.

While Bastion Falls included the rock on the map,
and the forest that cuts in and out of it, Bastion Falls is
really just the town and its immediate surroundings.
And calling Bastion Falls a town is paying a courtesy to
ghosts. There are a scant 613 persons registered as residents; roughly one-third of these residents are under
eighteen years. There are more men than women, but all
of the women—whether of age or just nearly—have children. Men swell the women, they swell the ranks, as the
local saying goes. Downtown consists of a mall-like
complex, a center; an architect's cold-weather experiment. The largest portion of the mall is given over to a
tavern called the Northern Lights—called that mostly
for the tourists. The bar is big enough for two hundred
and is often filled to capacity. Also in the mall can be
found a national department-store chain, famous in the
North, a cafeteria, various small shops, an outdoor skat-
ing rink and an outdoor curling rink. And an indoor
recreation center, but no one goes there, unless it's bingo
night. The residents are outdoor people, and are more
comfortable bundled up.

Bastion Falls is a winter place. For ten months of the
year, the town lives and thrives wrapped in blankets of
snow, ignorant of Hawaii and Florida and the south of
France. No one from Bastion has ever been to those
places, and so their existence is more a superstition.
When the tourists that come in from points south (there
are no points north) talk of such places with a January
that is so hot that people are in shorts, the residents are
polite (tourist money runs things), but scoff the minute
the outsiders are gone. "Shorts!" someone will snort,

and the others will concur. Shorts indeed. No one in Bastion owned shorts. What the hell for? When summer hits Bastion, the folks go around in shirts and jeans; if they want to cool off, they'll do that with a cold beer and maybe a skinny dip later. Shorts were something that teenage girls wore when they were asking for trouble.

Tourists come in the fragile months of early winter to see the wildlife of the North—polar bears, caribou and the arctic fox—all of which are real, and not those Walt Disney robots that some southerner or other sometimes claimed they were; they were real. The abundance of wildlife in and around Bastion is often commented upon, goodheartedly, as being suspicious. There were other northern towns. But the animals, thank you very much, have chosen Bastion Falls in spite of the hunters and trappers that lived in and around the town that used to seal an animal's fate. Those days were gone anyway. The few hunters and trappers left picked on the deer population, which never seemed to thin, and smaller game. And they no longer did it as a means to support their families. They did it for sport, to vary or supplement their menus, and maybe for a few lucky dollars.

A scant hundred and fifty miles away—a scenic two-and-a-half-hour drive—is one of the country's more popular ski resorts. Residents of Bastion are hardly the type to go in for that sort of thing, even if they could afford the expensive (dear—the colloquialism for the area) equipment that would take them up and down the slopes in appropriate style, which they could not. They are mostly hunters and fishers and freelance tour guides and trail guides, and government workers—most of whom have been in Bastion or a place like it for so long that they simply blend in with the townies. Once the northern weather sinks its claws into you, there is no leaving. Winter is forever, and by the time the good weather comes and it is possible to get out, you're too lethargic to move. That's how they stay. Few come, and fewer leave. Most leave the same way they came, through natural means: birth and death.

There is one church. It is a Protestant church, and since most of the residents through accident or design are either Catholic or something else, it is seldom used. The occasional wedding will be held there, and town meetings sometimes too, to give an air of formality to the proceedings that the rec center can't manage; otherwise it sits empty, even on Sundays. Everyone stays in bed on Sundays. Babies are baptized at home, if at all. There is, however, a spirituality in the town. A deep belief in and fear of God. God makes the gardens grow, brings rain for five days in a row, picks a good fishing spot and gives all your babies measles at once when you have a cold. God also makes you sorry when you slap your wife or shake your child; God is going to punish you for doing that bad thing. Once in a while, when you shoot your neighbor, or rape a town girl, God, you protest in the traveling court, sent you voices. God is omnipresent in Bastion, as much part of the town as Natty Spencer, the town's most obvious drunk. God might be scorned, hated, feared, worshipped, carried like a luck charm or dead, but he is a force, and his principles, if ignored, are still present, just like Natty.

Bastion has its other side, too, the side that people hardly ever mention to the tourists. For instance, the old fort from which the town got its name, built in the time of the settlements. About as far north as could be gone then, it served as a remote outpost, supposedly as a guard station, but was really the place to send those bad seeds that broke the laws of the settlement while serving the country. Murderers, thieves, rapists and drunkards served in Bastion, a punishment fitting most any military crime. Often by the time their sentence was up they had gone mad with cabin fever or killed themselves wandering around in the wilderness trying to escape but succeeding only in getting lost.

No one ever goes up there now, unless they're lost or crazy, or both. Old people say that it's bad there, that it's the place that belongs to another world, that the souls of the lost are there. No one says why, or has to, because the saying of it is enough to frighten the children or the tourists, or the new people from the government up from the city. Chances are, if forced to confess, most of the folks that tell the tale would laugh and say it isn't true, but no one goes there anyway and no one will. Truth be known, before the government made it their land officially, there had been more than one nasty skeleton, real or metaphoric, buried under the old fort. Some of their descendants reside in Bastion Falls, enough of them to ensure a conspiracy of anonymity; whether they discuss their heritage or not is privileged.

There are better places on earth to spend a lifetime. There are also worse. Bastion, in spite of being an isolated, condensed microcosm of human society, with its share of battery, substance abuse, child abuse, manslaughter and alcoholism, is comparatively sane. Some northern neighbors were far worse, and Bastion, compared to some, was a model of family morality. It went about its days in routine, livened up seldom, tales of woe and *maleficio* not counting after the first million told.

―――――

Natty Spencer hardly ever woke up in a bad mood. The part of her brain dedicated to bad moods had long since curled up and died from a lack of stimulus. She was always drunk. Being drunk made her pretty cheerful, and therefore she was. That's not to say she never woke up sick-hungover, but she believed wholly and entirely in the adage that biting back the dog that bit you would cure even the worst sick-hangover, and she practiced what she preached. Even if no one would listen.

She was half sleeping, not wanting to wake up from her dream. In her dream she was a hopeless eighteen-year-old, beautiful, with auburn hair that danced to her waist. She was dancing.

"Oh, Mr. Sandman, bring me a dream, make him the cutest boy . . ." A handsome man swung her by the waist, around and around, until the pleasantness had all but gone out of it and she began to feel sick to her stomach.

She moaned, and turned over, curling into a tight ball, arms on her stomach.

The man wouldn't stop spinning her. Her head felt lighter and lighter, and her stomach lurched.

Natty opened her eyes to a spinning room and a stomach very much in the lurch. She rolled over with practiced haste and dumped the meager contents of her stomach into a pail beside the bed.

"Uuuuuuhh. Yuck," she said, and wiped her mouth on the corner of the bed sheet. She flopped over, to get away from the warm, sticky smell of her vomit, and lay on her back, looking at the ceiling. She wished she was back in her dream. Even if it meant a bitch of a sick-hangover. Even if it meant vomiting again. It had been a long time since she was pretty. The boys had liked her so much. Too much not enough.

She smiled. A beer would taste goddamn good. There was no beer, though, only the homemade brew that she cooked up for herself, fermenting it as quickly as possible so it could be drunk in the same way. That was what was always making her sick, she told herself. She had to let it go longer. She was always telling herself that, and somehow could never make it stick.

She hummed "Mr. Sandman" to herself and rolled her fat self out of bed. As soon as she was upright, her head pounded with the last of the vomit. She closed her eyes, and got up anyway. It would stop. She knew the way to the drugstore, the drugstore being a huge vat underneath her kitchen table. Her eyes still closed, she stumbled to the table, grabbing the corner and shifting it out of the way. A cup hung on a homemade hook on the side of the vat, and she grabbed it. She had to dip the cup low into the vat, the homebrew just about gone. She scooped up the reddish purple liquid, drank it down in one fluid, almost graceful, motion.

Another taste would just about do the trick. Bite back that dog; nasty dog. Reaching down with the empty mug, she tried to get a bit more of the juice. The vat was empty. She tried tilting it over, but it was heavy and she was weak from last night (and the night before). There wasn't enough in there for any more than a sip. She got what she could and drank it down; it didn't go down quite as smoothly as the first. That was because she was a seasoned alcoholic, and an alcoholic isn't thinking so much about the drink she has as about the next one. There was no next one in the vat. Her heart and stomach both sank.

She rumbled over to the dresser beside the bed, pulling last night's sweater tighter around her. It could have been the sick-hangover or it could've been the cold in the room that made her shiver, but she didn't stop to think about it. Cold was cold.

A sealer jar on the dresser held a number of treasures: an old pair of earrings that she always meant to put on but forgot to right after the thought, broken chains, buttons from sweaters and shirts that she saved for reasons only she knew, and a collection of change panhandled occasionally. This was what she was after. She needed a drink. She could go to the bar. The coins would get her at least one drink. She could bum the rest, like always.

Natty dumped the contents of the jar out on the dresser and systematically separated the change from the buttons and jewelry. Not much there, but the thought of counting it made it seem much less. She poured what she could into her pocket.

She saw herself in the mirror above the dresser and chuckled. She saw a much younger Natty, once called Natalie, a beautiful, stupid girl.

She had meant to change her sweater, and forgot. She did remember to put the cup back on the hook in case she needed it right away later, forgetting—as was her way—that the vat was empty. Town was a far walk for her, her legs not being as speedy as they used to be. Natty was forty-five and had the body of an eighty-year-old. No matter, no one—including her—had so much as thought of her body in years.

It was time to go. She started on her walk to town, drinking in the beauty of Bastion just putting on its pretty fall clothes, without even thinking about it. So long had she been a part of it, it a part of her, she took comfort from it. Even if it was a little cold out.

Don Clanstar worked at the government-owned department store and woke up not to dancing but to music. The clock radio beside the bed sang a country and western song. He hated country and western, but it was the only shit they played up here. That and Elvis. He hated Elvis too. His arm reached over and slammed the infernal stuff off.

Beside him, his wife, Emma, sat up. "Leave it on," she mumbled, as she did every morning. He didn't answer, but plundered out of bed in the direction of the shower. Emma sat up, and as she did every morning, turned the radio back on. The Judds were playing. They were her favorite.

She got out of bed to make her husband's breakfast before the kids were up. She didn't bother with her bathrobe because it was warm in the house. They probably had the warmest house in town. It was electric heat, no wood stove for them, and Emma kept it cranked. It drove Don mad, but she liked it warm. She was from the city, down south—as far south as you could go in this country and still be living in it—and she liked it warm.

She slipped on her house-slippers and wandered into the kitchen to start the morning routine of coffee, lunches and breakfast. The clock on the wall said it was six-thirty. The kids would be up in half an hour; they needed lunch and breakfast quickly, because the school bus would be here to take them to school in the mall by seven-forty-five. She made the coffee first, because she wanted some right away. And Don would need it the minute he got out of the shower or else. Or else he would pout, that is, and she did not want that. He was a champion pouter, and it would put a crook in her day. She hated crooks in her day.

The coffee brewing, Emma hit the lunches. The kids were going to scream, but it was going to be peanut butter again. She reminded herself to ask Don to bring home some eggs. They could have egg salad tomorrow. She packed apples into their lunches and added a stick of gum to soften the blow of the third-day-in-a-row peanut butter. That would keep them quiet. Under her breath she hummed pieces of the song she'd just heard. She didn't have to make Don lunch since he would eat at the cafeteria in the mall. He thought it was a good idea to mingle with the townies. And lunchtime at the cafeteria was the best way—or as he put it, the most painless way.

This was the best time of the morning for Emma. The kids were still mercifully asleep, Don was up but occupied, and she was left to wake up in her own time. She pulled out her cracked favorite cup and waited by the pot for it to be done. Then the first cup was hers. A reward for working for others. The first cup of coffee. A small one-up, but one all the same.

She put some bread in the toaster and started the water boiling for oatmeal when she heard Don turn the shower off. He stepped out humming. As if by signal, once the shower was off, there was a chorus of "Mom's" from the back bedrooms. Her time was over.

She stood beside the coffee-maker for an extra second—the first cup of coffee denied her this morning, but jealously holding out for a second or two, until Don, from the bathroom, called, "Hey, Emma. The kids are calling you!" And she had to move.

Emma glanced at the wall clock in the living room on her way down to the kids and saw that in one hour and a half he would be here. He. He. He.

She hoped that missing that first cup that was supposed to be hers wasn't a bad omen, because she had big plans for this day, and they better go right.

"I'm coming! Keep your shirts on!" she called to the kids, smiling when she heard their giggles.

She trudged down to their rooms. The Clanstar morning always began with a racket.

Big plans.

Hickory had jogged the half mile to school and was there more than an hour before anyone else would be. He loved that. He loved clanking around in the big empty gym waiting for the day to begin. He methodically checked the equipment room (snarling as he did so, they had so little equipment) and then climbed into the school's one luxury purchase, his own personal shower. He soaped up and thought about the man, secretly, silently.

He didn't know why they called him Hickory. His real name was Allen. He didn't mind, though, he liked the name. He felt it suited the male image he had of himself. He loved to think of his male image. His hulking strength, his pumped-up muscles, his thick head of black hair. It all came together in just a lovely picture. Hickory fit too.

They called him Hickory because a sniggering twelfth-grader had once dubbed him Hickory Balls, said they were as big as hickory nuts, and the principal had overheard and let it slip during a staff meeting soon after. He burned red-faced, but dumb old Allen had liked it of course, and all the teachers sniggered behind his back about it but went on calling him Hickory anyway, since he didn't know it was their joke.

The soap was thickly lathered on his body. To get really clean Hickory stood out of the spray and soaped his glistening body and thought about a blank-faced, wholly anonymous man, glistening; he tried not to but did.

Before his climax Allen turned the hot tap off and stepped into the freezing cold water of the northern underground. His balls shriveled up with a scream, and he felt better. Aversion therapy, the only thing that worked, and even that was only temporary because it was getting worse.

He had to start his day.

The man was almost forgotten. Hickory combed his thick black hair and admired his body in the small bathroom mirror. This was something he still allowed himself to do. In his world—and mind—so full of don'ts, he took whatever small pleasures he could, without shame. Shame was a part of his being, his own shame, brought on himself. He tried desperately hard to keep it to himself, keep the thoughts and the shame something he only had in the shower, but whatever he tried the shame followed him everywhere and reminded him constantly of who he was and what he would have to do eventually. Eventually he would have to put a stop to himself. That too was a shame.

He took pleasure out of looking in the mirror, and tried to concentrate on that.

This was a morning routine. When his hair was

done, Hickory closed his eyes and tried to empty his mind.

Shame.

He breathed deeply, relaxed his shoulders, warming up from the shower. He counted: one two three four GOOD one two three four ALLEN one two three four TEACHER. Slowly the remnants of his real self came back and he filled his mind with classes, phys. ed. instruction, his good firm shape and the reminder that he hadn't actually *done* anything wrong. When he felt strong again he opened his eyes and looked at himself, taking pleasure once more that there he was, good old Allen, not a bad guy. *A mean sonofabitch when I wanna be, no sonofabitch'n sissies in my gym.*

Not bad.

Combed and primed, Allen decided to wait in the lunchroom for the other teachers. It was seven-thirty. He could start the coffee. Ms. Bergen, the principal, would be coming in any minute. Laurie Temtishion would come in around eight, and she would want to talk about inter-murals for this year, which hadn't had a chance to get started. She was thirty-four and single. Hickory suspected, but never alluded, that she was interested in more than inter-murals when she talked to him. He thanked god she was, because that meant that his shame couldn't be seen. He wished he felt the same. He carefully, and firmly, pushed those thoughts away.

On his way to the lunchroom, Hickory glanced out one of the many windows. He noted that it was snowing. That was no big deal, it was always snowing in Bastion.

He was the only one who noted the snow.

By eight the town was up and at 'em, as they say. The

few left in bed were sick children and the very old. Bastion was not a sleeping town. There were things to be done, jobs to be gone to (a few), traps to be checked, leftover canning to be finished and cheques to be picked up. The streets were not bustling, as they might have been in even a small city, but the citizenship was available, and visible. Women said hello, men touched their forehead if they wore no hat. In the midst of this, a gentle snow was falling.

Snow in Bastion comes about mid-September, disappears and comes back by the last week. By October, there is a decent six inches on the ground, and that's the usual. It got cold early and stayed cold, getting only colder. It didn't mean a goddamn thing. Nothing stopped because of the snow. It was a winter place. Nothing stood between snow and winter.

By ten that morning, there would be three more inches of snow added to the pile. That was quick, but not terribly unusual. *The Farmer's Almanac* said it was time, and it was cyclical. And if the robins hadn't shown up so bloody early, they wouldn't have had such a quick snowfall. But them farmers lived down south, and a quick snowfall in Bastion was just getting things started.

While Hickory was stepping out of the shower and Emma was denied the first cup of coffee, fifteen-year-old Shannon Marie Wilson was trying to wake up from a nightmare.

She didn't even seem to be in the dream. She was lost, no not her, but someone was lost and they were plenty mad about it, mad enough to chase after being found, and all she could feel was *cold*. She moaned in her sleep, the moan escalating into a scream that scared her mother half to death.

"Shandy! Wake up, honey," her mother called from far away. She tried to wake up, and moved toward her mother's voice, a familiar sound in the place where she couldn't see anything. Something black had wrapped itself around her eyes. Just before she opened her eyes in the black, there was white. All around her, trapping her, cold, white. Snow.

She screamed herself awake.

"It was a dream, honey. Just a dream," her mother chanted, holding her, rocking her like a child. "You're just like ice."

2

Don Clanstar had two local girls in this morning, giggling things, on the annual office practicum from the high school. He put them to work right away typing letters from himself to the head office and filing the papers that the store's secretary never really got around to. The girls clung together like puppies separated from the litter, each looking a bit uncomfortable in the skirts they put on this morning in lieu of the jeans they probably wore every day. Their heads were often together in whispered conversation that invariably ended with giggles. Don thought it would be a long two weeks.

"Girls," he said on his way onto the floor, "you don't have to whisper everything here. You can talk to each other. As long as you get your work done. Okay?" Their faces, so attentive when he spoke to them, broke into giggles again as he left the office. It was definitely going to be a long two weeks.

His real secretary, Marilyn, was late. He couldn't recall Marilyn ever being late before. He glanced out the window on his way down to the floor and saw the snow, but didn't think it anything out of the ordinary. He had the same thought as everyone else who noticed the snow this morning: this was Bastion Falls. Of course, Marilyn was coming from way out, and maybe the snow was heavy on the roads. The roads were bad in high summer, winter usually all but wiped them out. He hoped it was nothing.

"Let's get that dusting done before we open today, shall we, ladies?" he said to the two salesgirls chatting by the scarves.

"Yes, Mr. Clanstar," they answered in chorus, reluctantly but quickly grabbing for rags and spray kept under the counters. As he passed them, he could see them out of the corner of his eyes desultorily dusting.

Don checked his watch. It was 9:58. He went to the front of the store, the side that opened out into the mall, and dragged his keys out of his pocket. Monday began.

Marilyn called at ten-thirty, from the highway phone, just catching Don back in his office. Her truck had died. She had already called the garage and they were on their way, but it meant she didn't know what time she'd get in. "At least you've got the girls," she offered.

"Listen, you get in as quick as you can. I can't stand the way they jump when I walk into the office. I think they're terrified of me. Or amused. They giggle constantly."

"I'll get there as soon as they get me out of here. Hey, check out the snow, by the way. Looks like Christmas around here," she said.

When Don hung up, he walked to the window and gave the parking lot a look. It did look like Christmas.

There must have been three inches of snow. The nice light kind.

"Early winter, late spring," he muttered to himself. One of the girls behind him jumped. He wished he'd said boo.

Marilyn was losing her happy thoughts.

She was sitting in the cab—the rapidly freezing cab— of her ex-husband's ode to their marriage: a 1976 Dodge Ram half-ton. The damn thing died on a regular basis, and friends were always telling her she should either get another one or move into town so she could walk wherever she had to go. She wished she had, did, would.

It was cold in the truck, probably colder, she theorized, inside the truck than outside. Her theory being that surrounded by metal that gets colder faster than anything else, chances are that the truck would be colder than anything else. She entertained herself imagining that metal probably even stored up old cold—cold that it had experienced every year since it was formed, and that meant that there was probably 200,000 years of old cold, plus the new cold from today, stored up in the frigging doors, roof and floor. Just grand.

She looked at her watch for the twentieth time and wondered if it was frozen, or the battery dead—like the truck's (if that was the problem. God knew it could be anything). She had looked at it too many times, and time had barely passed. There was a blanket in the survival bag in the back of the truck, but she was too cold and too close to safety to brave going out there for it. Ten more minutes she would wait.

Forty-five minutes had passed since she had called

Don at the store, and that meant that at least forty-eight minutes had passed since she called the garage. So where the hell were they? It wasn't like it was deep winter here, in spite of the early snow.

"Come on, come on, come on," she said under her breath, and waited in the cold. Four more minutes and she'd get the blanket and start to worry—or walk.

It was not a winter parka that she had on, it was more of a ski jacket, the sort of thing everyone in Bastion wore before the worst of the snow set in and they bundled up in snowmobile suits—whether they had a snowmobile or not. It was a good enough jacket for September, which was supposed to be mild, not gut-grabbing; September seldom fell below the freezing mark. She had gloves but no hat or scarf with her. She was uncomfortably cold. A part of that was because she was sedentary; she should get out of the cab and walk; that might warm up the bones. But as yet she was too cold to move. If it got any worse she would get out and walk to town.

It kept snowing.

Ronnie Milgaard was not laughing. If he had been a smarter man, he might have been, but he wasn't, and so he didn't see the irony at all. He was on his way to boost Marilyn's truck with his own truck—because the tow truck was busy digging out a snowplow and he didn't see the irony in that either because the snowplow had fallen into a ditch—and his own truck failed to keep up with the road. Now he was stuck without a moving vehicle, and that was a sin greater than murder as far as Ronnie was concerned. But at least he had the radio and was able to call in.

He was worried a little, too. He had been raised by a kind woman, and although she was years dead, he couldn't help but hear her *tut tut* at the thought of a poor defenseless female out there somewhere stuck in the cold without a moving vehicle (a sin greater than murder). He had a heart full of guilt when he called in and told Chester, the tow guy, to get out to Marilyn first. After all, she was the customer; he was supposed to be the savior. Get her fixed up right and come get me, he told Chester. Chester said the plow was in good and it would take a while since Lawrence (he said it "Lawrinse" like they all did) was now sleeping one off in the truck, as usual, that's why he wound up in the ditch.

"One fucken job to do and the sonofabitch can't stay sober long enough to keep the goddamn plow outa the bloody ditch. Wasn't even plowin' anathin', just movin' the fucken thing from A to B," Chester commented and hung up. Ronnie didn't say anything, but if he had, he would have told Chester to watch his mouth when he picked up Marilyn. She was a lady. You don't use that kind of language around a lady. That was all there was to it. You watched your mouth around a lady. His mother taught him that.

Especially Marilyn. Because even if she was over thirty, or whatever she was, she was pretty. She didn't have a husband anymore either and it didn't bother Ronnie what his mother would have said about that. She would have said "Once burned, twice shy," and that meant look in another direction, but Ronnie knew Marilyn and knew that her direction was good enough for him. Ronnie was nearly thirty himself and he'd been thinking about Marilyn ever since the time she came into the bar and asked the whole place if someone would care to boost that damn truck of hers so she could get home. Ronnie gladly boosted it and noticed her when he did it, too. That was a whole year ago, but he hadn't stopped running into her around town, or finding reasons to go to the store hoping to see her. He found out she ate lunch in the cafeteria, so he went there whenever he didn't have a lunchtime job, which he usually did. She still didn't remember his name. She called him something different almost every time. But she was always kind, and always pretty. Sometimes she was prettier than the last time. One day she'd see him, he thought, and she'd say, "Ronnie, I noticed you . . . ," and that would be that.

While Ronnie waited for Chester, he kept himself warm thinking about Marilyn. It worked, for the most part.

The temperature had dropped from a tolerable 7 Celsius to a godforsaken minus 35 by noon, and five inches of snow had fallen on Bastion. Most people didn't even notice the drop in temperature; they were indoors. The few who did notice the remarkable drop considered that it might be their imagination, or maybe they were coming down with something. No one alerted the authorities, no one got out the deep-winter clothes; everyone knew that there was plenty of time for that. It was only September. Even this far north the weather was kind until the end of October. Halloween could be a bitch, but September was predictable. September still held the predictability of seasonal temps. Bastion or no Bastion, this was just a phase.

3

Already? Was all she could think on her way to school that morning. It was only September, for chrissakes. Welcome to Bastion. Candace, she told herself, you wanted a northern experience, and now you're getting it.

Candace Bergen had taken a lot of kidding about her name over the years, although, since she moved to Bastion, she took a lot less. The people who mentioned it were usually ex-city people who had seen a television in the last three years. Bastion residents didn't get much entertainment news, and certainly not a lot of TV, and so didn't make the connection. That pleased her, because she and the other Candace Bergen couldn't have been more different. The TV Candace had self-assurance and chutzpah; this Candace tried to have a bit of both, but sometimes wondered if she really knew anything at all, and worried that one day someone would tap her on the shoulder and tell her to move along, she was blocking the traffic of people who did. The TV Candace knew *everything;* this Candace knew only her own secrets, or so it seemed to her most of the time. She buried these feelings in work.

Candace Bergen, school principal, started graying when she was seventeen. By twenty-five, the top of her head (her hairdresser always called it her crown, but the last thing she wanted was a gray crown) was almost totally gray. The last five years had seen her hair go from salt-and-pepper to pure white, and though friends tried to convince her it was attractive, she didn't think so and was self-conscious to the point of paranoia. People seldom mentioned her head of white hair. Why would they? They simply assumed that she was old. She wasn't. At last count, the local Candace Bergen was thirty-two and in her prime. And peaking, according to Sheri Hite and Masters and Johnson. Everyone else assumed a well-preserved forty-five, or worse. It messed up the achievement ratio. No one praised a forty-five-year-old school principal. Had they known she was so much younger, they might have seen something special about her. As it was, no one had. She was, simply, on track.

On this day, she was feeling a little *off* track.

She *had* wanted a northern experience, but did it have to snow so early?

She had gone directly to her office and for the half hour before the secretary came went over her book and planned her day. It was still dark out when she had walked through the halls. Early was a big part of the achievement ratio: early to and late from. On her desk was the pile of reports—test scores, attendance records, any notes from parents that she requested from teachers and her secretary every day. The secretary sniffingly stacked them for the first couple of weeks that Candace had begun at Bastion, and after that it had been routine. This new year had brought more sniffs and finally a demand to know exactly why the principal of the school wanted to be bothered with such things; such things, it was suggested, better left to the teachers and secretary to handle.

"In the past, we have always let the principal know when something is worth looking into," the secretary had said. The teachers too had balked at the added workload, some of them remarking that they had enough to do without filing weekly reports on progress, test scores and student body. They came around once they realized that it wasn't the teachers that were of interest to Candace so much as the students.

Bastion Falls Composite School had just about two hundred students, ranging from the brand-spanking-new kindergarten kids to world-weary, attitude-heavy seniors. The majority of the students were somewhere in the middle. By studying student lists over the last ten years, Candace had found that for a while boys had outnumbered girls (and still did in the younger grades) and it seemed that over the last two years, particularly in grades eight to twelve, girls outnumbered boys. Girls stayed in school longer than boys, and scored higher on tests, until the crucial last year. That year seemed to take a general dip in grades overall. During her first year at Bastion, Candace had taken home documents and looked over them in order to better know the type of student body she would be dealing with. It became a habit and eventually fascinated her in ways that she hadn't realized. She even toyed once in a while with writing an academic paper on what she had learned from the documents and would learn from the next few years. It was still just a toy she took out and played with periodically, but it had encouraged her to pay careful attention to statistical realizations in the school, and to look at everything from attendance records to teacher-submitted reports on classes, as well as noted interests from parent-teacher meetings. They didn't know it, but she got to know a lot of the students this way. When a student's grades were falling, or their attendance was off for a while, she took note of it and watched for further signs of disruption in their education. If it went on, she would speak to the teacher and parents involved. Sometimes such knowledge could isolate a problem before it escalated into dropping out or something worse. Dropping out was a problem of unequaled proportions in Bastion.

An awful lot of the students waited impatiently for their sixteenth birthdays, marking the months before with chronic truancy, poor performance, missed homework assignments and bad temper, so that when they quit—sometimes the day after—it would come as no big surprise. Candace routinely called parents in after their children had made the decision to quit school and tried to counsel them as to the best way to get their kids back in school. Generally the parents were distressed. Meetings, however, ended on a positive note, with the parents (usually the father) remarking that they had no more than a grade-eight education themselves and they made out all right. Those were the lost causes. The closest university was over six hundred miles away, which meant a great commitment from families; the nearest secondary vocational school was closer, clocking in at three hundred miles. Candace could have, occasionally did, point out that eventually these kids would move to other places in search of work anyway, and wouldn't it be better to keep them in school and give them a fighting chance when they made their way to the city? The city was full of kids that *stayed* in school; she never pointed out that the city was also full of kids that quit. The parents would do their best, but invariably the ones that left right after their birthdays stayed gone.

The school had other problems.

Drugs were not as big a problem as in the city, because they were much harder to get out here. The growing season was shorter, so it was difficult to grow pot on a grand scale. There was also a suspicion about drugs, because the difficulty in getting them pointed directly to their illegality, in a way that was old-fashioned and good. Alcohol was the drug of choice in Bastion. And cigarette smoking. Their parents drank and smoked, and by example advocated the habits. Kids drank early. Promiscuity was not a problem, but most girls started sleeping with their steadies almost as soon as things got serious. Every year someone got pregnant. These things on their own were not disasters in Bastion. Pregnancy was still seen as a good thing, babies were much-loved and welcome additions to families. The kids got married or lived together and usually things worked out all right. The twentieth century was encroaching, too, and abortions were performed at the closest hospital, a hundred miles away. Abortions were looked upon with shame, though, and so if one was had it was hushed up.

Adolescent drinking and teenage pregnancy were old problems. The new problems had another element to them. They were darker, symptomatic of approaching bad times. A number of the kids were deeply involved in the occult. It was still only a few of the kids, but others were getting involved in a secondary way, through heavy metal music and the accompanying accoutrement of black T-shirts with devils' heads, skull jewelry, shaved heads and bad attitudes. The bad attitude was the worst to deal with, and it had the danger of escalating into something worse, like a fatalistic, apocalyptic approach to life; it took away the kids' future. Some of those kids really believed that the world was going to hell and that they were all going to die anyway, so why not have a good time if they could. (Candace sometimes shocked herself by thinking that maybe *some* kind of censorship was a good thing; the music sold in Bastion was never opera, classical or the hopeful folk music of her youth, but all the heavy metal to be had could be found—and was—and bought up as soon as it arrived.)

Basement bands that used to have names like Slick and Purple Praise now had names like Death's Head and Blood Bath. In Candace's day everyone was quite sure that they were making the world a *better* place, the world was full of hope and things to do. These kids took bad turns seriously and to heart. Last school year a boy had killed himself, leaving a note saying everything and everyone was going to hell and he'd see them there. Everything from vandalism to rape and assault had gotten worse over the last four years at the school, and while it could be said that things were worse all over, Bastion was relatively isolated and less at the mercy of the rest of the world. She saw the connection here between the music and the disillusionment, just as it was seen at the city school she came from. Kids just had more to be angry about here.

Overall, these kids at Bastion were pushing up against some sturdy walls. Unemployment and its accompanying poverty, alcoholism, isolation, lack of opportunity and a major division of labor were the things that these kids faced. The only thing she could do was prepare them for it.

In spite of the rest of the world, family was still a central force in Bastion, but as had happened elsewhere, the unit was eroding. She felt that it was a part of her job to make sure the children didn't end up without direction, lost. If she could give them skills to build a life on, then maybe she could catch them in time to pass those skills on to the children that they would have. Goal: no further victims of the erosion.

Her new project was something that was almost unheard of, even in the most progressive schools in the south. She wanted to bring in a new curriculum course called Life Skills. It was simple enough, a course dedicated to real-life issues like money, birth control, family management, parenting, relationships, self-esteem, planning for the future, dealing with change, the list went on. All stuff that never got taught to most kids but vital in the real world. So far the school board hated it or, worse, thought it was absolutely absurd. What they didn't know was that it only made her want the course in her school more. Her new project.

When the secretary came in at eight-thirty, Candace took a break, stretching backwards in her chair, taking a deep breath. She called through the open door, "I want to see the attendance reports asap, Mara."

Mara hated it when she said asap like it was a word, and Candace almost bit her tongue right after it was out. There were two students she wanted to check on, a new couple that had been coincidentally missing school on the same days. Had to nip that sort of thing in the bud.

The first bell rang and the halls got noisy. Candace waited for the day's attendance reports, because she had a feeling that she would have some calls to make.

David Millejour contemplated the snow outside the living-room window. He was looking at the school, looking to see if anyone came out. It was a precarious move; if a teacher came out and happened to look across the street, he would be seen and put on the truant list again this month, the fourth time. He had to be very careful to stay out of the light. In one hand, he held back the dusty, nicotine-stained curtain, part of the set that had been in the house since he and his mother had moved in two years before; in the other hand he held a cigarette. He hoped it would calm his nerves. He'd always had bad nerves.

He watched the snow fall between his house and the school for a moment or two, always expecting to see at any second Mrs. Bergen marching across the street to drag him back to school. She didn't believe him when he said he was sick. Go figure. With all the school he'd been missing, she should think he was dying of cancer, for chrissakes.

He let the curtain fall back into place and went to turn the stereo back up. He never should have answered the phone in the first place, but he thought it would be Shandy. It had been Mrs. Bergen and he had to fake sick. That hadn't been too bad, he was a pretty cagey liar, but she'd been persistent enough to want a note tomorrow from his mother. And that started a chain reaction that he'd rather not think about. He had to phone his mother at the hospital and tell her he was sick.

"You were fine this morning," she said, not a trace of concern in her voice.

"Come on, Ma. I'm sick now. I feel like I'm gonna throw up."

After a heavy sigh, thick with resignation, thicker with hoping he'd grow out of this stage, she said, "Well, David, I guess you're going to stay home anyway. *If* you're really sick, stay in bed, covered up. There's some juice in the freezer." She added, sounding a bit more like a mother, "If you're really not feeling well I could probably get Dr. Briggs to check in on you . . ."

"I'm not *that* sick. I just wanna throw up. I'll see you later," he said, and hung up.

He just hoped that she wouldn't give him a hassle about the note tomorrow, and that she wouldn't phone the school, which would make Herr Bergenmeister tell her just how much school he'd been missing and would tie it all into Shandy and his mother would never get off his back. It was getting harder and harder to fool her.

David was twelve the first time he got into serious trouble. He and one of his no-count friends, according to the great-god mother, had been caught red-handed in a break-and-enter. They had watched a neighbor leave her house and another neighbor had watched them sneak in. She might not have thought another thing about it, since the house that they chose to burglarize had been the home of the lady who babysat David when his mother worked, but, she told police, they made such a deal out of looking around, and sneaking to the back door, that she figured something must be up.

His mother picked him up at the RCMP detachment in the next town, sobbing the whole while. "He's a sensitive boy," she told everyone who would listen. Rather than have the sympathetic effect desired, it simply made the officers and the secretary roll their eyes. They saw a lot of sensitive boys.

They had been caught by the traveling squad car on a routine drive through town. The same officer who had caught the boys—red-handed, carrying a Sega game machine out the back door in a sack—took Mrs. Millejour into a small closed-in room to discuss her boy. David listened as best he could from his solitary seat across the hall, but hadn't heard much. Mostly he heard his mother crying. He cringed with embarrassment. After twenty minutes or so, he was invited to join them.

He went in and sat down in the only seat available, beside his mother. She clutched at his arm and held it tight, at an awkward angle.

"David," said the officer, "your mother seems to think that this is an isolated incident, that you were convinced to do it by your friend"—here he consulted a single-sheet clipped to an open file folder—"Jason Kilpatrick. Jason said just the opposite, however. What do you have to say about that?" This officer was not the same one that caught him and Jason in the act. The one who caught them and made Jason pee his pants and cry in front of David was Officer Brumheller, the same man that came to their school on Patrol Day. This one was some guy from inside. David had never seen him before. He was sitting on the desk in front of them, towering above them. The man's stomach was eye-level to David and his belly was soft, hanging over his belt all the way around him to his back. It made it hard to take him seriously, twelve or not.

"Well?" he said, a little more forcefully, and David jumped.

"You don't have to scare him!" his mother shrieked, yanking his arm convulsively. "He's already scared." The officer ignored his mother and stared at David, succeeding, finally, in intimidating him.

He mumbled a reply.

"Better speak up, son."

"I said, I guess so. I guess it was my fault," and with that he burst into tears. Tears he hoped would be seen as remorseful but were actually tears of utter frustration and boredom.

And it had worked. The officer sent his shrieking, grabbing mother out of the room and the two of them had a long talk about law and order and how things were at home and getting on the right track and staying out of trouble and the whole roll of patented cop bull-shit toilet paper. Everything was dismissed; no juvie record, nothing more than a slap on the wrist and David's sincere, tearful apology and promise to be good as required. Later he laughed about it to another friend. Jason wasn't his friend anymore; Jason's mother wouldn't let them be friends anymore, and Jason listened to his mother and the fat cop. Big deal, he thought then, and now, looking out the window at the snow, thinking about other kids that had passed their way through his life, never to return. They were punks, he knew, but he was just a little hurt when he thought about it.

"Punks," he said, cranking up the stereo.

In the sad little living room there was a chair and a sofa, both of which were never going to win any contests for durability or cleanliness. David picked the chair and flopped into it, dropping a little bit of ash onto the carpet.

It was already nine-ten and Shandy wasn't over yet.

David was cutting school a lot. He supposed it was only a matter of time before his mother figured it out; he and Shandy were cutting together, mostly. They would both cut and then one of them would go to the other's house, usually to David's. Then again, his mother was pretty blind these days. If she wasn't working at that two-bit fucking job cleaning floors and toilets at the hospital, she was cleaning herself up off the floor in the kitchen. She was drinking. It had snuck up on them both, and they were both still too startled by it to say much. She was watering down the booze now, too, supposedly so David wouldn't notice. What she didn't know was that he was drinking a bit himself. He didn't dare take any more; he'd have to try something else. If he added any more water to the stuff, she'd never get a buzz on and then she'd start getting suspicious. She didn't mind too much if David had a beer or two now and then, but there was no fucken beer in the house; she drank it as soon as she bought it. (What he didn't know was that his mother watered it down after she'd drunk too much and didn't want him to notice and he watered it down when he drank any and didn't want her to freak out and the neighbors thought they were a *lovely* fucking family and wished they would move the hell out.)

David was getting impatient, it was true. But Shandy wasn't to be pushed. She was like a cat: if you spent too much time coaxing it to come to you, it got pissed off and left. She was like that. He wondered over and over if she really had cut, or if she got nervous about how much school they'd missed and went. She had to come. They'd planned it.

He looked over at the clock on the wall: 9:12.

She was taking her sweet time about it and making

him nuts. He was nuts all the time now, ever since the first time they were together.

His feelings for her were very, very complicated, and something that he wasn't able to articulate even to himself; all of his feelings about himself and her and life in general were all mixed up together, and it came out in an unsettling manic kind of dependence. If she didn't call him every night, he freaked and wondered where she was, who she was with. The David he had been before Shandy—he tended now to divide his life into two parts, Before Shandy and Since Shandy—would have been contemptuous of this David, who mooned and sat by the phone. He was in love: horribly, terribly, typically. Like millions before him, he thought he was the only one.

She had been his girlfriend for one month, two days and counting.

It wasn't as if she was new or anything; David had known her, or at least, known *around* her, ever since she came to Bastion. A new kid does not go unnoticed by even the most senior of the school population. She had been in school with him, one grade behind, but in a small-town school that didn't count for anything. She had taken gym with his grade the one year that the administration decided to try co-ed gym, mixing up the grades in the hope that it would cut down on some of the recess-yard intimidation going on between the younger kids and the older ones. (What it actually did was provide the older kids with projectile weapons in the form of basketballs, volleyballs, floor hockey pucks and sticks, and anything else the animals decided to get their hands on; co-ed inter-grade gym was discontinued by December break, with Hickory squealing to anyone who would listen that it hadn't been his idea.) She had been somewhere in the playground whenever he had been there, and when David thought about the fragility of that, of the *almost* of her passing through his life completely—of never having even met her—it terrified him. Of her hovering somewhere, but not with him; of her being around, but not his. He shuddered and hated himself when he did it.

He'd never noticed her. He was in awe of that fact, too. All those years he spent in her presence, around her and not with her. He wondered how it could have been. Girls in general hadn't even caught his notice, it was true, until he had turned thirteen or so, and for that he forgave himself those years. But *after* that. Where had he been, where had she been? What if they hadn't ever met, what if she'd moved away before he met her, what if she'd met someone else before meeting him—where would he be?

That first time, that first day, they were sitting on a cast-off sofa in the basement of her mom's place, in the rec room she had made up as a place to sit privately. She was showing him some book about fortune telling or something. He'd kept his eyes wide and interested and whenever she would point out something of special interest, David would stare right at her breasts, always managing to look away just in time. She was wearing a black Led Zeppelin T-shirt with the arms cut off. When she moved sideways, the armholes gaped open just enough to torment him; he couldn't see all the way down. Once he saw a pink, tilted nipple, so close. It was an agonizing beginning to what would end up being the first girlfriend David ever had. When she said goodbye, he barely heard her whispered "We're soulmates,

David." He'd nodded stupidly, promised to call her and went home that night crotch-hot and happy as shit, to quote his mother.

Second date and third date and fourth and no counting after that. They necked a lot after that first date, and David could almost pinpoint the second, the delicious second, that he first put a sweating, trembling hand on her tiny breasts. Her nipple had been hard enough to feel through her sweater. He'd had a hard-on for four days after that, one that went away for only an hour or so at a time (usually during geography or history) to come back painfully when he least expected it. He spent a lot of time carrying his books in front of him so his cannon wouldn't show. The end of it actually got red and raw from rubbing up against his jeans. Whacking off never helped, at least not for long, and after a while he associated whacking off with Shandy and as soon as it was over he would think of her and like magic he might never have done it at all. He almost lost his mind until one night he tried to explain it to her and she told him she'd been painfully aroused much of the time too. They put an end to the waiting, which seemed stupid anyway because they were so in love.

There had been no turning back after that, and it was not *the* best part but it was pretty fucken good, and it was all tangled up and he never did get rid of his hard-on except during geography.

Shandy hung up the phone, contemplating the fact that she had *way* too much stuff to think about this morning. The day was not getting off to a good start, and now she felt guilty on top of all of it. Starting with that terrible nightmare first thing. Then Ms. Bergen phoning and sounding like she didn't believe Shandy was really sick. Of course, Shandy had planned all along to miss school at least this morning and go over to David's, but then after her dream and all she really felt *sick*. She told her mother it was just her period, and that she had cramps. That wasn't true, but she did feel sick because of her dream and because of those things outside the window.

Shandy wasn't afraid, at first, of the things she saw outside her window. Because she had spent all of her fifteen years seeing things that no one else saw, dead things, secret things, the misty auras that surround the living, the future. It was a part of her natural life. Like a person born blind, she had no idea what it would be like to *not* know someone's tomorrow when she looked at them, or not to see events before they happened, not to see the foggy shapes of leftover feelings that stayed behind when a person died. These of all were the strangest; they were like lost things, with no more purpose. She called them "leftovers" when she spoke to her mother about them. Eventually they faded away to some gathering place. Those left-behind and lost feelings were earthy, and therefore the easiest to recognize—even if they didn't look like what they were—because they were *feelings*; when they brushed past you while they floated, anyone would know what they were. Sometimes they were wonderful things, like love, or compassion; sometimes they were just everyday feelings like concern or enthusiasm. When they brushed past, she could tell they were leftovers because she felt them suddenly, even if her own mood had been completely unrelated. That happened to everyone, only most people never gave the sudden waves of feelings a name or even a thought.

Those things outside the window were something like what she called her leftovers.

She stood now, not unlike her boyfriend, at the window in her bedroom, one hand holding back bright pink curtains. But unlike her boyfriend, she wasn't looking across at the school wondering if they missed her. She was looking at the *things* out there in the snow. She had no idea what they were, she had never seen anything like them, but she had been seeing them—*shades* of them— for days. And then the snow came, and now they were even easier to see. She hadn't mentioned the shadows that weren't shadows to any one at all, not even to her mother, because she hadn't known what they were. And because she was fifteen and just didn't *want* to tell her mother everything anymore. Plus, she still didn't know what they were.

Sometimes this happened. When it did, Shandy just gave the things she saw some time, and eventually she could read them. She thought maybe she had to get used to them or something before they would let her in. It had happened with her uncle Jack. Shandy was just eleven when he died. Two weeks later she had been watching for him, and she saw him. But he wouldn't speak to her, and she couldn't get a feeling off him. She was hurt when he wouldn't respond. She gave him time. When he did let her in, she heard him—in her head, the only place she ever "heard" these things—she got the feeling that she was just a punk kid, just a two-digit midget to him, that he didn't want to talk to her because she had been just a child in his life, not an adult. He faded away from her life, as was usual for the dead to do, and she seldom thought about him anymore. They hadn't been close. That had been why he hadn't let her in.

She had been very curious about the black shapes because she hadn't ever seen *phenomenon*—what her mom had taught her to call the things she saw—like them before. There were literally hundreds of them, and each day this week they had become more distinct. They were shapes, though, not bodies, not people or animals; just shapes, floating here and there. And she hadn't been frightened by them. Not until today, after the storm started to get bad.

That's when they really changed. The floating black shapes had become slowly more distinct, and as they did, they moved a little faster, a little more determinedly. They began to disappear and reappear through the mounds of snow, leaving no marks. What frightened Shandy, all of a sudden like, was that the mounds of snow that they had disappeared into had been cars and houses, places where there were people. They moved in, fluttered out. Mr. Hawkins from next door had stepped outside earlier to look at the storm, and she had watched curiously when one of the shapes had approached him. It hovered around him for a bit, almost as though it was smelling him, or having a taste of him, and then, swiftly, it coiled and sprung into him. Mr. Hawkins had given a startled little jump, and then stood, very still, in the pile of snow that was growing at his feet. One hand came up and rubbed his jaw. He looked quite deep in thought. She watched him while he stared slackly out into the swirling powder. He was jacketless, she noticed, probably intending to stay outside for only a moment, to take in the amazing weather; a lot of people had done it, up and down the street, she'd seen them. She watched him for a good five minutes, each second expecting the black thing to pop back

out on his other side as she had seen them do. This one
didn't come out, though. Shandy was just beginning to
get anxious when she saw Mr. Hawkins take a great
step off his porch, into the ever-deepening snow on his
front lawn. Then he took another step and more and she
realized that this seventy-year-old man was going for a
walk on a freezing day in a storm where you could
barely see twenty feet in front of you. And that thing
was still in him and that was when she got one of her
enormous flashes that she hardly ever got (*dead dead*
like bells ringing), and she knew that flash was for Mr.
Hawkins. She ran to call out to him. That was when she
heard Mrs. Hawkins outside, screaming at the top of her
lungs for Herman to get in there right now. At the sound
of her voice, Mr. Hawkins (Herman!) turned abruptly,
and Shandy saw it. The black thing darted out of him.
But it didn't go away. It followed him into the house.
Shandy saw it happen. She saw it trail behind him while
Mrs. Hawkins held the door open kindly, seemingly for
them both. She knew better than to try to warn them.
She knew from most of her fifteen years that you just
don't call people up on the phone and say, "Oh, by the
way, Mr. Herman Hawkins, this is the teenager from
next door. This black thing—and I don't think it's a very
nice thing—just followed you into your house. I think
you better do something about it, because I've seen this
sort of thing happen before. Just thought I'd warn you.
You're welcome, goodbye." She had tried to tell people
things before and that was why they lived in Bastion
now.

Things had been pretty quiet over at the Hawkins
place since then.

Around nine she had called over there thinking that

she would just hang up when they answered. No one answered. She told herself over and over again that they could have gone out and she might not have seen them leave. She couldn't, after all, watch their house all day.

And where exactly would they go, Miss Shandy Marie Wilson? Where would they go? to the store? shopping maybe? visiting?

But she was no fool. These things had happened to her before. She *knew*.

Mr. Hawkins had a nice soft blue aura. That usually meant a soft person, sometimes just a little weak, or with some sort of character flaw that could put them in danger of being weak, but it also meant a gentle person at heart. Shandy had only seen Mrs. Hawkins a few times, since she hardly ever ventured out, and her aura wasn't as nice as his.

Now she was afraid. And David wanted to go out in the snow and come over to her house ("Or at least meet me halfway baby and then we can come back to my house") and be with her in that way that they were together. All of that was very fine and good but she didn't think it would be a good idea until she figured this whole thing out.

She still had half an hour to decide, according to the clock radio on her dresser, a gift from her mother's best friend from the city, Ellen Forbeway, but Shandy called her Auntie Ellen. She had given it to Shandy because Shandy had told her not to go on her vacation to California. Her missed trip to California had saved the woman's life.

There had been a terrible tragedy in 1990 in California, and everybody knew that had been the earthquake. It had killed a number of people. Shandy hadn't seen the earthquake; it was unfortunate, but her visions tended to be personal, hardly ever could she see the global causes of the vision, just the person's fate. And Shandy had seen the woman under a pile of lumber. Shandy knew later that it wasn't a pile of lumber at all but a house that had toppled. The woman, Auntie Ellen, she saw dead. She told her mother, and her mother tried desperately to explain the situation, the *situation* being Shandy, to her friend, and begged her not to go. She had been all set and ready, when her own intuition kept her from leaving, even though her husband threatened her with bodily harm, divorce and canceled credit cards, she told Shandy's mother in a postcard, but she didn't go. They went to visit her mother in Florida instead. They heard the news of the earthquake on the car radio. And the woman sent Shandy a clock radio, with no letter or note, just the package and a blank card with her name: Ellen. She hadn't spoken to her mother since. That was often the way it happened. They were grateful, and just a little bit repulsed, like by knowing that, you might know other things, like you cheated on your husband or you masturbate or you're a serious bigot or something else dark and nasty. The thing was, they were right. She generally knew that stuff too, but it took a long time to see it. It scared people off.

It hadn't always. When Shandy's mother became convinced that Shandy could see the future, she told her other best friend, the first one, before Ellen Forbeway. She startled Shandy one day in her bedroom, where she was playing with her dolls because she was only eight, by asking her to tell her fortune.

"Huh?" Shandy had said back. She didn't know what that meant: tell my fortune.

The woman held out both her hands and said, "Tell my *fortune*. You know, what's going to happen to me." So Shandy had taken the woman's hands and told her.

"Gloria. Gloria's going to happen to you."

At the time the woman looked at her strangely. A year later the woman was in divorce court and Gloria was, too. That was best friend number one, because in her pain (which Shandy could also feel) she blamed Shandy's mom. Once the pain was past, she told everyone about Lydia's strange child telling her all about Gloria before anyone ever knew.

Then they came in droves.

It was subtle at first. They would drop by to see her mom and chat in the kitchen about mostly nothing. Then they would ask if Lydia didn't mind if Shandy didn't mind if they didn't mind if she could just one little thing has been bothering me I'd sure like to know I've been wondering do you know if how when why where. After a while they didn't even bother with small, gentle Lydia. They became rabid packs, bringing cousins, mothers, sisters, neighbors, best friends. They wanted bingo numbers, lotto numbers, horses' names, boyfriends, lovers, cheating husbands, dying parents. Shandy was only a child and often didn't even understand what they wanted, and sometimes couldn't tell them. She could always tell them something, and she would. A lot of the time she told them honest things that were not what the women wanted to hear. This was not the worst part; the worst part was not the desperation she sensed in them, the *needing* to know. It was the "tell me something good" that she couldn't stand. She felt their feelings when she took their hands. Many of them had terrible, empty lives and wanted to know about this thing and that: the thing that would change everything and make their lives worth living for a while longer. One lady had spent twelve years writing a book that was bad from the start, but she had such a dream, such a terrible dream of publishing it, being famous, well thought of, rich. That was what she wanted to know. Shandy took the woman's hands and saw her life remaining unchanged: no publisher, no book, no nothing else. She was only nine then, but she could feel the woman's hope and knew that this was what it was for. She couldn't lie, so she told the woman, gently, "Why don't you write a different book?" The woman hadn't mentioned the book to Shandy at all. She got angry.

There are fortune tellers who get paid to "tell me something good." Shandy never got paid. She never told a lie. When the anger came, it came. Lydia and Shandy got angry, hurtful letters, crank phone calls, nasty looks and talk. Then they got calls from newspapers, and finally threats. Even a bomb threat. Shandy wouldn't let her mother drive even though she could see her mother going on forever, just about. She wouldn't let her mother drive because she was just a little kid, and a threat by a grownup seemed much more real than any vision. They moved away. To Bastion. They had lived in Bastion for six years, and so far only Lydia still knew about Shandy. They planned to keep it that way.

Moving away from the city hadn't kept any of the visions away, though. And here she was, standing, looking out into the front yard, watching the black shapes poke themselves in and out of places.

They hadn't scared her at first, but she was scared now. Too scared to even think about David, Ms. Bergen, skipping school.

4

The snow was getting bad, but Natty didn't care. During the worst of the storm several people had come in to get out of the snow, and the cadging was easy.

For now, Natty was content to sit at her table, with the sticky circles of beer glasses and grubby ashtray filled with butts, and listen to the people that had sat down at the table next to her. She wasn't drunk yet, but the voices she heard came and went in foggy breaths, and she wasn't picking up as much as she could have been. She was just listening, as if to background music against heavy thinking. Heavy thinking, however, was about ten years past for Natty.

At the table next to her were Hardly Knowles, Sam Treherne, Teddy Bastion (no relation to the famous Fort Bastion, but sometimes he put on the ghost), Lawrence Ross and Chester Hawkins from the garage—who were sort of a matched set, like bookends—and they were dominating the conversation, telling the garage and tow-truck horror stories that were rampant with this kind of snow.

Natty half listened and plotted another beer. The one in her hand had gone warm over the little bit of time that she'd been holding it, but she always had been a bit of a furnace. Once a fella in her bed—the name escaped her, but then they usually did—had told her, "Just a little furnace, ain't ya," and she had considered that to be one of the most romantic things anyone had ever said about her, even if it did mean that beer went flat and warm in her hands. It was something deeply personal, something noticeable about Natty-the-woman that few people would have the opportunity to know; it was an intimate thing, even if Natty wouldn't be able to articulate that it was *that* exactly about the comment that appealed to her. Still, romantic thoughts aside, another beer, a *cold* beer, would be nice.

"Wouldn't it be nice . . . ," she sang under her breath, and tried to focus on the guys at the table next to her. One of them would surely buy her a beer. If she listened. Men were real susceptible to a listening woman; if nothing else, she knew that. Careful not to drain the last drop, Natty sipped another sip of the warm beer, and listened. Chester was telling a story.

"So I tells Ronnie that Law-rinse is stuck, which you were, you old sot—goddamn drunk has one job to do and can't do that half right—but I says to Ronnie, it'll be a bit before we get you going, 'cause I gotta pull old Law-rinse outa that ditch. You know that ditch outside the dump, where he was moving the plow o'er to? No one in hell knows why the goddamn you gotta move the plow there when all these people in town gotta get theyselves home 'cause a storm's coming up—"

"I plow the way I plow for chrissakes I tell you that every goddamn—" Law-rinse, in spite of his recovery, was still pretty drunk, and so Chester continued on as if he wasn't there.

"So Ronnie was on his way, don't you know, to give that Mary-lyn a boost. Off his own truck, he's sweet on her, you know. Has been for a year or more now. His mother would have a kitten if she knew, good thing his old lady's dead. She's divorced, you know. But he's radioed in, the boy is stuck hisself, the truck won't go, and I'm thinking isn't that the goddamndest thing. You ever know Ronnie's truck to not go? He's so fine on wheels, he takes care of that truck like a mother. So I'm ta thinking that the snow must be one sonofabitch out that side a town to put down that boy's truck. I'm telling you—"

"Can't find him, neither," interrupted Lawrence. "We gone down once we got the plow out, to see if Mary-lyn and him's gotten out or what, and sonofabitch if we don't find the two trucks and no peoples," he finished, snorting up leftover tobacco from ten years before. When he turned his head to spit on the floor, he noticed Natty and caught her eye. Once, many years before the bottle got either one of them, they wouldn't have laid eyes on each other. They were friends of a sort now.

"Buy me a drink, Larry?" said Natty.

"Hey, Ed! Bring Natty a draught!" he yelled, and gave her a wink. She smiled.

Chester yelled out to bring a round.

"So where's Ronnie, then?" she asked, not knowing Ronnie from a hole in the ground, but knowing that she owed something for the beer.

Hardly laughed. "Holed up somewheres puttin' it ta Mary-lyn!"

Chester laughed too. "But it's the damndest thing. We drove up and down for a bit, couldn't see much for the goddamn snow, course, but we couldn't see them."

Ed came with the round, and the talk turned to the snow that wasn't a storm yet.

"That's fucking it!" she shouted, and moved, finally. She found it was colder to move and didn't that beat all hell.

Marilyn got out of the cab, which had become intolerably cold. She slammed the door as hard as she could, which wasn't very hard at all because she was so cold, and it gave a sad little groan before shutting. Once outside, she realized that it was much colder, and her breath came and went in smoke and her sudden exposure gave her goosebumps all over.

The blanket was much on her mind. With hands that were shaking with cold—her whole body was trembling but it seemed the worst around her hands—she made several attempts to grab the survival bag in the back of the truck.

She grabbed it, and dropped it, her fingers just about numb. She tore open the bag as best she could and some of the less important contents fell out, the candle and a can opener. She ripped out the blanket, flinging it open as she did. It was a big old smelly woolen army blanket and it was the most beautiful thing. She laughed when she saw it. She wrapped it around her head, like an old woman's babushka. Then she started to walk, pulling the blanket tight around her head and shoulders.

The light inside the truck had become gloomier the longer she sat, but she hadn't realized until she was outside how dark it had become; it was as gray as a clouded evening. It was the snow. It was covering the sky, swirling in great arcs, slow and sharply cold. She tucked the blanket worriedly around her face and started walking, using the nose of the truck as a compass, pointing her in the direction of town. She had waited for Donald? Robert? to come for over an hour. She wondered if maybe he'd had an accident or something, but the thought came and went much like her breath in the air. She guessed that just leaving the truck out here meant that the truck, at least for now, was toast.

Town was at least a thirty-minute walk from the truck, maybe more, because of the drifts that were piling up, drifts she couldn't believe she was seeing in September. With inadequate boots, she would be going slower than normally, and she'd never really had to walk to town from a break-down before; someone had always come and got her. Maybe it would take longer. What was it? A person walks two miles an hour. She tried to figure that one out, but she was too cold to think that way. The wind was light but sharp, not freezing wind but cold just the same. The feeling made her think of the Chinese water torture, and she wondered how long she could stand the little flakes gently hitting her skin before she went crazy and tried to kill them. She thought that should be funny, but she didn't laugh or even smile. It wasn't funny enough. Not with some hard walking in front of her, and not in her little dumb jacket. Never, since coming to Bastion, had she ever really felt the place cruel. She sort of thought that now.

Briefly, before she caught herself, she was scared.

———

Ronnie had started walking a long time ago. At least it seemed that way to him. The road was buried under the snow, and the ditches that ran parallel to the road had disappeared as much as the road. A veteran Bastioner, he knew how it could be in bad snow, and let the light flash of the sun through the clouds be his guide. He literally walked by his watch, and God's watch, the sun. He was heading toward where he had been heading in the truck, and couldn't know that Marilyn was heading toward town at the same time, would maybe get there before he found her. And even if he did, he still would have left the truck to find her. Marilyn was a damsel in distress.

Sometime at the end of summer, and summer ended fairly sharply in Bastion, he would begin wearing his long underwear; truth be known, he didn't actually shuck them until sometime in July, and even then he would feel naked and vulnerable until August-mid, when he would adjust to the nakedness and occasionally even feel a sort of freedom. He was unconsciously glad to be wearing them this day, and wondered what sort of clothes Marilyn would have on. He didn't think too much about the fact that Bastion was getting this kind of snow in September, but even he wondered about the cold. It was damn cold. He was glad he was dressed for working.

Dressed for working meant two pairs of socks, long underwear, a T-shirt (if he was wearing his long-pants-underwear; if he was wearing his longjohns, he skipped the T-shirt), a thick canvas workshirt, overalls, steel-toed boots, and a short army-canvas jacket that might have been called a car coat by one of the city people. On the hottest days, he was insulated as well as on some of the cooler days. That was his September outfit, and it was altered only by the addition of what he called a burglar cap and double garbos: thick leather mitts softened on the inside with home-knitted woolens, one of about thirty that his mother had made. He wished he had those mitts today.

Today, all he had were his work gloves, and although they were leather, they had no lining. They were cold as if he wasn't wearing any. He was glad even for them, though.

About every twenty or thirty feet he would stop and get his bearings, and at the same time, he would squint up his eyes and check to see if he could see the outline of Marilyn's familiar truck on the horizon.

Earlier, he'd tried to sing one of his favorite songs to make the walking seem better. About two verses faded off his mouth when he didn't feel like it anymore. It was too cold. When he realized it was too cold to sing—that was when he thought that it just might be a little early for this kind of snowfall. Then he heard his mother's voice, which he often heard, nudging him into figuring something out.

"Ronnie, look at that snow. In *September!*" And it gave him full stop.

"Damn straight," he muttered halfway, his mouth being too cold to form the consonants. He looked up into the sky, and decided then to put up the hood on his coat. When he did, snow fell down his back. He worried doubly about Marilyn alone in that stupid truck that never ran right, and walked a little faster. And at that point the light in his head burned overtime, and he wondered what the hell kind of winter Bastion was headed for if this was happening at the beginning.

The sun had gone past the top of his head and was working on his front when he thought he saw something up ahead. The wind had picked up some since the beginning of his walk, and though he was slow he wasn't stupid, but he was having some unrealistic thoughts running through his head. Kid thoughts. Dumb kid thoughts like getting caught in deep snow and not getting out, or getting caught in deep snow and not getting out after dark had fallen, or, getting caught while something bad was waiting in the white swirling in front of him. When he started having those thoughts, he would have to catch himself quickly because a funny panicked feeling would begin to rise in his chest and there would be nothing right about it.

The place where he thought he saw something, a shape or a truck, maybe, closed over with snow when he strained his eyes to focus, and when the wind blew again the other way there was nothing. He kept walking.

He noticed that, even with the midday sun pumping in front of him, it was getting mighty thick in the sky; sometime during the day it had clouded over. The snow swirled around him so hectic-like that he found himself stopping and getting his bearings again and again.

While he walked, his mind wandered over things that he hadn't thought of in years. Like this kid he'd gone to school with, grade four or five, who had been his best friend, who had moved away to the city. Ronnie had missed him something awful, and they even wrote a letter to each other before moving on to other best friends. But this kid, by name of Terry, had one bad ear. He'd been in an accident or something when he was really little, like a baby practically, and he couldn't hear outa this ear. He had a hearing aid, too, but was too embar-

rassed to wear it to school. So he and Ronnie had tried
to lose it. But they had a deal that if they lost it, it would
have to be, sort of, legitimate. No cheating. As a result
of wanting to accidentally lose this hearing aid, they had
done some pretty daring things, things like jumping off
of low roofs, hoping that the thing would fall off and get
lost on the way down. They never lost it, but Terry
broke his leg once, and Ronnie was the first one to sign
his cast. He signed it "Boss", because that's what Terry
always called him. He would say "You're the boss,
Boss," and that was partly why they had been best
friends.

His feet crunched methodically on the snow, lulling
him. His mind wandered further into the past. His feet
wandered further from the road, without his noticing.
He stepped in deeper and deeper snow as he left the
road—or what he supposed was the road—and entered
a field of white. All around him was white. There was
no longer a skyline, only a studio dressed in surrealistic
non-color, without angles or edges, without dimension.

*"Whatever you say, Boss. Let's go jump off the tree
by Toman Creek I bet you never done that yet eh. Let's
see if you can break your leg too you can get out of
phys. ed. for two months and it hardly hurts at all after
a while. Are you kidding my mom would kill me she'd
break the other one all cause of my dad you know let's
go look up girls' skirts under the bleachers."*

The deep snow posed no problems. Ronnie lifted
high his right leg, then his left in an awkward imitation
of the goose-stepping Nazis. His hands were stuffed in
his pockets to ward off the cold that was disappearing
from this white place. Way in the back of his mind was
some vague feeling of alarm, like a bell trying to wake

him up to go to school, but it stayed hidden behind Terry's cast and the girls up in the bleachers.

Mom when's Dad coming home I got a bad report I hope I'm not in dutch with him Dad's not coming home at all Ronnie you'll have to rely on me for everything now it's okay though because he was nothing but a worthless good-for-nothing drunk oh hold me I loved him.

He felt he should be tired, but he wasn't. He wasn't cold anymore, either. When he realized that he wasn't cold, he wondered if he might be freezing to death: hypothermia, the winter killer. But he was still walking. When you froze to death, you laid down and went to sleep, hell everyone knew that. His own old man had passed out in a ditch and froze to death but that had been in deep winter. No one froze to death in September. September was when kids went back to school and everything smelled new.

Once, Ronnie had tried marijuana. That's what this was like, *like the poppies in the "Wizard of Oz" that we saw at the Beaumont in grade five before TV came and it was on every Christmas.*

The snow was deeper as he walked. Ten yards from the road and he was wading. It slowed his progress, but he didn't notice, his mind was filled with Terry and poppies and the time he and some buddies got drunk and drove someone's wheels into the front of the department store.

Snow crawled on his skin, attaching itself to his scant beard and to his hair, sticking like ice that was warm and pleasant to the touch. Tendrils of snow crawled under his jacket and got somehow inside his underwear, squeezing his balls like a lover might. A not very nice lover.

Up ahead, the swirls darkened and Ronnie saw something dark. He stopped, in snow up to his chest. He stared at the ballet between white and dark, until the white gave way, opened.

"You," he said. The dark stepped forward, and the ice said his name.

The white became black. Seconds before the swirls and darkness took him, Ronnie saw his dad. And right after that, he screamed.

5

Emma was killing time. She had done the breakfast dishes ten minutes after everyone had left, had gotten dressed—nothing too breathtaking; after all, the news was bad—and was now taking the element plates out of the stove and putting them to soak in warm soapy water. The steam from the water was fogging up the window over the sink, and that was fine with Emma, since she wasn't looking forward to seeing him come through the back fence; it was just as well if she couldn't. Still, that didn't stop her from watching.

While she watched and swished the water around the burnt-food-blackened plates, she reflected on what an idiot she was.

This was not the first time that she'd had a bad affair. Not by a long shot. But it was time to end it.

In the beginning, she was mostly worried about Don finding out. After Tully left in the morning, her breasts full and tender from rough treatment, the smell of him in the bed and all over her, her hair messed and mistreated, her body aching for more, she would worry herself sick over if he knew, could he tell, what would he do. She never got beyond the worrying into the plan B stage of what she would do if he found out; she just worried over the maybe. When Don was home at night, she made sure that she was her normal self, not lapsing off into humming sessions, or absentmindedly fixing her hair in the mirror when she thought he wasn't looking. And she made sure to offer him sex, just in case he ever wanted it. He had caught her once because she hadn't been paying attention to her actions, and there was no way that she could be caught again. Yet another good reason for ending this particular sticky affair.

Emma finally took her hands out of the warm soapy water and grabbed her half-cold cup of coffee and sat at the kitchen table, to wait and plan.

Between sips, Emma leaned over and looked expectantly out the kitchen window. The window was too high, and she was sitting too low, for her to actually see him, but if he was coming up the walk, she would see the top of his head as he passed by the back fence.

After nearly ten minutes of this, she leaned back in the kitchen chair and decided that a watched pot never boils.

It seemed so remote from her marriage, the affairs that she had, as though when Don left in the morning that part of her life was in suspended animation until he came back at night. Almost as though she wasn't married at all. It wasn't lust, necessarily, although she felt that certainly. It was more like romance, or more specifically, adventure. Something to play over and over in her head when the place got to her. It was something that she felt defined her day, this inexplicable need to have something else going on in her life besides the kids, and

Don, and the kitchen and ironing and TV. Some people read. Having affairs, even if she wasn't proud of it, was her hobby, sort of.

She'd only been caught the once, and if Don ever found out about the others, he'd divorce her. She sometimes thought of divorce, and then having all the affairs she wanted, but she did love Don—it wasn't anything *personal*—and hadn't loved any of the others. She had hardly even *liked* any of the others. They simply were a part of that other life, adding a lift to her day. Her days were desperately lift-less, and her affairs were very, very important to her in their own right. She wouldn't give it up, didn't even want to think about it, even though she did, every single morning when the before of it all was happening and the excitement high and her genitals throbbing and all of it overwhelming her. She simply could not help herself.

It was over anyway. Things had gotten too far, too fast. And it wasn't just an affair anymore. Tully was bringing pot over and they were smoking joints and he was staying all day and she wasn't getting anything done anymore. And she suspected, but wouldn't admit just yet, that things missing around the house were not lost or misplaced but lifted by his strong, muscled hands and would be found in the nearest pawn shop, wherever that might be. It was getting hotter than any other affair ever had; she had lost control of things. It was unfortunate in that it was also the most exciting affair she had ever had, but excitement of this kind wasn't the point. She had to be in control; she didn't care what was going on in her lovers' lives, but she loved her husband and her children, and her life, most of the time. In any case, she was keeping it.

Telling him was going to be a whole other ball game. This was not the kind of guy who was going to listen to some weepy story about things getting out of hand and they can always be friends. This was someone that might get a little bit angry, might *argue* the point. She had to get rid of him before it was too far along. It had been, simply put, a stupid, stupid choice.

He was a handyman of sorts. He'd come by originally when Don was home and they just happened to be putting in a patio. That was last spring. Tully put in the patio, and put a seed in Emma—just a seed of desire at that point. When he came back just before summer was history, Don put him to work on the roof. Emma brought him inside to work.

There was no denying the attraction, especially in the beginning, when he was still being sweet and courteous. Everything changed once they fell into bed. Bed, of course, was great. He was beautiful, brown and muscled, inarticulate and therefore not much of a talker, with long hair that he kept pulled back and tied with a leather thong like some throwback from the sixties, but without the boring social commentary. Remembering the beginning was a bad, bad idea, and Emma stopped the thoughts, but the image of the naked-him remained in her head. She toyed with a for-the-road fuck, and decided that was not a good idea. For-the-road fucks just dragged things out, and she didn't have the energy for a long goodbye.

Firm, to the point, no wavering; this was going to take all of her negotiating skills. She tried to dissolve the picture in her mind. She half succeeded.

She had tried not to, but found herself leaning forward again and looking for the top of his head over the fence. She leaned forward like that for a long time, hold-ing her coffee in one tight hand. Then, she saw him, saw the top of his head over the fence. She couldn't help the tightening in her groin. Unavoidable. Had she been Pavlov's dog, this would have been her cue.

Tully had walked over to Emma's place thinking, as he did every time he came over, that he had it made. Here was a woman, a good-looking woman, who didn't want to trap him with anything, didn't cost a dime, had her own life and world, and he got all the good out of her and none of the bad. Plus, her house was full of little things to filch that she hadn't even noticed were missing. That was the first thing he thought of when she started her puling little speech: that she'd noticed some stuff missing and thought he might be taking it. He flushed guiltily when he thought of it, but then figured she couldn't know. When he realized she was just breaking it off with him, his second thought was for the stuff he had yet to steal. He had been making a pittance with the bits of jewelry and money that he'd been sneaking out, and had been hoping to figure out a way to turn this gold mine into . . . a gold mine.

He couldn't believe it. They were in the kitchen, sit-ting at the table with her dressed all prim. His jeans were damp where the sticky snow had melted after he came in. He'd been feeling friendly enough then to com-ment on the weather, something he never did. He hated conversation. Especially when he had to listen. Right now, he was listening because he was amazed. He stared at her, his face slowly trying to break into a grin with amazement of it all. She really thought she was running things. Her face loosened some of its screws when she saw he was smiling, or beginning to, and she looked at him softly while she rambled on about how things were getting too serious, she wanted to keep it light, and she was sooooo soooorrrry, they could still be friends, blah. While she was wrapping up he pulled out a plastic bag full of some homegrown that he had in his shirt pocket and started to roll a joint. She floundered somewhat on her point.

"Uh, Tully, I wish you wouldn't do that right now. Maybe you could wait until, um. Um. After, you know, when you, go," she said, smiling apologetically, leaning slightly forward, but keeping a distance.

"Not going," he said, running a wet pink tongue along the rolling paper.

"Huh?"

Her long hair was drawn back in a tail, like Tully's own, except hers curled around the side of her breast, framing it. He reached over and took her breast in his hand, gently running a thumb around the nipple. The nipple got hard. He felt around and took the nipple between his thumb and forefinger.

"Fuck you," he said, and squeezed the nipple, hard. Emma gasped in pain.

"That's better," he said. Then he started to explain to her who exactly was boss. He liked the way her mouth almost fell open before she caught it and clamped it shut tight. He didn't mind a challenge at all, just so long as she knew who was in control here and who was getting away with what. He started to make some plans of his own, and they made him smile.

What everyone in Bastion simply referred to as the mall was actually an experiment in northern living sponsored in the late sixties by a government determined to utilize all of its resources and land. It had been a fine idea.

"Making Bastion Better" had been the slogan to promote the mall concept. The township took the government people's money, gave them guided tours, and conspiratorially overcharged them on both food and accommodations. The town at that time had mostly consisted of folks escaping something. A huge majority of the people living in and close to the town of Bastion were the descendants and offspring of those unfortunates that had been confined in Fort Bastion. They had become mostly trappers and fishermen; some made a living moving up and down the rugged north with things to sell or trade at a healthy profit, such as the venerable Henderson, who had a river named after his family. Henderson sold cloth, beads, storemade shoes, trinkets and gadgets the likes of which were not found in Bastion until recently. His lesser-known but far more profitable businesses ran from guns and moonshine to the sale of women to lonely men through a rougher, and not quite as legal, version of the country's later mail-order brides. There were northern towns just like Bastion, and yet Bastion stood alone among them. It had in its earlier days a harder edge, a meaner desperation, a need for the fulfillment of some kind of darker order.

Things change; in that Bastion was no exception. The years piled on years brought it an air of civility that was inevitable. Its past was buried with the ruins of the old fort. What remains of the fort, in irony, are only its walls, the bastions.

The government moved in with what it believed would be the answer to such rugged living as provided by the north country. A "mall-like" complex, where everything the town needed would be in an enclosed structure, with new homes for new residents being built in a ring around the building, the farthest walk from home to the complex to be a four-minute jaunt. Architects of the highest order competed to design the project, and the winner was given a quick, well-dressed tour of the landscape and sent home to draw some pictures.

Bastion gained much, lost little. Homes from what would for a while be known as "old Bastion" were expropriated. Just about everyone moved into new tract houses provided by the government. In the case of several old codgers, entire homes were moved. The Henderson house—now the post office—was one of those homes.

The complex was completed in time for the start of the bad weather, late October. It was an impressive structure to the people of Bastion who had never been far enough south to see a mall of any kind. Letters to the editor around that time, when there was still a newspaper, complained that the mall would turn into a consumer trap for folks with little enough cash to spare. It didn't. The Treasure Chest was a staple for consumer goods in the north, and it had already been there; it moved into the mall complex. Larry Talgart took over the Variety Store when his brother moved to pastures that were greener for more of the year, and he had taken it over from the original proprietor when he died. There was the sewing notions store and precious few other places to buy things a person had to have. Bastion was still mail-order heaven.

It is an impressive structure. Sixty thousand square feet of indoor living, unnaturally cool in the summer thanks to good old Bastion Falls limestone, and warm and cozy in the winter.

Most people in Bastion didn't even know that the mall had a second floor. Not that the average shopper would be heartened by the news; there were no shops on the second floor, just a bunch of offices and places to keep administrative red tape. Joe Nashkawa was the mall manager, and his office looked out onto the mall, but you had to climb on a chair and peek through the window to see anything, just like a basement window would have been. Whenever he wanted to look into the mall, he would have to go downstairs. Thing about it was, he didn't have to look out, he could hear just about everything. The second floor seemed to have some sort of funnel effect on the lower floor, and the sounds of feet and conversation, sometimes even ringing cash registers, could be heard from his perch. Today he could hear the mall filling up with excited people.

It was the old-timers that came first, wondering out loud to each other if this snow was worse than that time in '21 when you couldn't get a horse out of the barn unless you took the door off. Or that time in early '50, or was it '49 yet? when the snow seemed to have brought the croup with it and every mother's child got it that year, and boy oh boy didn't we lose a few that year? It wasn't '50, it was '48, I remember because I was just home from over there you were never over there and anyway had a worse dog of a week over in '21 and no fancy plows were going to get anybody out you think you remember . . . It went on with those old boys and that was why they came. A little later than that, the regular shoppers were showing up whether they had to shop or not, just to gossip about how much work they should be doing but wasn't this exciting and how they always liked the first snowfall. By eleven o'clock the people running the places across the street like the post office and hardware store were dropping by with half-worried, half-amused expressions wondering if anyone was closing up shop. That was when Joe started getting worried and thinking about calling someone.

Besides running the mall, Joe was chief of the Bastion Volunteer Fire Brigade; in the winter he coached the under-six hockey team, the only team to play inside the rec center; and he was a band elder. He was also on the town's emergency services committee; it fit right in with fire chief and was mostly formed because of the small airport that ran during the warm season. Insurance costs were much lower if you kept the fire truck out that way by the airport and if the town had something written on paper about what would be done if there was an emergency of any kind. Joe and his committee had written it all down nice and complicated-like, and put the paper away somewhere. About now he was wondering where.

It was the emergency services hat he was thinking of putting on while he sat in his office and listened to his radio cut in and out of the static.

He had the CBC on, the only station he would play in the office, damn the others all to hell if they wanted to listen to their shit-kicker music, he liked his news. Now he listened impatiently to the blah blah on Quebec, union woes, and how goddamn hockey players were whining to beat the band again, and tapped his foot wanting the things he usually listened to with interest to end so he could hear the weather.

He heard it. It was cold front this, snow that, winds up to, the high, the low, tomorrow; not a lot. The thing was, Bastion was way up, the station was way down, and Joe suspected they didn't pay too much attention to Bastion even though he called them whenever something interesting happened. Joe suspected that they took most of their news from Springhill, up where the ski hill was. A bigger market. Everything was market these days, even the CBC.

It wasn't just his emergency services hat that made Joe want to know, either. He was just a curious man. He subscribed to every magazine that he could get up here, had the newspapers from Springhill and the city mailed up to him by friends, and he read them all too, and watched the early and late news and listened to the radio constantly. He liked to know things for himself. He liked to tell people the news, and there was damn little of it made its way up to Bastion naturally. So Joe told them. People probably didn't know it, but they depended on Joe to tell them things; thing was, he usually knew *exactly* what was going on, like he had some spooky sixth sense. He could smell when something was happening.

Like the folks coming into the mall just like this now. The last time this happened it was because of a forest fire and the entire town had been evacuated; for most of the town it was their first trip anywhere outside of Bastion. Joe had known something was going on then, too. There's a certain ring to the voice, and a step that's quicker. He believed that there was still an instinct for danger in people—whether they chose to ignore it or not was their privilege. He could *hear* it. He should have been a reporter, but there was nowhere to report here. Their newspaper had gone tits up a year ago, and so far no one had started one up. Now that was a bitch of a job that Joe had no interest in taking on.

There was a lady, Betty? Bonnie? down at the weather bureau in Altman, quite a ways south of Bastion, who had her baby the same day as Joe's wife had their littlest boy. Joe had made friends with her husband between dashes out for rest and coffee while he was waiting and watching their baby being born. Since the four of them had been practically the only ones in the hospital, except for some old old man, they had been real friendly.

Betty.

Joe thought he'd give her a call and find out the real poop. He looked up the number.

Static came free with any sound apparatus in the North, the phone being no exception, especially in bad weather. As soon as the phone was picked up on the other end, Joe hoped that he could at least get enough information across to find out if the storm was going to get worse.

"Envi"—static—"anada," said a voice on the other end.

Not knowing how else to argue with the static, Joe shouted into the phone, "Hello! I'd like to speak to Betty—" He struggled for her last name and couldn't find it. Apparently there was only one Betty, thank goodness, and the lady who answered told Joe to hold.

"Tell the static to hold," he muttered and listened to the patented government Muzak.

"Hello?"

"Betty! It's Joe Nashkawa over in Bastion!" He was still shouting.

"Joe! How *are* you! How's the baby?" The baby was nearly four. The static cut into this fact as he told her and asked how her little one was (nearly four, she laughed). The static was too much for small talk.

"Betty, what's the news on the storm we got out here? The snow's really heavy and it seems to be picking up. You got anything yet?"

"It's no cakewalk, Joe, but they're saying it won't last. But, then again, between you and me, the satellite's last picture was last night, and it's not working right. Might be because of the storm. Don't tell anyone I told you that."

"Betty!" he shouted. The static was getting louder. "I'm hanging up, can't hardly hear you. Thanks for the—"

"What's that, Joe? I can hardly hear you!"

"Betty! Thanks! Say hello to them all for me!" Joe hung up the phone, smiling.

So they were getting sold a bill of goods. No wonder the weather was so unpredictable. Anyway, Joe didn't need anyone to tell him when something was going on. He listened to the feet and the voices downstairs and estimated fifty people in the mall; that wasn't counting anyone in the shops, or the can, or on their way. People were gathering. That was a sign of something.

He thought he'd wander on down over to the department store and take a look out their big front window, have a chat with his sister who worked in the office, and maybe have lunch with Don. He felt like speculating, and telling someone about Environment Canada's broken satellite. Don was an okay guy, for a white guy.

Joe was careful to put on the office answering machine before he left. He hated to miss anything, even when the action seemed to be somewhere else.

Things might turn out to be kind of exciting. They hadn't had a good storm here since '49. Course, that was just his opinion.

6

Marilyn was nearly as excited by the storm as her brother was over at the mall.

The sky was thick with it, and she walked gamely for at least an hour before admitting to herself that she had lost her way. She began thinking that the best course of action would be to hole up in some place until it let up. After all, it couldn't go on forever, now, could it? If anyone had asked her yesterday how well she knew the town, she would have told them she could get around blindfolded, but she had gotten moved around somehow. She thought she knew where she was now, the stretch of road she was on. She thought maybe she had veered left when she should have been staying straight on the main road, and now she was off on the secondary road that was hardly used. It led up to the old dump site and if you followed it north long enough, to the old fort. That was the road she was on now, she thought.

"Bud where on thad road?" she mumbled through lips thickened with cold. Her hands were shoved deep in her pockets, balled into fists and still cold. Her toes in her neat fall boots were numb and she was starting to worry about her extreme limbs. She wondered how long before frostbite set in. She couldn't remember. Funny how stuff like that escapes you when you get used to living in a winter town. You're so used to the rhythm of the seasons and changing gears in time for the next one that you get lazy. Townies were probably much better at this sort of thing, she thought. Because they were soft. She wasn't soft, wasn't afraid of staying by herself in the that big old house in the middle of nowhere, wasn't afraid to drive around in her pickup on the lonely roads—like this one, for instance—in the worst of storms; she wasn't afraid of the dark, or escaped convicts, or what was in the basement, or getting too drunk to drive, or of drowning. She wasn't afraid, because she wasn't town.

The snow was getting softer, not biting into her skin. It felt almost nice, swirling around her, looking more like butter than sheets of ice. Her frozen lips curled up and she closed her eyes, relishing the soft darkness even after the soft light. The sun was dulled by the blankets of snow in the sky and she thought that was a pretty phrase and curled it around her tired brain while she rested.

It took another minute or two to realize that she was standing still. And that the snow had come down so thick and hard that she was blanketed nearly up to her knees. She came to with a start and found herself in the middle of who knows where, maybe the road, standing like an idiot waiting for a snowplow—for surely they were out—to hit her.

She had to move. With difficulty she started to walk again, wading through the snow as though it were a white swamp. She gave her head a shake to clear the fog. What the hell? She wondered where her mind had gone, and cursed right-brain thinking. Dusting cobwebs wasn't usually her style. She had to find a place to hole up. She thought of the truck that she had passed about a mile or so back, it was getting hard to remember how long, how far, and half wished that she'd stuck by that truck. It had obviously died on the owner, and at the time she had wondered if it belonged to Ronald? Donnie? who was coming to get her. It did look like his, he had boosted her truck once before, she remembered, but it was so long ago, she couldn't be sure. She could have stayed there since someone would eventually come and retrieve it. There would have been a survival kit in there somewhere with another blanket, maybe something to eat, and a candle to heat up the inside. It might have been cozy. She cursed herself for thinking she could get back to town on her own. She longed for the truck, even though . . .

"Was not scared," she told herself. *Were so were so . . . big empty truck was all dark inside and you thought—*

"Cancel that last thought," she mumbled. She didn't need any more of that crazy shit going through her brain, because she was still trying to get over what she had seen somewhere near that deceptively cozy truck. Or if she had seen anything at all.

Those eyes . . . looking through me. It was the eyes, the vacant, empty eyes, malevolent, it had been her impression. Where had such a horrible vision come from? Inside of her?

Marilyn felt a shiver go up her back under coat and blanket, a damp shiver; fearful perspiration and a pounding heart. She suddenly felt as though she might not be alone. Before she could resist the urge, she swung her head fast to the left, and then to the right. Around her was white. Everything. When the wind picked up and carried with it a load of snow, there was nothing that could see through the dense, thick curtain of white. In fact, maybe she *wasn't* alone; maybe there was someone nearby and if there was, of course, she would never be able to see them, because of the storm.

Her heart was now hammering in her chest, and instead of walking faster she stopped and tried to breathe deeply. When she stopped she thought she could hear—

Marilyn . . .

"Who said that?" she shouted into the depthless air.

She swung her body around in an arc, eyes frantically searching the faint skyline for shadows, outlines, figures . . . eyes. The panic inside her chest was reaching a bad state. Her breathing was ragged and shallow, moisture filming on her cheeks from the clouds of breath rapidly released.

She bent and rested her hands on her knees.

"Have to stop. Have to get control, Marilyn." She tried to slow her breathing, distracting herself with the matter at hand. When the image of the eyes and the sounds . . . *the wind it was the wind it was the wind* . . . of the voices came back, she pushed her mind to the forefront. Where am I, exactly? How long till I'm there? It worked after a while.

When she felt in control, the irrational panic was taken care of, and she could, if she forced herself, manage a little chuckle. Then she stood up straight and felt a little less shaky.

Concentrate on the matter at hand, she told herself.

Where the fuck am I now? She couldn't resist another fast look, right and left. Coast clear.

She pictured where she was, where she had been when her truck had died. She had tried to walk in a straight line, following the road, even though it had been impossible to see the road. If she had followed the road, however vaguely, then she'd walked about a mile or slightly more. Far enough that her feet were freezing.

The only thing she could think of up this stretch was an old cabin, half-hidden in the bush, guarded protectively by dense poison oak. Not to worry about poison oak, though. No problem in this weather. She wasn't sure if she would be able even to see the place in the dense white. She wasn't even exactly sure if this was where she was.

More determined now that she had a path, she pushed ahead and squinted into the diffused light, hunting for a glimpse of the cabin, or any building; any *thing* would do. She tried to keep the snow out of her head, because that's what it seemed to be doing, getting inside. It was like snowblindness. The way it seemed to take her focus away from the task, the way it did when you were driving, until you were only looking right before you, looking at your own eyes. No more of that.

There was something else that made you think that way, let's see there was snowblindness and what, what? Oh, yeah. Insanity did that. Like imagining you see a crowd of people waving at you, each and every one of them holding a cup of coffee, steam rising out of it. That's what she'd seen. She'd smiled and started toward them and they didn't stop waving or smiling, and when she got close enough she could see right through their eyes as if they were cardboard cutouts to look through, you could see the *snow* through their eyes.

Up ahead there was a shape that was slightly darker than the rest of the landscape. She thought it could be the little cabin she remembered from her youth. She walked as quickly as possible, the drifts and piles of snow giving her no quarter.

Marilyn could see only four, maybe five feet in front of her. She pushed ahead, plowing the snow with her legs—it was up to her knees, at least, in places. She walked until the smudge was almost visible. She thought suddenly about children who had gone to school this morning in little jackets, runners and no hats. Poor things. She reached out and felt in front of her. Her hand touched something hard, metallic. She felt to both sides. A wall. Leaning against it, she shifted to the right, toward the road, following the wall with both hands, freezing against the metal. She went all along the side of the building until she got to a window. This was not the cabin. The cabin was small and wooden. This was a building and she tried to shake the snow from her mind so she could think . . .

She peered through the glass blindly, until her eyes adjusted. Inside there were rows of cans, and a stand full of potato chips. In the corner, shaded, was a mountain of brand-new shiny tires. It was the Esso station. She was near town.

Marilyn moved faster now. She went to the door, careful to follow along the wall, and tried to open it. It was locked. She banged on the glass, hoping to break it even, but wasn't going to do that deliberately, and called. Her mouth was too cold to form articulate words, but she shouted, willing someone to come.

For nearly ten minutes she refused to give up. She tried the locked door again and again, each time thinking, hoping, that maybe she hadn't turned it hard enough last time. Her feet were freezing, she couldn't see, and it was getting darker somehow. The day seemed to have slipped away from her. She was afraid to look at her hands, and even more afraid to look at her feet in case there were little deadly black spots there. She would know soon enough when the warmth from inside that lovely—

"Open up!" she screamed into the empty dark, black building. When her hands felt bruised from the banging and she was near tears from frustration, she gave up. She would have to go all the way—so far, it seemed, with shelter that could be right here—into the mall. She would have to.

Resolutely, she walked to where she knew the road to be and stumbled up it on legs that refused to run, through snow that was too deep for it anyway. She was only a few minutes from safety, half an hour at most in this snow, from the mall. There would surely be people there, they couldn't have closed everything down.

She rushed, and looked behind her, and had the oddest feeling that she was running out of time.

Shandy was looking through her closets, supposedly looking for warm clothes but really stalling for time. She had gotten off the phone with David a half hour ago, and she said she would start walking in about forty-five minutes. She had fifteen more.

She had stood at the window—not that she could really see anything, because the snow was piled there, sitting on the windowbox that used to be filled with flowers. The flowers were still there, although dried shadows now, she supposed, under all that snow. She wasn't looking for dead flowers anyway, she was *feeling*. Several times she placed both hands on the glass and tried to get something from out there. She didn't know if they could hurt anyone but her. And even that was just a vague, uneasy feeling in the pit of her stomach, which might be something and might not. Sometimes she didn't know.

They couldn't hurt her anyway, not really, just scare her by hiding the way they were, not letting her in. Her own fear of the unknown, so different from everyone else's, was just that: not being able to know. Sometimes things were blocked from her. Or sometimes she could only get one angle on something, and not the whole picture, like Auntie Ellen's being hurt from a building falling on her, not the earthquake itself. Sometimes she could see just the ugly part. There were a lot of things out there that were ugly that Shandy had to see, like it or not. It was the way she was. She could see the dead anytime she wanted—she never did want to—and that ceased to be scary a long time ago. It wasn't scary at all until her mother told her everyone didn't see them, and until she was old enough to realize what dead meant.

Except for a slight shadow that darted near the window and away again, Shandy hadn't gotten a thing. She thought maybe they couldn't tell she was there. She got only one thing the whole morning that she stood there: *fire*.

She had no idea what that meant. It was like the dream. The worst part about it was if it was like the dream, it was bad. It was not just lost, it was mad.

7

In even the most isolated of institutions, Cover Your Ass is basic instinct, Candace thought as she slogged through the school's *Policies and Procedures* log to find out if she had to send these kids home from school. She had so far asked five staff members if they thought, knew, heard, would *speculate* on when the time came to make the decision to shut up shop. No one was really forthcoming. Mrs. Thurston, who had been *born* in the school and never left, according to some, had said that as far as she could remember (right up until the dawn of recorded time, the woman had to be ninety), the school had never closed on account of a winter storm.

"They do blow over, you know," she told Candace over the tops of her glasses. "The superintendent occasionally cancels school for the day, if the storm is really bad first thing in the morning, but I don't recall the school ever shutting down in the middle of the day." She then went on to explain to Candace that storms in Bastion were all blither and blather, and then they settle. The buses, she said, would follow the plows, and besides, all the children had billets in town in case of something happening to the buses and they can't make it out of town. But *that,* she stressed, had never happened either.

Candace finally called the superintendent in Altman, where he was in meetings all day.

"Candace! I heard we were getting some snow out there," he said. He didn't sound concerned.

"It's a little more than just some snow, Bernie. It hasn't let up in hours. Last time I heard, there was six inches."

Static was interrupting the conversation, and it was difficult to get her point across. It was equally difficult to understand what he was saying.

"Six inches isn't a lot of snow for Bastion. It's a little early, but have you called the town? Find out if the plows are moving, that'll give you some indication of if the buses can get out. That's the main thing, although you know, all the children have billets in town . . ." She let him ramble, she could barely hear him anyway.

Had these people not looked outside? It did cross her mind—about a thousand times—that she was overreacting. This was her first really bad storm, last winter had been relatively mild. Something tickled at the back of her mind, she just felt like something . . .

She called Johnny Nahgauwah, the mayor. He said the town had been spending the morning getting the plows oiled and gassed and juiced up ready for action. He sounded a little more concerned about the amount of snow; the plows would have to be starting soon or they wouldn't get the buses moving anywhere. He pointed out that it might be a good idea to start calling the billets in town. Candace thanked him.

Cover your ass. It seemed no one was going to give her the permission to send the kids home. She had the secretary start calling the billets just in case. It wasn't even noon, she might be overreacting, but she did want to be prepared. Early to work, stay late, be prepared: the career woman's creed.

She continued flipping through the *Policies and Procedures* book, a book she had familiarized herself with long before this day, but it made her feel better. She was semi–pissed off that everyone was reacting to this as though she was an idiot from the city who had never seen a snowstorm. She was being treated like the new guy again, and she had thought that was long past. Following the book was a way of asserting herself, and she was looking for even the smallest clause to back her up should she decide to do something rash. It didn't even have to necessarily apply *exactly*.

Forest fires evacuation procedure, the basement flooding in the spring, school fires, emergency numbers, everything was in the book, including what to do in the event of an air strike. Under that section, however, were the instructions for keeping students in the school if they could not be sent home. She kept the book open to that section. Be prepared.

She instructed the mall cafeteria to be prepared for the town children who normally went home for lunch to eat there. She had the secretary call the parents. There was some fuss, but she assigned three teachers to supervise in the cafeteria—they were really pissed—and succeeded by noon to alienate everyone: mall staff, school staff, everyone except the kids who usually went home for lunch. They got to eat cafeteria food and were on an adventure. The school was picking up the tab. There was no way she was sending those kids home for lunch in a snowstorm.

Don was staring at an inventory page, completed when the winter stock was put away last year and that had been out on his desk since he ordered the new stock a month ago. That stuff was on its way, but no help to him now. He was checking supplies for what looked to be a boom sales period. No snow shovels, but there were two snowblowers left; portable heaters were at a premium in the back room, but no one bought them last year, chances were slim that they'd go now. There were plenty of snowboots for men, but not much in ladies' sizes, or children's. That was going to be a problem. There was also not a child's hat or glove to be found in the whole store. There were ladies' scarves, of the diaphanous, decorative type, and they were better than nothing but wouldn't keep anyone warm for long.

The problem was, that last shipment should have been at the store in August, but something had gone awry, and the invoices had been misplaced or some such other shit—they constantly gave him trouble ever since the tree episode, which he'd rather not think about. So the shipment was late. Don still felt that the timing could work out all right, but here it was, the unknown contingency, plan B, the other side of the coin.

The window in his office looked out over the store. If he leaned forward far enough, he could see out the big picture window into the mall parking lot, and across the street. That is, if he could see across the street. Every time he looked he kept expecting to see Marilyn's crumbling old truck roll up into her parking space up front. He was damn worried about her.

When Don had first come to work at the store, replacing an apparently A-1 sonofabitch who was a bigot to boot, Marilyn had been determined to hate his guts. She was doing a fine job of it for the first month, and making his days an adventure in irritation. A dance through poison ivy, as Marilyn herself had referred to it since then. Things changed one night.

They were doing the first inventory since Don had come on board. He had told everyone at the monthly staff meeting that they would stay and do it all in one night, and everyone would get time and a half, or if they would rather could book time off at time and a half. This was standard procedure. No one wanted to do inventory.

The night the inventory came up, Don came down from the office after hours and headed straight for the back where the rest of the employees, including Marilyn, were. They looked at him like he was a ghost.

"Mr. Clanstar, what are you doing here?" one of the girls asked.

"It's inventory night. Please, for the last time, it's *Don*," he said.

"You're staying to count?" Marilyn asked him, in the voice that she had adopted only for him.

"Of course I'm staying to count," he told her, and then because he was starting to hate her back, and he certainly hated that snot voice she used, he added, "It's *my* store."

She later told him that she decided he was an okay guy when the other girls told her that when she turned around he stuck his tongue out at her back. Don still thought that it was because he stayed to count.

After that, things thawed. Things more than thawed.

Besides Emma, Don counted Marilyn as his only close friend in Bastion. And sometimes he wasn't so sure about Emma.

She hadn't called since the morning, and the morning seemed hours past, even if it wasn't. He thought he might just slip out and see what Joe over at the mall office thought of the storm, and see if he'd heard from Marilyn at all. Besides, Joe always had the poop.

"That stupid piece of junk she drives," he said aloud, and both students in the office looked at him.

"What's that, sir?" one of them asked.

"Nothing. Ladies, I'm going out for a minute. If anyone calls come and get me. I'll just be downstairs picking up a coffee at the cafeteria, okay?" The coffee in the office stunk. Almost no one ever drank it.

The phone rang just as he was on his way out the door. The student got it just before he did.

Don ran back and sat at his desk, shouting through the door, "I got it, Kelly!"

"Hello?"

It was the school secretary. The kids were all staying in the mall for lunch because of the storm. He could hear the contempt in her voice and thought about telling her maybe she should go home for lunch. The secretary added that this was on the Advice Of The School Principal, if he had any questions.

"I'm sorry to be bothering you at work, Mr. Clanstar. Normally with something like this, I would call your wife, but she's not answering her phone." This didn't please the secretary either.

Don thanked her and hung up. He looked at his watch. It was eleven-thirty. Napping? He knew she napped during the day, and even though it irritated him he didn't chastise her for it. He guessed maybe she did it because she was bored. God knows she told him often enough that she was.

Or she could be at that neighbor's place that she said she'd been visiting. Maybe she really did have a neighbor friend. He hadn't really believed her when she made a point of mentioning it, he thought she was telling him that because she wanted him off her back about doing something with her life, as long as they were stuck here anyway.

When Don had first suggested it, there had been all kinds of mixed feelings about moving their family to Bastion. What he hadn't told Emma at the time was that he had already put in for a transfer and knew he would get it—who the hell ever *wants* a transfer to these remote places?—and that he was going to go hell or high water. It had been an extremely tenuous time in their marriage. It was just after he'd found out about one affair, and he had been considering divorce, in spite of the pleading and her telling him that it meant nothing, that it *was* nothing, since it was over anyway.

Then there was the scene they'd had when he'd found out about her last indiscretion.

He'd heard a covert and cryptic telephone conversation, just her half of it, and like a fool, or the curious cat, he listened against his better judgment. At first he'd listened because she'd taken the call upstairs, though she had been downstairs when the phone rang. She'd dashed up the stairs shouting "I'll get it!" He had been on his way upstairs to get some papers he'd left in the bedroom. He passed by her sewing room and heard her say something odd.

"With," she'd said. Followed by a pause and "Bad."

That was enough to make him listen, a look of perplexity on his face. He was holding the papers, and his heart had been pounding because somehow he already knew. He didn't know the *what* exactly, but she had a secret those few months preceding the conversation, and when he heard her giving her one-word remarks over the phone in the secrecy of her sewing room, that was it, he knew. "Here," she said. "Can't," and then repeated, "bad." He didn't wait to hear her hang up, but walked down the stairs on legs that were shaking, taking no care to be quiet.

A few weeks later, he found out for sure.

He didn't find a secret love note, she didn't whisper someone's name in her sleep, he didn't catch her at it, and there were no men's underwear stuck between the bed and the wall. It was a series of things. She turned him down for sex one night after it had been at least a week. She said she was tired. He called her from work one afternoon too many and she wasn't there. None of those things confirmed it for him, even after he heard the conversation, because he absolutely did not believe it, even if he did. It was a little thing, a tiny thing, that convinced him. He came home from work early one afternoon and found her in the shower. Deciding to surprise her, he quietly snuck in, thoughts of nasty afternoon sex in his mind, thinking he might scare her a little. He got into the shower with her, his beautiful wife, that he loved, and wanted to love, home early from work for a change, in the afternoon. He got in, and she turned around, a big smile on her face, and she jumped a little when she saw him, the smile disappearing so so briefly. And that little startle, not much, barely perceptible, but there.

She fell into his arms, smile returning, hardly having left. But then it was his turn to be shaken.

He did what anyone would do. He got out and packed his things, naked and still wet from the spray coming off her back. She followed him out, still pretending. *Still pretending* that she didn't know what was going on, demanding an explanation.

"You surprised me!" she said. "You *surprised* me, that's all."

"You were *smiling!*" he sneered at her. "You were smiling *and* you were surprised! Surprised to see—" He couldn't even finish the sentence because his teeth had to stay clenched tightly together, very tightly, because he might hit her. Don pulled one of their bigger suitcases out of the closet and began filling it with his things, from his drawers.

It was his packing that made her confess. But it was over, she said. She begged him to forgive her, she begged him to stay. Finally she let him go, lying on the bed, crying.

She called around for him, found him at a motel. She had to call every motel in town, she told him. Didn't that prove something? Come home. She loved him. Come home. Please please please.

He went back. And he applied for a transfer to Bastion.

Don really believed that it was the right thing to do: start over, in a place that held no memories of how hurt, surprised, shocked and angry he'd been. Those feelings done with, but sometimes he was still angry. If he let himself think about it, sometimes he still thought about packing it in. It never seemed to go away. The slightest variation in a story he thought he already knew made him doubt her: something out of place in the house, an unfamiliar expression, refusal of sex (although she was pretty careful about that, he had to admit). But it was changing. He thought Bastion was a place that would bring a family close together, isolated from everywhere else, it would require a dependence on each other that they'd never had in the city. He thought it was working. Things were slowly healing; even the anger was disappearing. For long periods now he didn't even think about what had happened. Only when something like this came up, and he was determined to keep himself on track.

"Steady, boy," he whispered to himself.

He left the office to see Joe. It was lunchtime anyway, he could see the kids in the cafeteria, and he and Joe could have lunch together.

His hands were shaking.

8

He wouldn't let her go to the bathroom, and her bladder was bursting. She was going to wet herself, she knew it. Three cups of coffee, and no break. Emma was forcing herself to focus on her bladder, and holding it in, so that she didn't have to think about that other, worse, thing.

He was sitting on the bed with her, and he had both his legs thrown across hers. If she thought about it, the closeness of his flesh made hers crawl, and she would want to vomit again. She didn't think she had the energy to move just then. She was too sore. She had to go pee. She would ask just one more time—no, *tell* him that she was going—and if he wouldn't let her go, or tried to stop her, she would pee all over him. That would show him. The pathetic thought made her feel worse, and she could feel a sob coming up. That wouldn't do. She sucked at her bottom lip to feel that pain, and that would stop her from crying.

He said he wouldn't hit her in the face, and he didn't. But her lips were bruised, top and bottom, from him biting them, and scraped raw from his rubbing the beginnings of his beard on them. She didn't know what she'd tell Don—maybe that she'd had a reaction to the cream she was using. The thought of her husband did make her cry, suddenly and surprisingly.

"Are you crying again?" he asked her with mock concern. He was smoking a joint, his fourth in the last couple of hours. His eyes told how stoned he was, and Emma had hoped it would mellow him out like it usually did. Truth of it was, it was only making him meaner. She wished he would get up, go to the bathroom, so she could grab something, knock him over the head with it. Truly.

It wasn't the first time Emma had thought of killing him. The first time, after he dragged her into the bedroom kicking and screaming, she had looked wildly around the room for something to hit him with. As though he could read her mind, he pushed her hard onto the bed and told her if she tried anything he would tie her up good, and she wouldn't be moving at all when he left. It had scared her enough to stop thinking about it for a while. But now she was thinking about it again. She looked around the room underneath her eyelids, swollen from crying. On the table beside the bed there was a lamp. Too small. Besides, it was plugged in and she would have to yank hard and fast to get it quickly enough to use before he caught her. Same with the clock radio. Even in the drawer of the nightstand there was only tissue paper and some magazines. On the dresser there was a cut-crystal vase that had meant something to her before today, and it would mean something even more if she could get to it.

He had sat on her ribs and they were throbbing now.

She supposed she had big bruises on both sides of her rib cage. How would she explain *that?* Not just that, but her breasts had ugly red marks on them from the pinches he gave, she had pinch marks everywhere, and in some places he'd pinched so hard she thought he might have broken the skin. Every part of her hurt, or bore some mark or bruise that would hurt later.

While she categorized her injuries, the back of her mind ran overtime with how to explain to Don what had happened. This dirty, terrible business had started as a simple—very stupid, but simple—diversion and now no doubt about it, it would cost her more than just her marriage, and there didn't seem to be a way to fix any of it. It was, if not her fault, a direct result of her own stupid actions.

She had to tell. She could tell Don that he broke in and raped her. It didn't vary from the truth very far. After she killed him, they would believe her implicitly. And she had every intention of killing him. If she could get to that vase, or better yet to the hall closet near the bathroom where Don kept the rifle she had been so afraid of . . .

Tully looked at her. She opened her eyes wider and looked back, pretending more defiance than she felt. In her mind he grabbed at his stomach in pain after the sound of the blast and his face had the same look of utter horror on it that hers had had when she realized he was going to rape her. *Maybe I should shove it up inside him and let it go.*

The phone started to ring.

The two of them froze, and Emma recovered more quickly and made a desperate, futile motion to grab it before it stopped. Tully grabbed her arm easily, twisting the skin, making her cry out.

"Mmmm," he said, "I wonder who that could be." He pointed to his chest. "I wasn't expecting a call. Were you, Emma, honey? Were you expecting, say, your husband to call you this morning? Or maybe your kids? Gee, could be anyone on that phone. Too bad you're indisposed at this very moment." And he laughed.

The two of them listened in silence until the phone stopped. It stopped after ten rings, and that made her believe that it really had been Don. They always let an unanswered phone ring ten times. It was a family trademark.

"Oh, I guess they couldn't wait for you to answer," Tully mocked. He gave her arm one more twist before letting go. Emma stroked the reddened skin, trying to ease the burning.

Tears of anger filled her eyes. She glared at him, and spat, "You fucking bastard—"

He smashed her cheek with the back of his hand. Her bladder let go, and she could smell herself.

"I'm going to kill you," she said to him, through her tender lips.

He smiled and took another smoke off his joint.

Tully had never been a good guy in the respectable meaning of the word, but neither had he been distinguishable from the countless other ill-meaning bastards that populated the world. He'd broken the law, mostly property laws, stealing, and when he was younger, vandalizing homes and schools with the enthusiasm of anger. He bought liquor underage, drank it, pressured younger and younger girls into drinking it and then encouraging them to explore their sexual awakening for him. He'd laughed about it with his friends that were just like him. He hadn't made them do anything that anyone else wouldn't have been able to make them do given the same circumstances. Once with a group of guys from the bad school, he'd chased a high-school girl, with every intention of raping her, but she was too fast for them. She hadn't been able to identify any of the guys, but the cops seemed to know it had been them, and they got hassled for weeks. He'd shot deer and moose out of season, fished in private waters, shoplifted and been in fights. He was vaguely familiar with the police forces in several communities, but no more so than any other bad boy, and in more recent years as he aged he'd slowed down. He smoked a little pot, did some trapping, odd jobs, got drunk once in a while, and hadn't been in a bad fight in over a year. He hadn't ever been in serious trouble. Small pick-ups; he doubted if there was a cop who knew his name, even if they recognized his face. Until he murdered his common-law wife, he had been a prick on his way to being an older prick, but no worse than most.

That was his turning point. He had never been exactly patient with women. Women were for his pleasure, brief, sexual pleasure. He couldn't even remember being in love, at least not since he was a kid. Annie had struck his fancy. She'd been cute as a button, and clean. Not a girl that moved around from guy to guy, but a younger girl, from a decent family, poor but decent. She'd simply pleased him in some vague way. He took her with him on the trapline on a lark, thinking it might be nice to have someone hanging around with him, someone he could fuck whenever he got the urge, someone who would cook and take care of his stuff. He didn't think about it beyond that. He didn't find he considered her any more than he considered anything else he brought with him into the bush. It had been a mistake. But by the time he gave it any thought at all and realized that it had been a mistake, an error in judgment on his part, she had been dead for a week at least.

Whenever he looked at Emma he couldn't help but think of Annie, and it wasn't only pissing him off but scaring him just a little too, because once he happened to look out the window and thought that he could see her reflection in the glass, and she *was* Annie, dripping wet from the Toman, coming up behind him. He didn't let on. He kept his mental balance now when she looked at him, because he didn't want her to know what he was thinking about. He was thinking maybe she was Annie, Annie was her. He was thinking about killing her.

He didn't have to, but he might.

Natty wasn't nearly as drunk as she could have been, considering that she'd been in the bar for most of the day—all of the morning anyway. That was because all that time she had only had three beers, hardly enough for a buzz. On top of everything, her sick-hangover would be back if she didn't get another, and now her cadges were leaving.

Chester and Law-rinse had been in the bar nearly as long as Natty. Never two to work if there was an option at hand, even they came to realize that Ronnie wasn't coming back on his own and that the time had come to go out looking. Chester, the lesser of the two evils, had been forcing coffee down his partner's throat for the last hour and figured he had him sobered up remarkably. As for himself, he'd only drunk two draughts, and that was nothing for a big fella like him.

"Let's go, Law-rinse," Chester told the older man, giving him a sharp slap on the back to get him started up. "Gotta find that boy and maybe give him a screaming at. Tol' his mama I'd look out for him and I don't think she'd like his skipping out on a working day like this." He told this to the general bar population, missing out on the irony himself.

"Aaah, you don't think he's really out there doin' the deed with that Marylin, do ya, Ches?"

Chester rubbed his cheek, thinking about it while Lawrence put his coat and hat on. "Nah," he answered. "He's got to somewhere though. Gotta find him," he said with a final nod.

The two men said their goodbyes to others in the bar. Though it was just after lunch, the place had filled up right good. It was one of those days when the excitement runs high, and people feel like being with people. That was the atmosphere the men were so reluctant to leave. They wanted to be in on the speculation about how bad the weather was going to get, when it had been worse and if it meant it was gonna be shitty trapping again this year.

There were shouts of dismay when the men opened the door and let the storm swirl in.

"Damn you lazy shits," Chester muttered on his way out. "Cursin' at a workin' man."

The place where they had first found Ronnie's half-ton was about twenty minutes from town in normal everyday weather, on a normal every day. But this day, the men found they had to drive very slowly, the storm only letting half-light through, and the flakes driving so hard against the windshield they could hear them.

"Holy Christ," Chester muttered every few feet. He was driving, since he still didn't think Lawrence was up to it. Besides, he would say, Lawrence was plows, not tows. The two men drove in silence—except for Chester's whispered expletives—Chester bending his head so that he could see out the windshield, moving forward on the premise if he wasn't hitting anything, they were still on the road.

"Damn straight," Lawrence would mumble after Chester. "Son of a whore time to be out, you know."

It took them almost forty minutes to make the twenty-minute drive. Even when they got to where they'd last seen Ronnie's truck, they could only see the vague outline of a *thing,* and neither of them—between the earlier beers and the bad light—were sure if it was a truck.

"That's his truck," Lawrence said with the authority of having once had dinner at Ronnie's house, before his mother had passed on.

"You can't see shit. Your eyes is as bad as they ever been, don't tell me that's his truck. We gotta get out and take a look."

Chester grabbed a pair of leather work gloves to put over the mittens that he'd found under the seat. He wished for something better than the baseball cap he was wearing. He wished he had Lawrence's toque. Lawrence wore a toque pretty much all year round since he was practically as bald as a cue ball. It was as much from embarrassment as it was for comfort. He took a lot of ribbing for his hat—"Feared your brains gonna fall out, Law-rinse?"—but was snug and warm on this surprising day, and he would be smug about it later. Since Chester hated it when Lawrence got smug about anything, he let him keep his bloody toque.

"You know so much, you go see if it's his truck, I'm staying right here," Lawrence told him.

"T'right with me," Chester said, and slammed the door, mindful of the headache he thought Lawrence might be getting from his earlier drinking.

Outside was much worse than inside the truck, with the wind howling, and the snow blowing around him without the barrier of the windshield made it even harder to see anything. Keeping one hand on the hood of the tow truck as long as he could, Chester walked to the front of the truck, keeping his head bowed to avoid the flakes. He stopped on the passenger side, in front of their own truck.

Beside him was the bed of the half-ton, and he could make out the brown and white of Ronnie's two-tone. Pleased, he went to it, and got in, pulling hard at the door to crack the ice that had built up in the crack. The keys were in the ignition still, a habit that still permeated the small-town mentality that Ronnie had grown up with. That and knowing that sooner or later Chester and Lawrence were going to come and get the truck.

"Good boy," he said aloud, giving the key a twist.

Nothing.

"Geezus kee-rist, that sounds like maybe the starter's gone on you, old girl." The boy just changed the alternator in the summer, he thought, and tried to place in his mind when exactly that was. He argued over days in his mind. *That was that Tuesday after we spent time pulling the rig out of the ditch we all needed a snooze after that*

one the boy changed the alternator and we all shared a
six no Wednesday Tuesday we pulled the rig—

From behind him, Lawrence blew the horn.

"Hold yer fucken horses, old man!" he shouted back.
"This baby's toast 'n' jam."

Chester went around to the hood and felt. It was
cold. The boy had been gone awhile, although in this
cold weather it wouldn't take long for the engine to
cool.

The plan was to drive around until they had some
idea of where the boy might be. Chester didn't say a
thing to Lawrence about it, but he was just a little bit
nervous. "Ain't like him," he finally said.

"Yer right."

"Ain't like him to go off and just leave his wheels
thataway. He cares for that truck like a mother."

"Yer right about that," Lawrence agreed.

"Couldn't start it, no how," he said, just a little
guilty now about not trying to boost it. "Any-hoo, we're
gonna see him walking along any minute now." But he
was thinking about what happened to Ronnie's old dad.

Ronnie's daddy had pretty much got what he paid
for—as far as Chester was concerned—when he froze
away in that field. A no-good drunken sot was what he
lived and that was how he died. He gave Ronnie a job in
the garage when the old man asked him to, because they
went way back together, and while the old man hadn't
known it at all, it was like this: if things had turned out
just a little differently, Ronnie'd be his own son. When
Ronnie's mama had found out she had the big C and
there's never no way no how of getting out of the cancer, she figured she was gonna die. She made specific to
ask Chester to take care of her boy. He meant it when he

told her he would, and now he was worried about that promise.

"Maybe he is holed up somewheres with the lady," Lawrence said finally, picking up on the thread of worry in the truck cab.

"Now you know that ain't true. That's not what the boy's like. He'd set her some-a-wheres and go get a ride from someones. No one's seen the boy t'all," he snapped.

"Don't go screeching in your daddy's voice to me, Chester, I ain't your kid."

When Chester turned sideways to give Lawrence a look to kill, he saw something, something small and dark, lying just as far as he could see through the storm. He slammed on the brakes.

"Holy shit, that might be—" He pushed the truck into gear and jumped out before shutting it off. The truck shook itself into a stall.

"Whaaat . . ." Lawrence was twisting to look out the window while his friend jumped out. There was something in the snow, it was covered everywhere, but when he squinted up his eyes he could see the shape of a boot. A big shit-kicker boot, like Ronnie wore. He got out of the cab.

Chester shouted to him, "Shit, shit, Law-rinse, help me brush him off and get him up, he's done froze out here, his momma's gonna kill me when I get upstairs, help me get him home, maybe he's all right he couldn't a bin out here more'n a couple hours—"

Lawrence beside his friend. Chester was brushing the snow off the boy rapidly, as more fell on almost in defiance.

"You sure it's—" The jacket on the boy blew open

with the wind, and it was a flak jacket, green and white with the snow crusted on.

Ronnie was lying on his stomach. Chester fell to his knees, sinking into the powder. "Turn him over!" he shouted above the wind. The two of them grabbed him by the right side and rolled him. He rolled like a pile of blankets.

"Oh god!" Lawrence screamed. The beer he drank all day came up in a sudden gust.

Ronnie was gone. Chester stared at the boy, transfixed. It didn't even look like him. The skin had turned a dark brown, and it was rumpled inward like a crumpled-up piece of butcher's paper. The eyes, where the eyes would have been, were hollows that disappeared sideways into his head. One glove had fallen off his hand, and all that was there was the skeletal outline of what had been fine muscled hands. Hands that had worked on cars.

"Ches, we gotta get outa here, he's been kilt we gotta go get the RCMP, he bin murdered or something—oh god, Ches!"

Chester couldn't move. He stared into the face, thinking, he coulda been my boy if things had been different.

The body moved. Lawrence grabbed Chester's shoulder, but Chester yanked himself away.

"He's still alive!" Chester shouted.

The chest swelled slightly, and the movement pushed the body up from the snow. The cloth pulling away from the frozen snow underneath gave a scritching sound. The swelling moved up, slowly.

Lawrence shook his head. "Ches, he ain't alive, something's wrong here . . ."

"He's breathing, you old fool," he shouted, helpless hope taking a hard grab at him. He reached over to pull the boy up to him. "Help me carry him to the truck we gotta get him to the doctor's." He struggled to lift the body. Lawrence, who could see things more clearly, didn't move to help him. The swelling seemed to crawl slowly up the boy's body, into his neck. That's when Lawrence screeched, and stumbled back from the two of them.

The neck swelled and got huge, the skin stretching until it was shiny, pulled as far as it could go, as if someone were pulling the innards out of it.

Lawrence backed away, picking up momentum, never taking his eyes off the two of them, while the boy's head swelled suddenly, and filled out, a terrifying caricature of what he had once looked like.

Something black burst out of Ronnie's mouth. Chester looked at Lawrence, once, terribly surprised, his jaw opening and moving as though he wanted to say something to his friend. The thing, huge and black, paused, then darted into Chester through his own open jaw.

Lawrence backed away, bile rising again in his throat, and turned, ran so fast for the truck that he fell and had to grab the handle to pull himself up into the cab. He was crying and blubbering when he slammed the door shut, too terrified to look and see what happened. From through the window of the closed cab, he could hear a terrible sucking sound, and the sound Chester made, his friend, giving one fast cry, before silence.

"Ooohh . . ." He moaned on and on, hiding his

eyes with his hands, and closing his fists against them too.

It was some time before he could crawl over to the driver's side. It was longer before he remembered how to turn the truck on. But by then, his mind had gone to a place far away.

9

"Oh, come on, Shandy."

"David, I'm sort of scared to come. It's really blowing."

"Shanny! It's a little snow! What the hell is there to be scared of?"

"I *mean*, I just have this weird feeling, you know, like I told you about?"

He laughed.

There was a deep pause on the other end, and David thought, horrified, that she might have hung up. He was sorry he'd laughed, but it was just more crazy mumbo jumbo that she'd been talking.

"Sorry, Shan. I'm sorry. Don't be mad. I'll meet you halfway. I'll meet you . . . by the hardware store, okay?" That was more than halfway, plus he was truant so much this month that if anyone saw him he would be in deep shit. That was more than compromise, that was *sacrifice*.

She was thoughtful at the other end. "Well . . ."

He wouldn't laugh again at her, he would promise

her anything now, she'd given him such a start and then taken it back, he felt generous and relieved.

"Come on, by the hardware store. I'll leave in fifteen minutes. Okay?"

"Half an hour. I want to find my winter stuff."

David didn't even hear the serious reluctance in her voice. He was simply ecstatic that she was coming and he was meeting her and they had about three glorious hours to spend together before his mother got home from work.

"Dave," she said before hanging up, "it's really, really bad out there. Not just the storm, but, you know . . . I feel like . . ."

"Don't be scared, babe. I'll keep walking till I meet you."

"Really, it's a weird storm. There's something . . ."

He could see her in his mind's eye with her lip curled under her two tiny top teeth, her forehead all scrunched in a frown. God, he loved her. He thought about the time he made her come, and her face got all red and her freckles stood out and she wouldn't open her eyes after because she was too embarrassed . . .

"—not listening to me!"

"What?"

"I *said,* don't you think it's weird to have this in September like this?"

"Shandy, I'll leave in half an hour. I love you," he told her firmly and hung up before she changed her mind. He thought about taking the phone off the hook in case she tried to call back and cancel, but that would be too cruel. He left the receiver on the table anyway, just for a little while, he'd put it back on just before he left. If she freaked he would tell her his mother called. If she didn't show, he'd go to her place even though her mother got home a good full hour before his.

He walked over to the window.

Scared of a little snow. He remembered when he was a little kid, he and his friends would play street hockey every day, no matter what the weather. Once a kid up the lane got frostbite. He had been in goal and hadn't moved around as much as the rest of them, and he hadn't even said a thing. He didn't even know until he got home. Winter was what you made it. In a town like Bastion, you couldn't let a little winter keep you down.

The big window faced their front yard. He hadn't really looked out all day. The yard was buried. Their cracked concrete sidewalk had disappeared and his bike was nowhere to be seen, even though he knew he'd left it at the end of the driveway last night. He knew because his mother told him he better move it before she came home that night or she'd run over it. Mrs. Rupert across the street had a small picket fence around her yard so that her dog couldn't get out and chase what little traffic there was on the road, and he couldn't see the fence. Could the snow be that high, or was the white fence just harder to see in this surrounding? It was everywhere, deep and white, and this was only September. And it was still coming down, in absentminded swirls, slowly and comfortably, as though it had all the time in the world to finish its work.

It wasn't until later, when his mother phoned, that he really got to wondering. She wasn't coming home, she said, sounding mighty pissed off about it, because the plows weren't out and she was scared to drive with the summer tires still on. Besides, Dr. Briggs wouldn't let her risk it. He probably smelled the booze on her breath, David thought.

After that he thought about calling Shandy and telling her that his mother wasn't coming home and they had all the time in the world, and maybe her mother would get stuck too. It was too perfect to imagine. He didn't call. He figured it might just make her more determined not to come and that would ruin everything. He'd tell her once they were safe inside his house and she'd be as thrilled as he was. He'd *make* her be. He got dressed and watched the clock tick off the minutes.

He'd talked her into it. She tried to tell him she was sick—anything—to get out of leaving the house, but he talked her right into it. That made her angry, and she didn't understand her own reluctance to just tell him no and be finished with it, instead she just dealt with the angry as this part of their boy-girl thing she would have to get used to. It wasn't like she could explain herself to him.

She hadn't *exactly* explained herself, but she'd sort of tried. She'd hinted around at what she was like, the essential part of herself, akin to the way people will explain that they have a terrible temper, or dye their hair, lie about their age or are allergic to animal hair. She never did tell him, oh by the way David I see things all the time. I saw what your dad looked like from inside your head and I know that you can't figure out if you like your mom at all and I know you cheat on tests at school and that once you thought about killing yourself, and while all of this *knowing* just makes me love you more, I will always know more about you than you know about me. She tried to tell him some of this, taking it slowly, by telling him that sometimes she saw the future. Only problem was, a lot of kids at school were really into the occult. It had more to do with heavy metal music and the devil than anything Shandy felt, but it made him less open to the *reality* of herself. He would only nod and agree and not really listen at all. That made it harder than if he just didn't believe her. She knew that all she had to do was to tell him something that she knew that she wasn't supposed to know, but years of training had kept her from being able to do this. It was a little like pointing out to a good good friend that they were lying. It would be rude.

There was also the whole pressing problem of him meeting her halfway. That meant he was going outside. It didn't mean that he was going to be dead, but she still wanted to know what those things were before he wandered out into the middle of them. She had tried to call him one more time but his line had been busy. He had taken the receiver off the hook; she wasn't that stupid to think he was actually on the phone. He was skipping school, like her; his mother was at work and they weren't that close. Who exactly did he think she would think he was talking to for half an hour? He just didn't want her calling and changing her mind about seeing him.

She called her own mother before she left to tell her that she was going to nap, just in case she tried to call and there was no answer. A year ago it would have bothered her to lie to her mother, but things were changing between them. Her mother was concerned—well, worried sick—about it, Shandy could feel the concern coming off her in great hectic waves, but she could feel that same feeling coming off the mothers of her friends in the same waves, and so philosophically decided it was normal. She and her friends were just growing up.

Lydia told Shandy not to worry if she was late coming home. The snow was just as bad in Trefort as in Bastion, or so she heard, and Mr. Remfeld was doing what he could about getting everyone home before it was too late, but so far no luck. She may even have to stay over. "Don't you worry, anyway, honey. If I can't get home tonight I'll be home first thing tomorrow, all right? We can keep in contact by phone." She sounded far more worried than Shandy could imagine herself ever feeling.

"Mom, I think you better stay where you are," she cautioned, hoping she would take it as concern for her driving.

"Well, we'll see . . ."

No one was going to be driving in this weather. Because she could, Shandy closed her eyes and stretched forward to the evening, when she expected her mother home. The door stayed closed, the lights stayed off. Something else . . .

Never mind. David.

"Mom, I don't think—"

"Honey, I'll *see* you later," her mother said, cutting her off. Her mother thought that firmness could change the facts.

She ruffled through the things in the closet and realized that David would be leaving. She had to hurry.

The only thing she could do was meet him, get to the halfway before he did, meet him sooner, so that she could protect him. *I don't even know if they're bad.*

———

It was much worse outside. From the moment Shandy stepped into the thick of the snowstorm, she had the distinct feeling that she shouldn't be out there in the cold with those *things*. Her back and shoulders tensed against the compelling need to run back into the relative safety of the house.

She was standing on the front stoop, facing the yard. Where she should have seen grass, still fairly green, there was only white. The wind was blowing the snow around, not quite in a one-directional drift that was usual for Bastion, but in a circular pattern that seemed slow and lackadaisical, as if cruelly enjoying the shutting down of things, the blocking out of the sun. A silly thought, she reminded herself: snow has no feelings. Weather has no feelings, and if it did, it would feel efficient, she thought, with a built-in work ethic. This part of the world gets sun today, tomorrow there will be tidal waves in the west, rain in the east, and it's winter in the north. It would have to be efficient, because the weather of the world seemed a complicated, cyclical job. Rotational. Rain, sleet, now spring is here, heat heated hotter summer now, cool things off the trees are tired of growing put them to sleep here comes a winter storm. Did it know it was early?

At some point in her reverie of weather, Shandy's eyes had glassed over and she wasn't really looking at anything. She didn't have to, someone told her, someone sitting way, way back in her head. You don't have to, Shandy, because you can't see anything anyway. Just stand still, until it all goes away. Are you sleepy? it asked her.

Shandy was dressed moderately well for the weather, considering that most of the winter clothes had been packed away by her mother in June and not unpacked for the season yet. She had managed to gather a pair of her mother's driving gloves that had been a gift one year from Shandy: a standing joke since her mother had an average of four speeding tickets a season. She had a decorative scarf, also her mother's, that was supposed to go with the London Fog coat she bought on her last trip to the city. She had a sweater on under her ski jacket, which had luckily been hanging in the hall closet because it was slim and didn't take up much room. But all she had on her feet was the standard teenage-issue high-top running shoes. (It *had* been an issue, all right, her mother freaked: Everybody had them! But where in hell did everybody get sixty bucks to buy them from, answer me that, young lady! This is your *birthday* present.) White, fluffy snow, tiny and sneaky, slipped down around her ankles, her body heat warming and melting it. Her feet started to get cold.

As was always the case, she was aware of the other-world activity around her. In the cold sullenness of this particular day, she realized that it was very quiet, very still. All around her were barriers to the seeing of the world. One eye was kept out for those black shapes, and every now and then there would be a movement to the right or left of her—not necessarily a sighting of anything in particular, but a movement—and she would swivel her head to see. Her body was electric with awareness, with the *wanting* to see one of those things, as if that could prevent them from touching her. She kept an eye out, as it were. And still she felt within herself, as though the swirls and patterns of the snow were so close, she had nowhere else to be but inside her head. She watched for them, but fell deeper and deeper inside herself, her mind wandering here and there.

Her feet were cold.

She shifted on her feet, and that brought her a little more forward from the place that she had slipped into. The back-of-her-head voice whispered something too quietly for Shandy to hear. She didn't hear it, and stomped her feet, blinking two or three times.

"Shit!" she said into the icy air. Her lips were cold already, what the hell was she waiting for?

Snow had swirled around her legs and snow was indeed inside her runners. She wondered about going in the house and finding something else for her feet, but knew that if she went back in, she wouldn't find the nerve to step out again. And David was meeting her. Would have left by now. Had to go meet him.

She seemed utterly unaware of how long she had been standing on the stoop lost in some other world until she stepped down to where a step should be and sunk into more snow. She would have to wade all the way to the hardware store. It wasn't far. Still, she had to watch out for—

That was when she heard it. She was suddenly *entirely* aware of her stiffened back, and the feel of something around her, and she flipped her head around to look over her shoulder, pulling the makeshift scarf out of her collar. There was one nearby her. *Is it in me?*

She did a mental feel-around inside herself, as if feeling for leeches after a swim in a bad lake. At the same time she kept her head swiveling, eyes wide and aware, looking for those black things, the ones that got into Mr. Hawkins and followed him into the house. She couldn't see one anywhere. Her mental feel-around turned up nothing.

"Holy Christ." There was panic building up inside her, and that frightened her as much as the voice she *swore* she heard. Her heart was beating so fast she felt slightly faint. Her breathing was shallow and fast.

"Calm down, calm down," she whispered to herself, as much to hear only her own voice as to settle her heart. As her breathing slowed, she opened her ears slowly, ready to hear it again—not wanting to, but ready.

She looked around her. Starting at the front yard, she looked to the right, and furtively next door to where the Hawkinses lived. *I don't want to see Mr. Hawkins because I don't think he would be Mr. Hawkins at all I don't think I need to look over there too long I probably didn't hear a thing.*

The first time it had sounded snotty and mad. But the second time it sounded scared.

Now she wanted to know. And she would find out.

David buttoned up the top button of his denim jacket, something he never did. He wished he'd thought to pull out his scarf; it was somewhere in the back of the closet where winter things belonged when it was only September. It was damn cold.

He had made it through the yard, walking alongside the grass where the snow was softer, where it had fallen unevenly over the blades of still mostly green grass. Once on the road or the sidewalk—each was indeterminable—he was having trouble walking.

It was still light out, but the sky was overcast; the falling snow wasn't helping much either. It made everything sort of glow, the sun trying to get through the gray clouds, the snow still as white as it would be freshly fallen having had no opportunity as yet to grow brown and dingy with exhaust from plows and trucks and snowmobiles and every other vehicle that was a winter must in Bastion. Between the clouded sky and the white snow, everything seemed to melt and glow into one solid mass. The road was covered evenly, it didn't even look like anyone had tried to get through yet. The whole landscape was variations on a gray and white theme and it was really tough to see where he was going.

David pretty much knew Bastion like he knew the shape of his hands. It was a place that he had lived in always, and they had lived in every neighborhood in town. All four of them. They'd lived everywhere.

When David's dad died, they'd been living in what was called "town" by most of the folks around Bastion. That was right in the center of things, sort of like where they were living now, across from the mall. Except, they'd been living on the other side of the mall, in one of the nicer houses. David's dad had been a town employee, working winter and summer keeping the park clean and the grass cut down at the cemetery and collecting the garbage on Wednesdays, hump days. His mom had been a homemaker, and David went home for lunch every day.

In the winter, his old man had trapped. Everyone trapped in the winter, it was a good, honest way to make a few extra bucks.

One afternoon, it was a Sunday, never forget that, David wouldn't forget that it was a Sunday and he'd hated them ever since. He was out to check his traps and he took his rifle with him because it was deer season and he thought he might see something if he just walked a little bit north of where the mink traps were. Darby Blanchard had seen a great big eight-pointer there just two days before. David was on his way out to play hockey in the street; Cal Bud Ken Butch were going and he was getting his stick when his dad said, "Play fair, now."

David's last image of his father was the old man reaching up into the back closet, pulling his rifle down, and giving him a nod. Saying "Play fair, now" the same as always, and David "yeah, yeahed" him the same way. As if playing fair had anything at all to do with playing. You played and the game was fair, period. The best thing about sports was that the game ended up being played no matter what. You could fair yourself to death and that hardly ever had anything to do with the outcome. It wasn't like if you didn't slapshot or slash with your stick your father wouldn't end up dead because some hunter had too many beers and wasn't seeing straight. It wasn't like not tripping would make sure that Day-Glo orange was orange and deer weren't orange. *It wasn't like he was perfect or anything he always said the same stupid thing play fair and he wiped his nose on his sleeves because he was raised in the bush and there weren't no such thing as Kleenex or toilet paper you used the Sunday paper and that was that he said he fell asleep once when I was trying to tell him about the theory of relativity and when I got mad he laughed he wasn't perfect and sometimes I didn't love him at all.*

All around David it snowed. As though it didn't care at all.

David didn't know what made him think of his dad, because he hardly ever thought about him at all. He'd been dead a long time. If he ever thought about it, it was to think, in his limited way, about how quickly things could change on a person. One day everything was the way it ought to be, and the next day his mother was sloshing back rum like it was a new fashion and working in a hospital. He got in lots of trouble before his dad died. After his dad died, it seemed like no more fun anymore. Almost like it didn't matter if he got in trouble at all. It certainly wasn't making it special. His mom drank and forgave him for everything, telling him that it was all because his dad died. She would smell like a brewery and suck him into herself as though she didn't so much believe that he was him as he was her.

He shook his head, not liking the way his thoughts were running. It was a weird day, for sure, but that didn't make it a bad day, and he was on his way to meet his girlfriend.

His head had taken him farther from his destination than he'd thought and he stopped to get his bearings. It was so damn close out in the storm, he couldn't see anything really, without *really* looking. He did.

He was heading for the hardware store, and that was down the street from him, turn right, head south for about three narrow blocks and then on his other right would be the store.

From where he stood he could see . . . nothing. Straining his eyes, narrowing them so they let in a minimum amount of snow and a maximum amount of light, he thought he could see . . . the something that it might have been was a stop sign. He should be almost at the corner, and there was a stop sign at the corner. Was that it? He walked closer to it, finding that he had to get almost right up to it.

It was. He was at Hintertown Avenue. It was the corner, and he turned right.

He wondered how far she'd have gotten by now. It seemed to be taking him a long time to get anywhere, the snow was much thicker and heavier than it looked, as always. He had put the receiver back on the hook just before he'd left, waited a respectable three or four minutes and left while his luck was good. He sure hoped she was on her way, because the way things were going, getting to her house in this weather and then staying only until her mom got home from work at four would be a total drag, not to mention a waste of what could be valuable time. It would be absolutely much much better if she was right now waiting at the hardware store wondering what was taking him so long.

There was something about walking in this totally white world that left him free from distraction. It was almost . . . peaceful. He felt sort of good. It was like there was nothing else, just this walking, this trek. He wondered if this was the way his father felt when he was alone out in the woods trapping. One job to do and doing it.

David reached the post office, or at least he thought he might be at least there, and there *was* a hulking dark thing right next to him that had to be a building. For a moment, just a moment, fear gripped him, the sort of fear when you're under water and you can't really tell where the surface is.

This was crazy, this storm. It was almost dark, and he hardly felt he was anywhere. If he didn't know the whole place so well, he would swear he could be anyplace, it all looked the same. For a moment the stop sign wavered in his view as though it were any stop sign anywhere, in the city even, where there was practically one on every corner. But he'd seen it and it was the corner and this was south and he had to be at the post office, which would only be a few short, tiny almost, blocks from the hardware store where Shandy would be waiting.

Stopping again to get bearings, he stared into the gloom to his left, trying to make it out. He finally stepped through the mounds of snow up to the building.

There was a window. No lights were on in the front, only in the back. He reached up with his gloved hands and scraped the ice away. Snow fluttered down, blending in with the mounds covering the window ledge. He peered inside.

Up front there was a row of counter. Barely, he could make out the little sign. He thought it said—and he thought it more than saw it because he saw it every day—"Next Wicket Please." It was the post office. One more block and cross the street.

It was elating, really. He turned away from the window and walked instinctively one more block. One more short, tiny almost, block, even though he could barely see two feet in front of him.

After four or five steps he found he had to stop again, to figure out where he was. It occurred to him then that he wasn't scared, not even a little nervous. He probably should be, he told himself, since he couldn't really see a thing, and he'd never in all his years in Bastion, all his years of *life,* been in such a storm. He decided that he must be made of sterner stuff to be in such a situation and feel no concern. He felt instead utterly independent, strong, capable of this kind of suffering. He falsely worried after Shandy, worried that she was frightened, but that too was a part of his fantasy. The storm was giving him an adventure. His mother was nowhere as far as he was concerned at that moment, might never have existed at all, except for his own presence on the planet. He was an island. He was going to his girl, and taking her home with him—saving her almost. He was full of pride, full of the storm riding over him, his adventure a prelude to derring-do.

He had to continue to squint into the faded light to get glimpses here and there of buildings and shapes cars? trucks? that would have to serve as landmarks in the most civilized portion of the North. Nothing was moving on the street, and all he could see clearly was the fog of his breath. He walked, trying to imagine he could feel the sidewalk beneath his sneakers.

When David got to where the other corner should have been, where he would be across from the hardware store if he could see it, he called.

"Shandy!" His shout stayed right in front of him, as if frozen in the icy air. He took a deeper breath and tried again. "Shhan-neeeee!"

Across the street, he could see nothing. No one answered. In the dense air there was not even the illusion of an echo. His voice seemed to have carried no farther than it had the last time. He listened intently, thinking maybe it had and it was just hard to tell, but he heard nothing. Nothing. While he stood, listening and concentrating on hearing *any* sound, flakes of soft snow gathered on his face. The first of them melted, the ghost of it freezing to his skin; as it gathered, it stayed there. He felt suddenly compulsive about hearing something, *anything*. It seemed that he couldn't hear his own breathing, and knew it was there only from the little gasps of fog it left behind. It was like this sometimes in the bush, where there was not a human sound for miles and miles; only the animals to slink silently past, and the breeze, if there was one, to rustle nature. In the bush, he had often been frightened by the silence, the stillness. This time, he began to feel a peace. The longer he listened, the less he needed to hear something. He wanted to just stand there and listen forever. Because it was futile, and he knew he would get no answer, he whispered her name, as though a part of him needed an excuse, still, to listen. It sounded just like the shout to him.

"Shanny," he whispered. And waited, not wanting to hear anything back.

David stood, waiting, listening. His eyes staring blankly into the whiteness blinding him for everything else but. He felt suddenly tired, listless.

A shape moved slowly in front of him, coming clearer as it got closer.

Standing stock-still in the muted air, David knew there was something else in the snow, in the midst of the peace. As though the peace was covering up something that wasn't peaceful at all but confused and determined. He had closed his eyes, and when this underlying feeling began to creep up on him, he opened them. At the same time that he did, he could *swear* he saw something, peripherally, moving to the right and left of him, indefinable shapes. He could not say what they were but had a feeling that they were ultimately a part of something other than the storm; shadows and shapes whispering around him.

Something brushed past him. He felt a sudden chill, not the natural, even-tempered cold of winter, but a clammy, damp, finger-cold—like a hand that had been once part of a body that had frozen.

When it spoke his name he jumped.

"David!" Shandy said. He screamed, and jumped. She was so glad to see him, to find him waiting, that she forgave him for scaring *her,* standing there like he couldn't (or wouldn't) move, staring off into space, his eyes darting side to side, even though she had stood right in front of him saying his name.

She had thought for a moment that she had seen one, through the dense fog of the storm, its black sharp against the white of the snow. But it was brief, and then it was gone. It had tugged at her, too, like it had before. It seemed to have been chased away, maybe when she came. She had felt it, and then it disappeared. Lost.

"Da-*vid!*" she repeated sharply, and stepped even closer to him. The storm stood between them still, and she grabbed his shoulders. He squinted, recognized her, let out a deep hold of breath. It fogged and fell between them.

"Oh god! Shan. Fuck. You scared me," he said, covering his heart dramatically with one hand. He inhaled deeply again, and let it go.

"What happened? What happened to you?" she shouted into his face, but like his before her, the shout sounded small and forceless in the air.

He looked around him quickly, almost guiltily, and put an arm around her shoulders. "Let's go. This frigging storm is not to be believed." He started them off in the direction of his house.

She was with him all the way. Together, without another word, they ran as well as they could, which was *very* slowly, past the post office with its empty wickets, past the corner with the stop sign, past the storm as it swirled and danced in front of them. Shandy had the distinct feeling—as distinct as any she'd had all morning—that in the storm they were laughing at her, playing with her. She pushed the thought away, along with the sound of chuckling, which she was sure was just the sound of her skeptical side enjoying a joke at her other side's expense.

David's house never looked so good. By the time they reached the front door, she was shaking from the cold and the exertion of running. From the feel of David's arm as he pulled it off to open the door, she knew he was too. Things would be much better inside.

"Hurry up," she said through cold lips. She felt so much better just being with someone that the feel of herself trying to talk through the cold mouth, like when they were kids, made her laugh.

"Cand talk, my mouf iv frove," she said, giggling. She even felt better knowing that the school was across the street. The authority of all authorities, parent of all parents. Even knowing that there were people there going about their business made her feel much better. Everything was normal, copesetic. If a hell of a storm was going on, Shandy didn't think that would get Mrs. Thurston's class out of grammar today. Maybe they would get stuck there overnight, like Shandy's mom getting stuck at work. That's when it occurred to her that she might have to stay at David's overnight.

"David, you know my mom might get stuck at work. Did your mom call?"

David didn't answer. He held his keys to the door—

his mother always insisted he lock the door—and his other hand was holding the knob.

"Come on, hurry," she prompted. He wasn't looking at her. He was looking behind her.

David fished around in his pocket for the keys. The locking of the door hadn't been an always thing, but this was a different part of town, and not a better part either. He reminded her that Bastion was Bastion and neither of them had seen the irony of the only thief they knew actually living in the house with them. His fingers felt cold through the thin fabric of his pocket, and they brushed against his flesh, sending a shiver that drew his testicles up and out of the way. That was when something touched the side of his face, a slight buzz, like a mosquito. He tilted his head to brush it away, his hands otherwise occupied. It wouldn't go. It moved around his head, he could hear it, *feel* it almost, not like a mosquito but more like the violent feeling of a hockey puck blowing past your ear, narrowly missing.

Play fair, now, he heard his dad tell him, and he answered *you bet.*

The door and the keys were forgotten. The winter world around him disappeared too, and he was all by himself. There was no Shandy, no school, no mother; just himself and the game around him, the wind sounding like his friends cheering a goal.

David smiled slightly, because he could smell a whole mess of mink, freshly dead; a pungent smell, a *good* smell, the one that wavered in and out with his dad passing him in the hall, whistling and bragging, David only half listening then, but now sucking up the smell as though he could eat it. Wanting to eat it. He kept his eyes open but couldn't see any winter, any snow, anything white. Instead he could see his old kitchen, and underneath the smell of the mink and his dad's cigarette, he could smell something cooking. It was good at first, but a frown crossed over him as he realized that it was burning, or going bad while he smelled it. It was too faint to trouble him; and besides his dad was right there, holding up his mess of mink and bragging dollars in front of David, even though he couldn't understand what the man was saying, could hear him, and knew that it must have been that, because it was always that way when he came out of the bush.

The keys in David's hand elongated and felt smoother. They weren't keys at all but a hockey stick and they'd won.

He was cold, though. His dad said all that playing in the snow heating up and cooling down and sweating up a mess of mink you better take yourself some ass-prin.

His dad good old dad . . .

His good old dad, tall, big strong-smelling like something rotten rose above him suddenly, changing and *smelling* like the mink gone bad turned over crawling with maggots, the old man's face changing, going white, horrible white, large and black holding a mink except it wasn't—

David opened his mouth to scream when he saw the faceless black thing like an animal.

His eyes went round and his mouth dropped open. He started to say something that sounded like "Da?" In a flash in her head like a volcano erupting Shandy saw what he saw, a wide whitened face, familiar . . .

She swiveled around, knowing, and then a surge of

anger flew at her so strong she fell to her knees as if punched. In her mind a series of lights were going on and off, red, orange, white, flame blue.

Shandy screamed.

David fell beside her, on the stoop in the daylight of his yard. He was choking, his mouth wide as his eyes, a look of utter pain and confusion on his face, finally disappearing with a strangled sound.

In the corner of his mouth, for just a second, Shandy saw a black tail-like thing, attached to something bigger, but like a shadow. It moved down his throat to the center of him, she followed it with her eyes as it moved into his chest.

It reversed. The swell disappeared.

"David?" she whispered.

David's body shrunk into itself, the blood disappearing from his flesh leaving it the color of corn husks, the flesh shrunken.

In what felt like slow motion, Shandy got to her feet, shakily, and very slowly stepped down the stairs, clamping her hands around her mouth, keeping the scream in, afraid that if she screamed she would lose all control.

David was dead, she could hear the sounds of him dying right inside of her, dying with him.

She stumbled into the white, frosty air and let it swallow her.

10

English 101 was an obedient class. Mrs. Thurston was the teacher and she was fond of saying that she put up with no, absolutely no, crap from any of the students. She gave hard detentions. When a student from English got a detention, it was a week of cleaning the staff room, or getting the ink off of the desks in her room. It was always something that a person definitely did not want to do, something boring with no decent result. Other teachers made you study or something like that, extra work, but Mrs. Thurston made you waste your time doing something for her. Hers was a most obedient class.

Unfortunately, this afternoon's students had just come from a double period of business math with the ineffectual Mr. Thiesson. He was hard of hearing, and when his back was to the classroom, many of the kids would continue their hallway conversations with their neighbor. A good number of students were failing business math. On this afternoon, rather than talk to their neighbor, the students had been watching out the window. Mrs. Thurston had pulled all her blinds down. At first the kids thought that meant they were going to get a movie, and sometimes Mrs. Thurston got great movies, all from books. They were studying *Animal Farm* at this point and they figured they would get to see it, or maybe even *Nineteen Eighty-four*. It wasn't until they sat down and no movie came on that they figured out that the blinds were down so that they couldn't even look out the window while she droned on. She never even mentioned it. She was a firm believer in knowledge is power, and kept a lot of information to herself.

"And so, what was Snowball's role in the sabotage? Anyone? Maria?" It was the perfect timing of high school, and the stuff of which class clowns' careers are built on: when Maria opened up her mouth to enlighten one and all, a terrific groan sounded in the room, a groan of magnificent proportions. The class cracked right up, since everyone had been dutifully listening, and looking at Maria. She flushed, but laughed too. A boy in the back told her to cover her mouth when she burped; someone else questioned her manners and added, "Excuse you!"

"That's enough! That's enough. That was just the boiler in the basement," said Mrs. Thurston, and because hers was a most obedient class, the laughter died out quickly, as though someone had pulled a plug.

"That's better," she said. "Maria?"

And Maria started to give the answer, but not before the groan sounded again. Mrs. Thurston gave a huge groan herself, impatient with the distraction to the *point* of distraction.

"Read chapter ten and I will be right back." She stopped at the door, just before opening it, and repeated firmly, "Chapter ten." Then she stomped away to find the custodian.

The students in Mrs. Thurston's English class opened their books to chapter ten, except for a couple of the more daring ones. Billy Brandskin's book was still in his book-bag, but he was a bully, and an exception. After the first fifteen seconds, the giggles came and one of the boys teased Maria about what she had for lunch. One of the good kids said "*Shhh*" and then that was over with. It wasn't long until somebody got up and walked over to the window, to peek through the side of the blind.

Tom Carson was first, sauntering up to the window on the far end, as far from the door as possible, so if Mrs. Thurston came in he had a fighting chance at not being noticed. After a careful, quick look at the door, he reached out and opened the first blind. It rolled up with a quick snap, and the kids jumped. After the first few made the move, there was no stopping the others. The last few desks were emptied, the kids moving over to the window. They could always fall back on the traditional excuse, that they didn't start it, when they were all caught. The pull to the window, in any case, was extraordinary. Mrs. Thurston and hard detentions and washing the floor of the staff room were all forgotten when twenty pairs of eyes looked out into the swirling whiteness. The room became utter silence; Mrs. Thurston might never have left.

The sight was a surprise to many of the kids, most of whom hadn't looked outside since the noon hour, two hours ago, when there had been seven inches less snow to see. Now, as they stared out, they really saw what was going on.

The grounds were no longer divisible from the sky.

At lunch there had at least been a tree line to fathom, a line that grew faint with the swirls now and again, but a line just the same. Now there was nothing, just the impenetrable whiteness, familiar not even to the kids who lived far outside of town on farmland without trees for miles. Even during the worst snowstorms, some form of darkness or lightness was visible, even if only at intervals when the wind would drop or rise. Outside the school there was nothing.

"I think I want to go home," said Kath. She sounded like she really did want to go home, but she didn't move. Like the others she continued to stare out into the dread whiteness, searching for some shape to latch on to, so she would know that the school had been suddenly picked up and transported to heaven? *Gramma are you there?*

The light outside the window was bright in the way that a fall day is bright; a pleasant, natural light. Kath stared out into the brightness, and where there had been fear, a slow warmth crept up inside her and she realized with a silent, internal giggle that she had the stares, the Sunday-morning symptom that you got after staying up too late Saturday night watching horror movies on the VCR. Her face tightened with the need to chuckle. The laugh stayed put, however, and under the silence of the classroom, there was more giggly tension. She wasn't the only one, it seemed, who felt suddenly heartened by the blinding white. Something else had replaced the fear, and that, she thought, was the familiarity with snow, and the rememberings it brought with it, *when we skated and Gramma made us chocolate and Gramma told us stories about the Great De-*

pression in Winnipeg and how to make bannock. *Gramma are you in heaven out there?*

Kath fell deeper and deeper into the snow, and she went further and further away from the classroom. All around her the giggly tension that she had felt before vanished, and vanished unnoticed, as the teenagers watched the snow fall and swirl and as they looked, farther into it, for shapes.

Someone whispered a name that sounded like "Bahara" but might have been Barry. Jerry Callwell had a brother named Barry, but he'd been killed four winters ago, in what everyone said was an ice-fishing accident but what everyone knew was a drunken-brawl-while-ice-fishing accident. So it couldn't have been Barry who was called, even though Jerry was standing at about the right spot, and it did sound like "Barry," but it was a whisper and really could have been anything.

Linda Barefoot reached out and touched the glass. She kept her hand there for a long time. Her mouth formed some words, and one of those words was a name, but no one else noticed because they weren't looking at her. If they had, and if they could read lips, they would have seen who she was talking to.

Kath most definitely called for her grandmother. "Gramma," she said quietly, but loud enough that any-one listening would understand. No one was listening to Kath. Her gramma died six years before, but had been the closest thing Kath had ever had to family. Now Kath lived with a family that got welfare for her. "Gramma," she whispered.

Sandy Dressner, a goody-two-shoes gay-boy, as some of the worst boys came to know him, climbed slowly and deliberately onto the counter that stood underneath the bank of windows. He too was saying something to himself, but his mouth was just moving up and down in a way that looked like a fish's might. You couldn't tell what he was saying, but from the staring look on his face you could sure tell that he was *eager* to say it, and to get closer to that window. Once up, he got both hands pressed up against the glass, and it wasn't long before he had his face pressed up against it, too. No one had any way of knowing that when Sandy looked out the window what he saw was himself, pulling tight on the end of the scarf, his breath coming in sharp gasps, his right hand firmly and desperately stroking his plumped-up teenaged penis even after everything he read about that kind of sex made him want to stop, it seemed to be a disease with him and he only could until the next time; in the snow he saw himself, red-faced and coming. He called a name that no one heard; no one was listening.

They all saw faces in the snow.

No one saw or heard her come back into the room, and when she snapped the first blind shut and shouted "All right, get back into your seats!" in her angry voice, the whole lot of them just stood there, rooted, and blinked; they did that until she shouted it again. Kathy almost started to cry, making a little mewling voice inside her throat, but they all returned to their seats. From the outside it seemed that it was business as usual, books, blackboard, teacher talking; but some kids were still blinking blankly and wondering.

Joe Nashkawa had piped the CBC out over the speakers in the mall, replacing the dull, mind-voiding Muzak. He felt it was prudent to let people know what was going on outside. It was a full-blown storm. Apparently Environment Canada had got their satellite pictures, because the forecast was more alarming than it had been in the morning. None of that breast milk and pablum they'd been feeding them about cold fronts and scattered flurries. Bastion was on the radio. In a way, they were famous.

Folks that had come in just to shoot the shit and talk about the weather had found themselves quite suddenly in a situation. Many people had left soon after arriving, after lunch when the table talk turned seriously to digging out and stuck for the night. But a lot of people, the old-timers with not much to go home to, the ladies caught up in the excitement of a break in routine and of course the men who believed that they could get out any time they wanted. Between all of the folks that decided to stay, for whatever reason, the mall was full of people.

The thing about it was, Joe thought, they just aren't afraid of a little snow. Folks in Bastion, in northern towns all over, *respected* the storms of winter, but they were not afraid. A storm was a storm and there was a big one every year. Not like down south in those cities— even though they were winter cities, like every place in the country—where they got a storm and it was a big emergency, with keep your car off the road, cancel school, stay home from work, shut-ins on your block might need something, go do this, don't do that, whatever you do don't leave shelter. Sure, people got caught in storms and died. It was a fact of the country. How often did it happen? When people died from exposure to the elements in Bastion, they did it of their own accord: drinking and fishing when they were supposed to be fishing and watching the sky; drinking and falling down dead drunk on their way home—taking the cold way to sober themselves up some for the wife, kids, dog; solitary dips in a river too cold to swim in just yet; driving a bad truck too far on a cold night and trying to walk to better shelter. Those were the people that died by their own hand, as far as Joe was concerned, and if he did a survey he knew he would find that everybody felt the same way. Stupid might not be a crime, but it was as good as a signature on your death certificate.

Joe had more to think about than stupid ways to die. He had about fifty people in the mall, and things were looking like they might need a place to sleep.

He looked at the clock and thought about calling the weather bureau again. But he didn't have to. He knew. Still, he was going to give it another hour or so before he rallied the shops to prepare for overnight guests. He started making a list.

The kids, of course, would get the hotel rooms. It would just have to be that way. What worried Candace most was what to do with the seniors. That last thing she wanted nine months from now was a whole bunch of babies born courtesy of the Northern Lights. Who needed supervision more, the little ones or the big ones? The big ones needed the supervision, but the little ones really needed the comfort of an adult presence. They could split the girls and boys by floor and put a teacher on duty at both exits, but that didn't seem quite as safe as having the whole bunch of them separated not just by floors but by buildings.

Candace looked at her watch. It was two o'clock. She would call a staff meeting for three. Just her and a few of the more relevant teachers. It would have to be.

She made a list, wrote out a memo for all the teachers, and gave it to the secretary to type.

"Mara, just so you know, we might have to be calling parents about an overnight stay. I think you better start that about the time I go to the meeting, okay?" It wasn't a question. For once, Mara didn't answer snidely back. She had eyes. She could see.

Don was not exactly *frantic* with worry, but he was surely wondering why Marilyn hadn't called if she'd gotten to safety. He'd tried her house, and then tried the only neighbor of hers that he knew of. They hadn't seen her either. Joe had shown some concern over lunch, but reminded Don—suspiciously, Don thought—that she was a big girl and knew enough to come in out of the rain when she had to.

"Even if it's snow," he added with a chuckle.

The lunchroom had been so full of children, but none of them Don and Emma's; they had stayed for lunch in the regular lunchroom, and he decided to drop by and see them at school. They'd been pleasantly surprised, and Debbie had strutted around the room, importantly introducing Don to her lunchroom friends. *Their* daddies hadn't dropped by for lunch. They talked about the storm and Debbie told him that everybody was saying that they might have to sleep over, "at *school*," she stressed with disgust. Bobby, only six and still trying to figure the world out, asked him if that meant they had to do work the whole night. Don started to tell him no, but Debbie interrupted.

"You can't have school *all night,* stooopid," she said.

Don promptly told her not to call her brother stupid.

"Daddy, if we have to stay, is Mommy going to be scared to be all by herself?"

Jury's not in, kid, maybe she ain't alone, he thought. "No, I don't think so, honey. She's a big lady."

"Maybe we should phone her?"

"Tell you what, Deb. I'll give her a call and tell her we're all thinking about her, howsabout that?" Maybe it was the excitement of having her daddy and her friends together, but that seemed to satisfy the child. It took Don several kisses and about ten minutes to get away from the kids.

Back in the office, Don gave it a try. He felt mildly guilty that he was just calling his wife now, when he'd spent nearly twenty minutes trying to remember the name of his secretary's neighbor and another ten looking it up in the complicated town directory encompassing the twelve small towns and villages served by the northern phone company. It seemed to Don that everyone who lived even barely beyond the town limits was on a different exchange.

Someone had told him once—probably Emma—that if you let the phone ring ten times, it was about a minute and anyone that was home could make it to the phone in a minute. He let his own phone ring ten times before giving up, realizing that either Emma wasn't home or she wasn't answering.

Not answering made no sense. He hadn't heard from her all day. Ever since the time they'd had their difficulties, she'd made a point of calling him every day, even if it was just to say "Bring home some bread." If she didn't call, he usually called her. So, maybe she wasn't home. If she wasn't home, why didn't she call him from where she was to let him know that she was not home, shel-

tered, stuck. Images started running wild-fire through
his head: maybe she hit her head in the shower . . .
was showering with a friend didn't hear the . . . accidentally slit my wrists . . . over at a man's place he
doesn't have a . . . fell coming up the walk broke my
. . . house burned down burned it cooking lunch . . .
driving to the car broke down ran into Marilyn we're
dead beside the road.

He stopped himself before he started to believe any
of the pictures and tried to think sanely, reflectively.

She could have been over at that mystery neighbor's
place having a cup of coffee the first time he'd called;
now she's come home and is having a nap. Just missed
her. Logical, sensible. He didn't believe it. Hours had
passed since he'd tried to call. The guilt because he'd
tried almost frantically to find his secretary, not nearly
so worried about his wife, flushed through him now,
same as the desperate thoughts about what might have
happened to her. The thought occurred to him that
maybe this was why she had the affair and he wondered
if he ignored her often.

Don realized he was much more worried about
Emma than he was about anyone else. He started thinking about going home. Finding her. If Don had been a
woman, he would have realized that his intuition was
tickling at him, because he was thinking that something
awful had happened, or would.

He had to find someone to get him out, through the
storm and home. He would have pursued it right that
minute, but one of the girls from downstairs came running up, calling to him.

Marilyn had come in from the cold.

———

Way, way, far away, Marilyn could hear someone with a familiar voice, Don? Dad? Baby? calling for another blanket. It was cold in the house. The fire must have gone out. Fire? There was no fire in their house. Their house had an old black gas furnace with a tiny flame that burned all the time.

"It can't ever go out, Mary-girl. If it does, you come get Dad," her father's voice. The flame flickered and danced in front of her eyes. But it was so cold, the flame must have gone out.

"Flame—Da," she said out loud. She tried to shout it, because it was so cold. Her mouth was too cold to make the words, even when she tried very hard. Her dad didn't come. "Pa—" she tried again. The tips of her fingers were maybe going to fall off, because that's what happened to Grandpa in the war, the tips of his fingers fell right off when he was in Russia during the war.

No wonder her dad didn't come. She was in her own house, the one with the pink bathroom and blue bedroom and yellow kitchen. She was married to Stan. He turned the heater off in the bedroom. It was only September. That's what he said, "It's only September, babe." He was laughing at her because she was cold already. She told him she would get frostbite and her fingers would fall off. He said they were divorced anyway.

She told Stan in no uncertain terms that she was damn cold. He put another blanket on her and told her, "Shhhh." It wasn't his voice, but it was a voice she knew; it tickled her, but she couldn't place it. It was a good voice, not the wind. She wanted to ask him if they got her but she forgot.

She went under and under and under the blankets where it was black; it was warmer there.

She was so glad to go there. There, she couldn't see the faces. She couldn't hear the wind or the voices. It was too dark, too warm. Marilyn fell away, into the dark.

After Don had tried to reach Emma, and Marilyn came in from the cold, and Candace had her secretary call all the parents (she was up to the H's), every phone in the mall was occupied. There were a lot of folks who had kids at home, husbands at home, parents to call, friends to check up on. There was a lineup at the public phone beside the Variety Store, and all the shopkeepers, secretaries, inside the clinic, the notions shop, the department store were letting lineups of people call home, office, other towns. People were getting concerned about those not present. The phone lines around Bastion were buzzing with last-minute calls, last-minute checkups, last-minute instructions.

"They're just little knobs inside the heater part, on either end, just give them a twist. It'll take a ways to click on but you should hear it and don't put it up too—"

"—well there are beans in the cupboard but I think you better have something better than—"

"—called her earlier and she's trying to get the stove—"

"—you can't go to Bonnie's you're supposed to be—"

"—not sure when I'll—"

"Isn't this exciting? The last time this—"

"—sleep in the hotel I guess—"

"—*No*, I'm not drinking—"

"—he's probably hiding under the porch, don't worry about him. He'll come in when it stops snowing. They have big thick coats and they can dig it's nothing to—"

"—get upset. One night won't kill—"

It could have been the overload of calls, but most people thought the wind, or just the penalties of a winter storm knocked the lines down. Whatever it was, for better or for worse, the people of Bastion lost their connection to each other and the outside world at 3:37 PM. There was nothing could be done but wait out the storm.

11

He had tied her up because, he said, she was getting too frisky. He said it like it was funny and for her own good, but tied her up tightly. A fuzzy feeling was sweeping up her wrists to her elbows; her hands had gone to sleep.

She had rolled off the bed when he tried to grab her again, and managed to get to her feet and run for the living room. Before he caught her she had a good-sized ceramic ashtray in her hands and she brought it down hard. It hit his shoulder. It only succeeded in making him mad and he broke his promise and hit her in the face. The last thing she remembered was the smile on his face that came after the grimace of effort it took to knock her out. She woke up tied.

"Frisky girl," he said, mockingly.

The phone had started to ring around, what time was it, in the afternoon. Emma knew it had to be Don, and begged Tully to let her answer it, using the negotiating skills she thought she'd had earlier in the day.

"I won't tell him you're here. If I don't answer, he'll think something's wrong," she threatened.

"If you don't answer he'll think something's wrong," Tully repeated. "And then what will happen, Miss Emma? Frisky little Emma with such bad aim—I should have broken your nose. Maybe I did, huh?"

He looked at her expectantly. When she didn't answer, he told her what would happen if Don thought something was wrong here at home base.

"He'll come looking. He'll come checking up on you. Won't he? He will." When he said that, Emma felt a surge of hope starting up in her. *Of course!*

Tully saw the sudden light in her eyes.

"And when he does, he'll first see us in bed together, very cozy. And then he'll jump to some conclusions, won't he."

Her mouth dropped open, and without thinking, she blurted, "And he'll see me tied up—he'll see me hurt! Do you think he's going to think I *want* to be here?"

He slapped her again, and it started her lip bleeding again, after it had crusted over.

"You think I'm stupid?" he screamed in her face. He grabbed her by the hair at the top of her head. "*Do you?*"

"No!" she screamed. And he let go.

"That's right! When your hubby-baby comes home, he's going to find us in bed, naked, *making* love. That's what you call it, isn't it? Or is that just what you call it when you're doing it with him? What do you think he'll call it when he sees us together? Making love?"

Her face was a mess, there was blood on the sheets, on her face, her lips were cut up, her body was a relief map of bruises and swelling. Did he think?

He was crazy, it occurred to her. The thought of it made her feel like any attempt at getting him to go away or just to *stop* was going to be futile. She felt hopeless. She had been thinking about trying to be nice, to pretend . . . but she didn't think now that it would work. Probably nothing would. She couldn't even get away with her hands tied behind her.

She would have to think of some way to make him untie her, her mind said. But the rest of her was unwilling to do any more thinking. Part of her just wanted to give up. In the meantime, Tully got up off the bed and walked to the bedroom window, placed high on the wall. She couldn't really see outside, just the layers of snow that had piled up on the windowsill. Above that she could see the swirls of snow still falling. The sun must have been getting low because it was cloudy and dim from what she could see. Or maybe the storm was just so thick it was standing between light and not. Tully stared silently out. Looking for Don?

Her mind whirled away taking chances her body never would, and she tried to close a part of herself off from everything.

Tully was staring outside at the storm. Earlier, when Emma was out like a light, he tried to get the radio to come in, but the static was so bad it only irritated him. The TV too was cutting in and out. He didn't need a weather report to know that it was bad out there.

Things had gone too far, but he was beyond thinking about any of that. All that was coming out of him now was anger and fear. He was scared. He was scared be-

cause of the stuff that was in his head. The things his
rational mind told him were crazy, but he saw anyway.

Annie.

She was out there. He saw her. Every time he looked
outside, he could see her outline, coming closer to the
house. Once, he glanced up from watching Emma being
passed out—making sure she *stayed* passed out—and he
saw her face, full and round and as pretty as she had
been the first time he spotted her on the street in town.
She was looking in at him, looking . . . fetching. Then
she stepped right up to the window, and moved up, as
if she wanted to get a better look, and there, then, he
saw, the bruises on her throat, in the shape of his hands.
And he saw the ice collected in her hair, and the water
dripping off her as if melting from her flesh warmed up.
He heard her in his head too.

Come out here, Tully. Her mouth hadn't moved, but
he heard her, and he could see her.

He hadn't meant to kill her. It just had come over
him somehow, her nagging, throwing up; she ended up
being good for nothing and got herself knocked up on
top of it. She wanted to go home, she wanted this, why
wouldn't he take her, talk to her, help her. He stared out
the window at her while she smiled and preened and
wormed around inside his head, saying things. He almost went to her. Then Emma started shifting and
moaning and he got himself distracted.

She was dying of thirst. She was feeling lightheaded. She
felt she was fading in and out of consciousness. But
mostly, she wanted something to drink.

"Tully," she whispered, not wanting to startle him.
"Please . . . ," she said. He turned abruptly from the

window, a strange look on his face, as though he expected to see someone else. Emma didn't notice. His face softened and lightened when he saw it was just her. Just her. But just a little bit of that came out, because he was beginning to be unsure.

"Tully, please. Water?" She gave him a look of pleading, hoping that it would appeal. It did appeal, to his sense of control.

He took steps to the bed. In his ears, in spite of what he saw, what he knew to be real, he still heard *her*. She came from different directions, all inside his head. She was the window, she was the doorway, she was the living room.

Tully's eyes drifted away from Emma to the doorway, holding that same look of expectancy. Hope again. Was he losing it? Would he drift off somewhere and be harmless?

Emma didn't tell him again that she wanted water, or anything. He didn't look as though he would hear her; he looked as though he was listening to something.

Don!

He could hear something. Emma crooked her ears to the doorway too and listened in painful stillness. She waited to hear the sound of a car, truck, snowmobile— given the weather he could be on a snowplow—she didn't know what. Footsteps was what she desperately wanted to hear.

Annie.

Emma had all but disappeared for Tully. She *was* calling him. He didn't want to go to her, but he didn't want her sneaking up on him, getting him when he wasn't ready, kicking him when he was down.

"Out there?" he asked the hallway beyond the door. Emma's eyes followed him. He walked slowly, cautiously to the doorway, looking ahead of him the whole time. The images of Annie and her dying flew around inside his head mixing and melting with the feeling of ice-cold water that he held her under while he squeezed with his hands. He closed and opened his fists now as he listened.

Beyond the doorway was the hall. It was darker in the hall—no lights were on and it was getting darker outside with the storm—and colder too.

He wished he could see better, see right into the kitchen, where he could hear her. Was she in the kitchen getting something to hit him with when he stepped around the corner?

From in the bedroom, Emma heard him say, louder, "Do you think I'm *stupid?*" She wished she could see, but she could only hear his footsteps on the carpeting. She went through a list in her mind and it panicked her, all the things in the kitchen that he could kill with: knives, all the knives, cleaver, broken end of vase, bottle, sharp can opener, Don's Swiss army knife, all in the drawers.

The kitchen too was dark. He didn't know where the switch was, but with the instinct of modern man he felt around just the right place until he had it. In his head she sounded—just slightly—closer, just slightly more like she wanted to die again by his hand.

Light flooded the kitchen, mechanical and bright. Outside there was still some light, which might have been from the sun and just seemed not; it added to the gloom of the electric bulbs. An afternoon storm, which is what it was, the strange light made inside seem small and safe. From where he stood, still in the doorway, he could hear the wind whistling through the back door. He slipped his eyes quickly around the room—sink dishes table counter blender pantry cans garbage carpet doorway—with the practiced eyes of someone who has looked for trouble before. The whistle kept on and he recalled vaguely Don asking him about fixing the back door before winter set in. He said the sweep had fallen off the bottom of the screen door and the air, the bugs, mosquitoes, blackflies, passed right through and weren't the bugs a bitch out here?

Instead of drowning out the sound of her voice, the whistle sounded like a woman moaning, or crying. It gave the voice in his head a whiny quality, very like the way she would say his name when she was begging him for something *take me home please I'm sick Tulleeeee gonna have a baby don't know what only fourteen . . .* It was the voice he couldn't stand. He had to go to her, had to make it stop.

The door. That was where it was coming from. Of course, she was outside, where he'd left her. She'd walked a long piece to come here, but she was there, right outside the door he bet. He walked swiftly to the back door where he had come in hours before, when he talked about the weather because he was in such a good mood. He was gonna get laid, pilfer her wallet and maybe grab one of those what he thought to be expensive silver candlesticks from out of the living room when she was taking her gotta-wash-him-off-me shower.

His hand on the door, he pulled. Outside the light was dim and fading. The whistle was coming from underneath. He took a look. Under the door, a two-inch space—the missing sweep. Snow drifted in while he held the door. He stared for a moment, mesmerized by the drifting. Outside, the dark began to close in, blending with the swirling white. He lifted his eyes, slowly, having to *make* himself look.

Emma listened carefully, body and mind attuned to the most silent of sounds, wanting to hear Don, Tully, anybody, not the silence. It seemed to fall around her, like doom. Frayed from a day on edge, and anything seemed better than the silence. She listened and heard everything, nothing.

Tully's eyes ran over the gloom, dragging shapes from nothing, turning them into Annie.

From behind him, sudden enough to make his nerves jangle, came Emma's voice, intrusive, *whiny*.

"Tully?"

The spell sprung, he slammed the door shut with might. There was no satisfaction in the sound, muffled by the drift of snow that had gathered between the doors. The inside door didn't quite meet the frame.

He turned toward the bedroom, fists still opening and closing rhythmically, strongly, he set toward the sound again. This time it wasn't Annie but sounded the same. Toward the source.

Snow drifted in from outside, under the door, into the house.

12

Following is the minutes from the Emergency Staff Meeting of selected Staff Members, Bastion Falls Composite School:

MINUTES
Emergency Meeting Bastion Falls Composite School Staff September 21, 3:00 PM, Teachers' Lounge

In Attendance: Candace Bergen, Principal; Mrs. Gertrude Thurston, grades four, five and six, plus English, serving as Acting Secretary (this instance only); Killian MacGregor, high school; Allen Tinsdale, all grades, Phys. Ed., Acting Chair (this instance only); Dan Hack, all grades, History; Miss Alice Loopol, high school, Home Ec.

Quorum waived (this instance only)
Call to Order, 3:03 PM

(It was understood by those present that due to the nature of the Emergency Meeting, the formal agenda

was discarded, and the agenda set informally by Ms.
Bergen and Chaired by Mr. Tinsdale)

Item One: It was moved by Ms. Bergen that the chil-
dren of Bastion Falls Composite School be allowed
to remain in the school's care overnight, from Sep-
tember 21 to a time as dictated by prudence—allow-
able, a twenty-four-hour minimum, or until the Cats
can get out to return them home. Seconded by Mr.
Hack. Carried.

Item Two: Put forward for discussion, the overnight
sleeping arrangements for Bastion Falls Composite
School students. Ms. Bergen suggesting that girls and
boys from grades four to twelve be separated for the
purposes of discretion.

NOTES FROM THE DISCUSSION:
It was raised by Mr. Hack that there was no need to
separate the boys and girls from his class as they
were all fine children. Miss Loopol allowed that
many of the girls from her experience should not
only be separated but some of them (she offered to
provide a list) should be watched very carefully. The
secretary recording these minutes (Mrs. Gertrude
Thurston) agreed with the motion that the children
should be separated and offered the further precau-
tion that they all be given chores or extra gym time,
thus making them so tired they would have little en-
ergy to think up mischief. This suggestion was met
with approval by Mr. Tinsdale, Miss Loopol and Mr.
MacGregor, but Ms. Bergen said that such a situa-
tion would be difficult to schedule given the short

amount of time they were dealing with. The secretary recording these minutes would like to go on record as saying that this was a better idea than some and when it comes to light, she will be on record as saying so. After several minutes of discussion a motion was made:

> *That grades five to twelve be separated for sleeping, with the girls and the younger grades accommodated in the hotel (with the cooperation of the hotel management/owner, Ed Thibedeau, as Ms. Bergen promised there would be), and the boys from grades five to twelve sleeping in the gym. Seconded by Mr. Tinsdale. Carried, with 4-1, Mrs. Thurston abstaining.*

Item Three: A motion was brought forward that the teachers be paid time and one half (as guaranteed by their contract, 1991) for the duration of time spent due to the continuing weather conditions, not to extend past twenty-four hours. No discussion. Seconded by Mr. Hack. Carried, unanimous. (The secretary would just like to add that there was only cautious approval from Ms. Bergen.)

Item Four: Brought up for discussion, the need for additional sleeping bags for the boys (grades five to twelve) for accommodation in the gymnasium.

DISCUSSION:
Mr. Tinsdale allowed that there were enough sleeping bags for approximately fifty children, but that

there would be need for about seventy-five. It was suggested that someone (Ms. Bergen) approach the Treasure Chest Department Store Manager, Don Clanstar, about the borrowing of sleeping bags for the boys. Mr. Hack allowed that he had a bag in his car, and if he had to, he would go get it. Miss Loopol said that—providentially—the Girl Guides' sleeping bags were stored in the Home Ec. room, since Miss Loopol is also the Guide leader for Bastion, and that the boys were welcome to those, adding only that Jenine Jasper peed in hers last time and that she thought it still smelled even though it had been cleaned. Ms. Bergen thanked her and the Guides, and added that if there were not enough to cover the numbers at the Treasure Chest, plus with the Guides' sleeping bags, then she was sure that Mr. Thibedeau at the hotel would be glad to lend out blankets. A motion was made including all of the above. Seconded by Miss Loopol. Carried, unanimous.

Item Five: Brought up for discussion, the feeding of the students of Bastion Falls Composite School while on School Property.

DISCUSSION:
Miss Loopol offered the use of the Home Ec. kitchen and offered to grab a number of the grade twelve girls to help out. She only said that she would need a couple of hours to plan things and get set up, and that additional groceries would be required, as they simply did not have enough on hand. She suggested Porcupine Meatballs for the entree, simple mashed potatoes with a bouillon gravy, and a variety of

steamed vegetables; she said she would have to see about dessert, but could probably whip up enough peach cobbler, she thought, for everyone. Miss Loopol called for a motion. Seconded by Miss Loopol, and then by Mrs. Gertrude Thurston when it was pointed out that she couldn't call for a motion and second it. Carried, unanimous.

Ms. Bergen would speak to the proprietors of the Treasure Chest and the Northern Lights.

Mr. Tinsdale would make a plan for sleeping arrangements of the boys in the gym.

Mr. Hack would work out a schedule for supervision shifts, for teachers and staff in the gym and at entrances and exits in the hotel, including some of the more responsible grade twelve girls, adding that most of the boys were too risky.

A motion was put forward at the last minute regarding sleeping arrangements for Teachers and Staff. All that got out before the meeting was interrupted was that the Science Lab, the Teachers' Lounge and the Home Ec. room after supper would be open to the Teachers.

At 3:40 PM the meeting was adjourned.

At 3:40 PM, Mara interrupted the emergency meeting to tell Ms. Bergen that the phones had gone out. She added to everyone present that she had only gotten up to the H's in parents before it happened.

"It should be all right, though," she added. "They know there's a storm. They'll have to hope for the best. They have eyes, they can see," she said, in her own defense. It wasn't her fault the phones had gone out.

Of course if she hadn't called Donald she would have gotten to the J's, but she couldn't help it. Even prisoners get one phone call.

13

It might have been a party, except for the fact that you couldn't really come or go as you pleased. It had been hours yet since the last person had come tumbling in the door, looking for all the world like a half-dead zombie—like the ones that used to be in the movies they showed at the Park Theatre before it shut down.

Oh, those zombies used to scare Natty. If she'd been a better-educated woman, like a university-educated Ms. Bergen, then she might have made the connection between the zombies who lived for only one thing maybe and the alcoholic monkey on her own back, but thankfully she wasn't. She could live in a healthy, connectionless world where things were exactly as they seemed. But when that last guy, Natty didn't know his name but had seen him around, came tumbling in the front door, he'd looked to Natty exactly like one of those zombies from the Park Theatre. She'd even given a little jump, and she hadn't been the only one, either. Some of the men at the next table jumped up too. But that had been hours ago, and no one had come in since.

Natty wasn't as drunk as she could have been, considering that she had been in the Northern Lights an entire day and some of the night. She hadn't even tried to leave. She never tried to leave, but usually at some point Ed got a little tired of her cadging drinks and told her it was time to go home. But Ed had hardly come near her except to drop off drinks at irregular and torturously few intervals. Her sick-hangover had long since left her and was being slowly replaced by another one. If she didn't get more drunk soon, she had a feeling that she would be sick. Someone would buy her a beer. For the hundredth time she thought about searching through all her pockets to come up with some change, and try the more honorable tactic of borrowing enough. She'd done that, though, and there was no more change. She rolled herself a Drum cigarette from the rapidly emptying pouch on the table.

She knew why no one had asked her to leave. She couldn't leave. No one could, because of the storm outside. Being stuck in a bar because of a storm seemed to Natty an amazing stroke of luck, and if she could get another beer, it really would be.

She checked around the room for new people. Maybe someone who had just come in. Through her dim alcoholic haze, Natty didn't think that many people had left, or any, maybe. Except Law-rinse and Chester, but that was a long time earlier. She scouted around the room, knocking people off her list of those who had bought her a beer and those who hadn't in search of someone to cadge from. It seemed to her everyone looked familiar, even if she didn't know their names. They, too, had been in the bar all day long.

Over in the back, sitting alongside the wall like some

throwback from the Old West, was Johnny Nahgauwah.
A million thousand years before, Natty and Johnny had
been schoolmates, but now he didn't even look at her
with anything resembling recognition, maybe because he
was Mayor Big Whup Johnny. In fact, if he got in her
general vicinity, he seemed to shrink up and slink away
as though Natty might actually care to tell anyone about
the time she let him have a kiss that time when they both
had to stay after school and the teacher, Mr. Purdue, left
the room. He had been some cute stuff in those days,
but since he didn't like to look at Natty, she hardly
looked at him. She had her standards, too.

The table next to her that had been filled with old
friends had broken up and moved closer to the pool
tables. There was a less than friendly game going on.
Three men were playing the table, probably eight ball,
the only game Natty understood, so she always assumed
that they were playing it. Natty had to squint to make
out who they were, partly from the booze, and partly
because her eyes were a casualty of her body. Hardly
Knowles, Teddy Bastion and Sammy Treherne were
playing. Sammy and Hardly were having a little dis-
agreement. She could hardly break up their game to ask
for a drink.

Just as it seemed futile for a while yet, and just as she
started to formulate a plan to get credit from Ed, the
table next to her was filled with the boys that weren't
playing pool anymore. She didn't know a one of them,
but that hadn't stopped her before. She smiled a bright,
gap-toothed smile at them. One of them was bound to
buy a girl a beer.

———

Ed Thibedeau looked at the clock and for the first time that whole day started to seriously wonder what the hell he was going to do with all these people.

It had been a profitable day, to say the least, and at first he'd been happy as a pig in shit—to quote his dear departed old mother—but things were starting to get out of hand. A handful of the folks in the bar were drunk past the point of removal. Fred Foley—and him from a good family and a man's gotta wonder what his mother was going to say to him—had just fallen over and took three goddamn tables with him not to mention the half-pints of beer and shots on them. It looked to Ed like it was maybe time to ask Sam Treherne and his buddy Hardly to take it easy, too. Just about all his regulars were there, having been in for most of the day. But a lot of folks were people he hardly ever saw, the twice-a-month folks, the once-in-a-while folks, some of them were in the bar. Most of those folks had come in out of the storm for refuge and found it in booze. There was no helping that: he couldn't exactly start throwing people out into the worst storm he'd seen in years. That Marilyn barely got herself into the department store made it for sure that this was one storm that was nothing to be laughing at. Therein lay the problem. What was he going to do with all these people?

He wished to hell he'd never made that deal with that principal lady, but what was she supposed to do with a bunch of hormone-happy teenagers, he supposed. But that took care of putting everybody up in the hotel. Those kids took up just about every damn room he had to offer. The girls at the hotel were on his case about it, too, talking overtime for the whole night—he supposed he'd have to give it too, so that school better come through with the money. He muttered a curse to himself, thinking of the hotel. He was no hotel man, and wouldn't be at all if it wasn't attached to his bar.

Ed had few morals regarding what some had called, just after he got his liquor license, the demon liquor. If a man, or a woman for that matter, wanted to get soused on his premises, they were certainly within their rights. A person needs to let go once in a while, and Ed was more than glad to provide the means. He had no problem with drunks. He didn't like cleaning up after the messy ones, and he didn't particularly like it when they got violent in the bar, but these things went hand in hand with letting off a little steam. Better a good, long, hearty drunk than a dead family. A few years back—ten or fifteen if he stopped to think about it, but seldom put dates or clocks on things except Last Call—a man up north a ways yet hammered his family to death. Now there was obviously something wrong there, that fellow had needed to let off a little steam. Perhaps if he had been a drinking man that family would be alive today. It wasn't his job to preach to the masses, even the masses of Bastion, that was some teacher's job. His was to provide a place to let off a little steam. He was a drinking man himself and although he seldom indulged at work, he was happy enough to spend Saturday afternoon in front of the TV working his way slowly through a twelve of Bud, his beer of choice. He thought that you could sure take the hard stuff, though. It gave him a terrible hangover.

A few choice customers were drinking on credit, and they were good ones too. The government didn't approve of such practices, but Ed didn't mind one bit. He was careful who he gave credit to, and since the mayor was here enjoying a bit of it, he didn't think he'd have to worry about the liquor inspectors just yet. No, he was making a bit of money, it was true. But the drinking ended at one sharp, that was Last Call, and Last Call was not exactly drinking on credit, it was a Major Fine and Loss of Premises if it was broken. But if he was stuck with a bunch of people who couldn't leave, how the hell was he going to cut off the drinking? He had to get these people out of the bar and somewhere else to sleep off their regrets.

"Sheeee-it," he muttered. He was as busy as shit to boot, and if he hadn't managed to slip out into the mall in the early afternoon and collar a couple of locals to help him, he would've been nearly at the end of his rope by this time. He sure hoped the customers were tipping because if he lost his help, he might just walk out himself.

The bar was filled to capacity, and that was something else. Except for fight nights, when he could get something in on the satellite, he was hardly ever filled up like this.

Ed wiped the bar off one more time and started filling the beer glasses in front of him.

"Here's four more, Cherry!" he shouted to the harassed red-haired girl giving him an eyeful of harried on her way over to a table full of people that should be cut off. He turned away from her evil looks; he'd pay her well for her work this day and close the bar for a day or so after. It had been a while since he'd worked this hard. If he'da had a wife, she'd be divorcing him for the mood he was going to be in in the morning.

"Sheee-it," he said. How the hell was he going to get

these people out of here, and better yet, out of here to where, exactly?

At the rate people were passing out, it might just be best to let sleeping dogs fall where they may, or however t'hell that saying went. It was starting to sound like a really good idea.

Ed was thinking about it while he poured another beer from the barrel, and was thinking too about how he'd have to get another one happening soon, when something big—something *huge*—smashed into the side of the building, like a bomb exploded, and he slopped the beer all over his hand and the floor.

"What the fuck was that?" someone cried out.

Ed dropped the half-empty mug to the floor where it hit with a crash and ran to the door. Most of the bar followed him.

"Move outa the way, you guys, lemme see," he said, pushing folks aside until he got to the big glass door. He gave it a yank and stepped into the little cubicle that separated the inside from the outside. Behind him, the bunch at the door squeezed in with him, everyone craning to get a look. They speculated loudly over whether it was a bomb or something hit the wall outside. Somebody laughed and said it was probably some poor duck got lost in the storm.

"One fuck of a big duck."

Ed pulled at the outside door, having to *really* yank on that one, thinking that the ice had got hold of the bottom. Maybe the top too. Ice coated along the bottom of the door kept him from opening it too far, and besides that, as soon as he opened it, too much of the storm started coming in.

"Back up, back *up*," he shouted to the guys pushing

behind him. He peered into the whiteout, *one bitch of a storm worse than—*

Under the howl of the wind he could hear a human voice, sounding like crying or choking, or something.

He gave everyone behind him a wave of his hand and a loud "Shhhh—" so he could listen. The silence lasted just long enough for him to hear it again.

But by that time, a huge, shambling figure had come into view, first vaguely, because it was so white-covered with the snow and bent up over itself like it was going to fall. It took Ed a second, but finally he recognized him.

"Oh, for goddamn chrissakes, Law-rinse, what the hell did you do to my—"

Ice on his face confirmed it for Ed. He had been crying.

"My god, Ed! Ed!" Lawrence cried and fell into Ed's arms. Ed stumbled and backed up. Behind him, people started grumbling and backing up.

Inside the bar someone called back, "Fucken Law-rinse drove the plow into the wall."

Ed dragged the man into the cubicle, and inside the bar, where the warmth hit him and brought him weaving to his feet. Everyone stared, alternately disgusted and amused, depending on how well they knew Lawrinse and how much their insurance was going to go up.

Ed's insurance was going to go up. "Goddamn, chrissakes—" he began again, but Lawrence cut him off.

"He's *dead*, Ed. Ches's *dead!*"

The bar fell silent, and Lawrence started a moan, a cry, genuine and frightening in the silence.

Ed got the man a chair and yelled for someone to pour him a whiskey. There he sat dripping melting snow on the barroom floor, telling a shocked bar full of half-drunks what had happened to Chester.

Behind them, the outside door stayed open about an inch and a half, clogged with ice and falling snow. The inside door pushed open and closed with the rhythm of the wind.

Once, many many years ago, Natty had seen a ghost. A real live ghost, out in a marshy area far behind her mother's house, sneaking behind the few trees that had tried hard to grow on the other side of the sloughy water. There had been a forest fire there, and the land around was just starting to come back, the trees still spindly and young. It had been about five miles from the old fort and she wondered ever since—whenever her mind was clear enough to remember the incident—if it had been someone from up there. There had been a lot of people die up that way.

She'd been about ten. That sloughy area was a good place to sneak off and get away from the house with fourteen people in it, most of them Natty's younger brothers and sisters, whose tender care was usually placed in her hands. Sometimes when she snuck up there she'd bring along a kid or two, and they'd smoke stolen cigarettes and talk about how much money they were going to have when they grew up and ran things, and how they were going to have meat every day for supper, and cake after, and how (Natty particularly) they were never going to have *any* kids. On the day she saw the ghost she had no witnesses with her, because—as she remembered now—she was in trouble with her mother for leaving one of the little ones alone when she'd been distracted by something outside. That little one had fallen and broken his arm. After school that day, knowing she was in trouble, she didn't bother going home, just snuck off to her spot.

She had been sitting on one of the big rocks that sat upright in the water, dipping her feet in and out, 'cause it was too cold to leave them in very long. She was smoking a cigarette too, one of her mother's and dry as dead grass because it had been stolen long before.

Out of interest sake, and because it gave her a peaceful feeling, she had been staring into the forest on the other side. She was thinking maybe she'd see a deer, or a wolf, or even a skunk. That was what she thought she saw, shadowy and slow from one tree to another. It was coming closer to her, still across the slight expanse of slough, but in her direction. As it got closer, Natty could see that it was a person, a man.

She called out, "Hey! Hello!" and the man was certainly close enough to hear, unless he was deaf, but didn't acknowledge her at all. She decided that maybe he was deaf, and jumped off the rock, into the cold slimy water, waving her hands, still calling. She thought he might be lost, because he looked to her like he was in town clothes, with his shirt all done up, and wearing shoes.

"Over here!" she called, and started to step closer to him. He was standing by one of the skinny trees, just standing there, sort of weaving back and forth. She noticed something else about him. He seemed kind of, almost, *see-through*. That was when Natty stopped waving and calling and started looking real closely.

He had on a blue shirt, and pants about the same color. This seemed to be more of an impression than an actual fact, because in actual fact she could see, behind him, the spindly trunks of trees and the determined underbrush giving way.

He was a ghost. She stood silent and still, staring at him, terrified that she would scare him away, he seemed so fragile and jumpy, like a doe. She was scared to move, as if standing still was the thing keeping him there, and one false move . . .

They stood that way for about fifteen minutes, with him moving side to side now and again, but mostly hovering, only fifteen feet or so from where Natty stood, her feet slowly freezing in the calf-high, cold, displaced water.

It was her family come finding her that chased the poor ghost away. They knew about her spot and when she'd turned up missing, her mother and three of her brothers came to the slough to flush her out and give her a licking. Even then, he didn't disappear suddenly, but just faded away, as though he had been thinking of leaving for several minutes and the time had just come up.

She tried at first to tell, but the licking was much more important to her mother than the ghost, and she gave up soon after. But she'd seen it, she'd seen a ghost.

That was why, after thinking about that ghost in the bar so many years later, she decided to believe Lawrence when he told what happened to Chester and apparently first to Ronnie.

Lawrence had tried to tell the story to a bar full of drunk, irritated people, stuck too long in one place, in a limited vocabulary, after a bad experience, with his own reputation as a drunk standing right in front of him. And he was sipping the whiskey while telling it. After the word *monster* had come out one too many times, people stopped assuming that he was talking about a murderer and started remembering who was doing the telling of this tale. They drifted away, disgusted, and Ed had told Lawrence he could stay but he couldn't drink.

"I can't get the authorities on the phone," Ed told Lawrence, pointing a finger at him, " 'cause the phones are down. But as soon as the lines are up again, I'm going to try, because I guess something *did* happen to Chester and that boy. But I'll tell you this: you better not be telling tales to the cops, because they'll lock you up!" And then Ed disappeared behind the bar. After that folks started looking at Lawrence like he was some piece of business, but later on were laughing at him. One boy came up behind the old man and yelled "Boo!" laughing to split a gut when Lawrence almost had a heart attack.

Natty felt terribly sorry for him. He was sitting at a center table, sipping the original whiskey, or at least bringing it up to his lips because the glass was dry. Having nothing to drink herself made Natty even sorrier for him, and she eventually picked up her empty draught glass and went to sit with him.

He had his face buried in his hands, his elbows propped up on the sticky table. When Natty put a hand on his shoulder to give it a pat, he jumped.

"I believe you, Lawrence," she told him. Then, in a spirit of generosity, she added, "I saw a ghost once."

"This weren't no ghost, Nat. This was a—" He searched for a word that it was, and came up empty. "This was a big black thing, like a shadow, looked sort of like a eel, or a . . . well shit, a *tadpole*. But meaner." It was the very same thing he had said earlier, and everyone had laughed.

"I think it ate him up—Ronnie, I mean," he went on. Natty hadn't laughed. "He looked all sucked out, his face just folded up and dry looking. I guess the same's gonna happen to Ches," he said, and gave a small, dry sob. "Poor Ches! He was just trying to help out Ronnie. When he saw him moving, you know, he figgered he was alive. I knew he wasn't alive, I just knew. Ches loved that boy like he was his own, I think. Might not a let on that was so, but I could tell. He was like my own *brother!*"

Natty leaned a little closer. "So what do you think it was, Lawrence?"

The old man thought deeply for a moment and finally shook his head slowly, an apologetic look settling. "I don't know. I just hope . . . you know, I figger one a them cops or somebody's gonna find their . . . them, and it's going to happen to *that* person too. I don't know what to tell them, old Ed says not to tell them what I told you, but what can I do about it? It's the truth! The god's honest, Natty!" He buried his face in his hands again and began to cry quietly, but in earnest. Something he'd said was sticking in Natty's mind.

His faltering story had painted a picture of sorts in her mind, and she reconstructed in a way that someone with a lesser imagination would not do. Something that he'd said struck a cord inside her foggy mind.

"Was it see-through?" she asked him suddenly.

"Yeah, I told you! Almost like a shadow, but it was black, you know, black," he said.

"Maybe it was a ghost," she offered. That explanation seemed more highly palatable to Natty since she'd seen one herself, and two made a story confirmable. "There are ghosts. I seen one."

"This wasn't no *ghost!* This wasn't no person float-

ing around mumbling or scaring. It was more like a
. . . I don't know! It was black, I tell you!"

"Maybe it was a black man's ghost," she offered.

"Too small to be a ghost. It was like the size of a
head, just a bit bigger, maybe." He was starting to perk
up somewhat, glad that someone was believing him. He
was beginning to see Natty as a comrade, a friend. He
leaned in closer to her.

"I just hope it didn't follow me back here," he told
her.

She nodded, not believing for a second that it did.

"You got any money, Law-rinse?" she asked. She
was getting dry. And her headache was coming back.
Lawrence reached into his back pocket, beginning to tell
her again how it all happened, how they went looking
for Ronnie's truck, but Natty by this time was distracted
by the prospect of a beer. She listened anyway, knowing
that this was sometimes the price of a beer. She forgot
about ghosts and listened the way she usually did, with
lots of nods and smiles.

When she went up to get her beer from the busy girl
who took over behind the bar while Ed did tables for a
while, she noticed the draft coming from the front
doors. She even mentioned it to the girl. The girl was too
busy to do anything about it yet. Besides, she thought
after, it was getting warm in there with all those bodies.
A little fresh air never hurt anyone.

14

The atmosphere was more like a slumber party than a crisis. People had been heard to remark that the mall looked more like a few days before Christmas, when everyone in town is out and about doing last-minute shopping. Gerry and Phyllis, husband and wife who ran the cafeteria, had set up a table—actually several tables pushed together—with coffee, tea and what looked like the day-old doughnuts they sometimes sold. There didn't seem to be any charge for them, and people were wandering around with styrofoam cups half-filled with coffee. Groups of people were mingling, chatting in excited tones, or hushed tones, or everyday tones, whatever befitted the conversation they were having. Town folks were sitting on the benches provided for them by courtesy of the mall, a number of them, sometimes six or seven, close together, not the maximum of three that you would see on an average morning in the mall. Most people, even people that knew each other as well as the people of Bastion knew each other, usually left a good bit of space between their neighbor and them when they sat to have a smoke.

Gerry was sitting with Samuel Burton and having a smoke. He'd given up smoking at least a year before, but it was a special occasion. Samuel had closed up shop and made his way across the street when things had started to look real bad, about noon, and had spent the rest of the day in the mall. A lot of people had wandered in when things had started to look bad, and such was the way of the small northern community.

Lynn Lake, the lady that ran the notions and craft store on the other side of the mall, was sitting with a pile of cross-stitch in her lap, not touching it, and talking earnestly with Betty, one of the students working in the department store on her school work-experience. No one noticed what they were saying, but to the casual observer, they looked like mother and daughter, perhaps having a serious conversation about sex.

Kelly, the other girl working in the department store (Betty was her best friend, and she often got called Veronica because they were always together, like the comic book girls), was talking to Calamar, the girl who used to be plain Janet but changed her name, and so when you thought of her, in your mind you thought Janet/Calamar, and Calamar usually came out unless you were over forty and she made allowances for such things. Calamar sold a brand-name makeup privately and that was obviously what the two girls were talking about since Calamar was touching Kelly's face at intervals, with a serious look about her.

Over in the corner of the mall, Jake Freisen from the Economymart and the man that stocked shelves there—Roger—were having a coffee and counting people for the heck of it. Jake was a very organized man. At home he had his workshop tools numbered and outlined in magic marker; everything had a place and everything in its place. His wife, a big, fat bossy woman, sometimes borrowed things and just put them on the workbench when she was done. When she did this, Jake would stomp into the house and drop the tool/scissor/knife into the wastebasket and promptly go out and buy a new one. A big-city shrink would probably say that this was the way Jake dealt with stress, or that he was compulsive; people around Bastion just figured he hated his wife: most people did.

The mall was rampant with odd couples and strange bedfellows, but that was the way things were when something odd or strange happened. What mattered at that point was that people were bolstering each other up and keeping the faith. Everyone thought like this: it would all be over in a few hours, and why not enjoy the company, especially if the coffee's free?

Larry Talgart owned the Variety Store, the store that sold cigarettes, combs, lotto tickets and newspapers, and he was standing and talking with a group of men. Every now and again one of them would wander into the store and take a slug of something. It was hardly noticed, except that they were getting bombed. It was sort of funny, since it was really still quite early in the evening, a fall evening, even though the light from the mall windows—there were quite a lot of them—had faded and left a long time ago. It might have been midnight in the middle of winter.

A few people had been wondering about things, such as what happened to Marilyn, because most everyone had either seen or heard that Don had to carry her from

the front door of the store over to the beds in the furniture department to lie down, and that she'd been hyster-
ical/unconscious/hypothermic (depending who you
talked to). Everyone agreed that maybe she was sick.
Rumors about what that no-good drunk Lawrence had
been up to were running around too, but far more interesting than that was the fact that the principal was using
tax-payers' money to put those children up in the *hotel*
for the night because she apparently thought the children of Bastion were raised with loose morals. There
was a lot to talk about, in any case, and so far everyone
was getting along just fine. Some people thought it was
the most fun they'd had in years.

That's what people were *saying*. Every now and
again a laugh sounded forced. Folks still left the middle
of conversations, where people would stand in a groups
of two or three, coffees in hand like at a cocktail party,
and wander over to the set of four glass doors and look
outside. They saw mostly nothing, if you could call the
tall drifts that had come to settle against the doors and
walls nothing. There were the swirls of falling snow, but
you had to look up, at the top of the door where there
was still some glass that hadn't been covered over with
the piles. Earlier, if you had stepped out into the foyer
that separated the two doors, where folks would normally wait for their rides, out of the cold, some people
said you could hear the tap-tap of the flakes hitting the
glass if you listened closely. It was not a soft snow anymore; it was ice-hard, the kind of snow that would tickle
on your face at first, and then hurt, and after enough
time would begin to feel like little pellets of glass. They
knew this from experience, because who in Bastion
hadn't been caught in a snowstorm at one time or an-

other? It was a claustrophobic place, and a worse sound. People didn't listen long.

Underneath the party sounds, the laughing and gossiping, was a feeling a growing unease. Even an hour ago, some people were thinking that they still might make it home, that the snow would let up, that the plows would magically appear outside the doors of the mall and everyone would go home, joking about being stuck for hours and hours inside a mall.

Because they were in a mall, a number of people felt compelled to buy things. One lady, Margie Wilks, clutched and guarded four bags of non-essential items purchased at regular intervals throughout the day. She would wonder about them; she wondered what she was going to do with a Thighmaster, being sixty-five and the prospect of thin thighs long behind her; she thought she might give it to one of her daughters for Christmas. She also wondered if her husband really needed sweat socks, since he worked in the bank and wore black socks or brown ones, depending on his suit for the day. There were always the weekends, she supposed, paying $5.99 plus taxes for them. She had bought a fancy wreath in the craft store, and a set of coloring books in the Drugs. The coloring books were better, they could be used and reused by her grandchildren when they visited. Her bags didn't bother her quite so much as the little brown bag, right beside her own. It contained her friend's favorite face cream and a package of Juicy Fruit gum. Margie had peeked. Her friend, Emily, had forgotten the bag, hours ago when she stepped out into the storm, telling everyone she just had to try and get home because she was caring for her mother, a woman of eighty, who forgot things and couldn't be left alone too long. She had left, oh, four hours before. Margie had called her just before the phones went out to tell her she'd forgotten her bag. There had been no answer.

She looked at the bag now, meaning, every time she did, to put it inside one of her own, so it wouldn't be misplaced in the kerfuffle that was this day. Emily only lived two blocks from where they were. *Four hours she's been gone.*

She looked at that bag a little funny, like it might be evidence, or at least the last things bought by a dead woman. So far she hadn't mentioned this to anyone.

Emily hadn't been the only one to try to make it home before nightfall. There were others that had gamely struggled out into the storm, cracking jokes about search parties and wishing people luck, some even asked if they could check on so-and-so, it's on your way home, just see if my windows are shut, if it's too far the door's open, etc. These people were viewed as sort of foolish sort of brave. When the doors had opened and closed on these people, the others left in the mall had the feeling that they were making a mistake. No one said that, because it was a stupid remark. The most that could happen was getting lost, or falling and breaking a hip. There were houses all along the way; people were wise enough to stop in and stay if they thought that things were too hairy outside. This was a winter town, and people knew how things were.

Most folks thought it was better to stay. The mall was warm, there was food, and there were friends and neighbors around to ward off the feelings of claustrophobia and nerves. For instance, it was pretty dark out, seemed almost *black*. That was setting some people to wondering. If one fretted too long, and was so inclined, you could have a drink over in Larry's shop, but he had to know who you were, and they were still keeping it pretty much under wraps. If you got bored, you could pick up a magazine or newspaper and read, as a lot of people were doing. Most weren't thinking about the prospect of sleeping in the mall just yet, and anyway, Joe was in charge and he was a heck of a good man. He would figure something out. Already a lot of people were turning to him and asking if he'd heard about this or that, and he was doing his best to keep people informed. He was setting up a meeting.

By four-thirty, the mall was very active. The school had given the children a one-hour break, during which the younger ones would be subjected to the supervision of the older children. The whole lot of them were under express orders to remain in the mall at all costs. Candace had circulated a memo, passed out by one of the highschool students, asking shopkeepers and all other adults in the mall to please be on the watch to make sure children did not leave the mall. Junior salesclerks were given the odious duty of acting as "security" at the mall doors, some so remote that the clerks hadn't even known they existed. By three-forty-five, all were at their posts. Troublemakers were being kept in the school, given jobs of responsibility, in order to protect them from themselves. They were not pleased, since a band of older kids had decided to break out, moments before being collared on cafeteria duty or some other trumped-up job. Everyone, so far, was present and accounted for.

Joe had spoken briefly to Candace and they discussed the children. A number of parents were in the mall, and some were with their children over the break and were expecting them to stay with them through the night.

"I think things would go a bit smoother if all the children were kept together," Candace told him. There were about six mothers and two fathers who had their children with them. Joe was thinking by then in terms of sleeping arrangements.

"We've organized the gym into games and some of the others are doing crafts and skits, and that should keep them occupied and happy until it gets later," she added. Joe agreed. It was going to be a job and a half just to settle the big folks in and he had an idea that a lot of people weren't going to sleep for much of the night. It would be better to keep the kids where they could at least get some shut-eye.

"I'll talk to them. I'm sure they'll agree," he said. "I want to assure myself of just one thing, though. And that is that the kids stay the responsibility of the school and the mall will take care of these folks. Hope that doesn't sound cold, but I'm going to have my hands full . . ."

"Agreed. Just as long as I can count on you for help if something comes up," she said.

"You bet. You need anything, you come to me. One thing, how's everyone on your side set up for sleeping stuff, you know, blankets, pillows, that sort?"

"We might end up using towels stuffed into pillow-cases because there's not a lot extra. But we have the boys with sleeping bags in the gym. I think we have enough, but it hasn't really been confirmed yet. Any extra on your side if we need?"

"Not much. Sorry."

She turned to go, stepped out of his office into the stairwell, suddenly remembering.

"Jesus! I came to ask for volunteers. We're going to need maybe four people for exit duty in the school, and maybe two others for in the hotel."

"There's your answer right there, lady. Use the parents," he said.

"Good, right. I'll go talk to them now. Thanks, Joe." She stepped quickly and effectively down the stairs.

Joe watched her through the high window, stepping down when he saw her approach the first parent, with a six- or seven-year-old boy on her lap. He liked to see something through to its completion.

Over his shoulder, on the table in the corner, was a citizens-band radio, with a hook-up to the police unit in Altman. He'd had it on for most of the day, and the cops there were certainly aware (that was how they put it, "We're *certainly* aware of your situation there, Joe") of the storm and everybody stuck in the mall. He'd mentioned the folks stuck in the bar, knowing how those guys like to bust up the bar once in a while, but had gotten little reaction, just the usual and obvious there's a storm going on, what do you want us to do, *float* over there? That had been hours ago. Now the radio sat silent for the most part, with only bursts of static coming through, like a live wire. He hadn't been able to rouse anyone over there. He thought maybe a new doughnut shop had opened up, or they were in the middle of a game of four-card.

He tried once more. "Breaker! This is the Mall-borough Man at the Shopping Box, come back?" He waited while tantalizing static came and went. No response.

It was time to rally the troops. A dinner meeting with

the guys that owned shops in the mall. He'd check out Don first, and they could get the rest of the shop people in the cafeteria. They had a table booked. Phyllis was going to sit in for the café, leaving Gerry the overwhelming job of cooking for the masses. He chuckled, wondering how had she swung that.

On his way down he took one last look at the radio, and heard its static and hoped that those guys took a piss break and remembered that there were a whole bunch of people stuck in the storm.

The cafeteria was as busy as could be expected. Some of the teachers had decided against the food cooked by the kids and had taken their respite in the café. The end of a massive lineup at the counter was just beginning to disperse and a number of people that hadn't been able to get seats had taken their food into the mall. Every table was full, but true to her word, Phyllis was jealously guarding a table in the back against the wall, large enough to accommodate Joe's meeting. She was sitting in the first chair, with one arm spread across the table to the other side, her whole posture proclaiming "These seats are taken," and you wondered how far she'd go if someone tried to sit in one of the chairs. No one was chancing it, anyway.

"Phyl!" Joe called to her. "You look like a bear with cubs."

Everyone sat down with their food, a mix of burgers and meatloaf, the special. Joe smelled like whiskey, but aside from a slightly red nose, he didn't appear incapable of thinking, and besides he usually had a red nose and smelled of whiskey.

He started by saying, "Listen, this is no big deal, I

just want to make sure that everyone is together on a
number of things so that there isn't mass confusion out
there later. There's a couple of other things that should
be worked out, like say contingency plans in the case of
an emergency, who's going to borrow what from whom
and the returning and stuff. Also plans for credit and
that sort of thing. Larry, I know that you've been giving
credit to people on cigarettes and things, and I guess
that's personal, but I hope you're keeping track. We got
a long night ahead of us and I don't want things to get
out of hand, and I don't want anybody whining in two
weeks' time about how this cost that and that was this—
you guys know what I mean. First off, to get it out of the
way, let's figure out a game plan for everybody to get
some shut-eye."

A tally of beds (from the department store), cots
(same, except Larry had one in back and the drugstore
kept a cot for customers in the throes of insulin shock
and stuff, never used) and blankets, pillows, sleeping
bags was discussed.

"We've got a few sleeping bags, and a couple of air
mattresses," Don told them. "But this is end of the season for that stuff, so it's limited. We also have those
blow-up pillow things for in the shower—"

"I always wondered what you did with those things
in the shower," Jake said with a leer. "How about tell us
that, Don?"

He laughed. "Maybe later. But those could be used
for pillows. My only problem is that using this stuff
makes it second-hand, and I'd rather not discuss what
head office is going to say when I tell them about our
little 'emergency' here."

Joe passed it off with a wave of his hand. "They got

insurance. Ahh, just tell those people to talk to me, they been behind in their rent before, I can pull some rank."

"Okay, any medical emergencies that anybody know of? Anybody gonna freak out without their medication, any epileptics, any diabetics, any really old people about to expire?"

That made Don think of *Emma hit her head in the shower fell coming up the walk broke my house burned down cooking supper—Emma and where was she right then?*

If he was home, if this had been a normal day, he would be in his living room right now, the news on the tube; the kids would be fighting in one of the bedrooms and he would be waiting until it escalated before going and breaking it up. He might decide to have a beer and get up from his chair during the commercial, going into the kitchen. Emma would be at the stove, her back to him, stirring something, thinking about things, what she did that day, what she would do the next. Her body would be moving slightly with the stirring, and maybe she'd jiggle a bit in her jeans, a little tighter with the weight gained last winter. Maybe he'd step up behind her and surprise her with a hand on her breast; she'd jump and tell him to stop that, she was cooking supper. But she'd turn around and slip her arms around his belly (a little looser with the weight gained last winter) and hug him back. He'd probably whisper something obscene in her ear about what he was going to do to her later, but he wouldn't do it later. But she knew the joke and would dare him to try. He'd go to the fridge and get his beer, offering her one, and she'd say no, or maybe yes; the news would be coming back on by then, and he'd maybe give her a pinch on his way past. It was how the evening went at their house. Normal, suddenly wonderful, cozy, warm.

He drifted further away from the meeting, keeping only half an ear on Lynn Lake droning on about old people sleeping in the beds because they'll get piles sleeping on the concrete floors in the mall. No spring chicken herself, Lynn Lake.

Emma could have got stuck at a friend's place, Don thought. She could have been like most of the people that got stuck, waiting for it to pass, and by the time she realized it wouldn't, she *would* be stuck and the phones were out by then.

But she would have kept in regular contact. She would have called anyway, just because of the kids. Whatever her faults she was a damn good mother. It didn't add up. She might not have called if they'd had a fight, or at least left it until later, but they hadn't. Everything had been as usual this morning. An image rose in his mind, of his wife standing at the coffee-maker pouring coffee, in her robe, the smell of coffee in the air, the kids making noise at the table.

Then another image. A stupid, defeating image came to him suddenly and unbidden, of her lying dead on the floor in the kitchen, the morning coffee cup in her hand, spilled all over, her eyes glazed but open, somehow admonishing him. *You could save me and you* aren't.

Christ!

He hadn't even thought of it and felt like a coward and an idiot for it.

"Hey! Does anybody keep a snowmobile here? Anybody?" Six pairs of eyes and six mouths turned toward him, one pressed tightly shut, annoyed. He'd interrupted

Carole the drugstore lady in a litany of the ills of those present in the mall.

"Sorry," he said, red-faced.

"I think Ed's got an Arctic Cat behind the bar," Joe said. "But you'd never get to it, man. It'll be under twenty feet of snow. Besides, the medical help is all here. No one's going to get so bad that we'll have to get them out, if that's what you're thinking." From the distant look on Don's face, Joe realized that probably wasn't what he was thinking. He said, "Man, you'd have to be Indiana Jones to get home in this weather, and Indy you ain't."

"No, no. I was just wondering," Don said.

The picture of Emma hurt and alone wouldn't go away. His dinner continued uneaten in front of him, spoiled by his cowardice. Or was it cowardice, he wondered. Was he afraid of traveling through the snow, rushing home against gale winds, in blinding snow, only to get there and find . . . Did he believe she was hurt, or did he already know something, and was *he* hurt? The thought shocked and surprised him, unprepared as he was to start thinking of truths, the truth being what exactly? That she was having a . . . *don't even think the word.*

His face set itself in a stern line. He would hope she was fine, *believe* that she was fine. And if he couldn't stand it any longer, there was the option of giving the snowmobile in Ed's back shed a try. He wouldn't be foolish. There were people here who needed him too.

Don tried to focus on the meeting, and at intervals did an admirable job. But mostly the voices droned and faded, just a voice-over to the pictures in his mind of his wife, hurt, or worse, not alone.

———

Everything was running smoothly. The home ec. lab had been set up into a makeshift diner, and what's better was the kids were having fun cooking and serving. The breaks were all over now, and several of the teachers were in the gym and the multi-purpose room setting up for games and distractions. Two more were helping the hotel girls put extra cots in rooms at the hotel. Everyone was setting up for the long night.

Candace had about a half an hour in which to do little things that had to be done in her office. She was keeping a detailed log of the whole experience, both for her own records to be viewed through the clearer lenses of retrospect, and for the board, which would surely want to see a detailed log. While there she checked the phones, to see if they were still dead. It was such a strange dead, hollow sound that she listened for a moment, remembering a prank call she'd had once in the city, where the phone rang and when she picked it up, the person on the other end just . . . listened. It had the same hollow sound as the dead phone, and she found herself listening for the breathing that would come at the other end.

She left her purse in the drawer and locked up the office. Before attending to her clean-up shift in the kitchen (she'd taken a dirty job hoping to win points with some of the staff that didn't want to be there) she would go around the school and check all the exits for kids smoking, kids necking, kids hanging out.

Unlike in the morning when Candace arrived, all the lights were on in the halls. It still seemed to her, though, if she used her imagination, she could go back and be in the same place. It seemed like morning, because of the darkness outside the windows, the echo of her shoes on the tiled floors, and the empty hallways. She had the same eerie, alone feeling she sometimes got, a little bit jumpy; she stopped and listened. When she did, she could hear, faintly, the sounds of pots clanging from the home ec. lab, and people talking.

She had been a Candace all her life; no Candy for her. Her parents, both retired school teachers now living on the coast, had been strict but warm. There had been little physical affection, but lots of praise for achievement. One replaced the other quite well and the only hangover from childhood that Candace had was an apologetic uncomfortable feeling for physical affection. Not that she was standoffish, just uncomfortable. In her personal life she was a warm, giving person, like her mother, and at the office she was a hardworking, efficiently organized person, like her mother and father. She had little patience for illness, in herself or others, since she never got sick. If someone else was sick, if a teacher called in ill, her first response was to assume they were goldbricking. Who couldn't work with a little cold? It was also difficult for her to imagine real misery, having never truly experienced any. She hadn't been a popular girl in school, nor had she been particularly special in the peak years. She'd always been just a little bit uncomfortable, burying herself in schoolwork, using that as her niche in society. She never felt like she'd necessarily missed out on anything, but she never really felt like a big part of anyone or anything, either. A lot of girls at school reminded Candace of herself. A little on the edge of things, trying too hard to fit in some hole, finding one finally and pursuing it with gusto, or never finding one at all, and finally no longer looking.

Misery had not really been a part of her life. Not real misery. Outside of a broken heart (not something she wanted to think about now) when she was still in her twenties, she'd led a charmed, if conservative, life. Misery was foreign. But she was learning an awful lot more about it since she had been a principal.

The city school that had given Candace her first job as principal was typically—for first principals—in the worst part of the city. Abuse and neglect were as common as kids getting a cold, and the real disasters were kids bringing weapons to school, and threatening teachers, girls as young as thirteen getting pregnant, drugs that helped or hindered kids in the daily grind, which as often as not included substance-abusing parents, grandparents, neighbors and family friends. Assault and rape were not unheard of in the halls of the school, and permanent damage done by assault to some eleven- or twelve-year-old kid was more or less taken in stride by parents and administration.

Hardest to deal with wasn't the fighting or the assaults, or the violence. It had been the little kids. It was hard to see anything innocent in the faces of the older kids; most of them were simply mouthy and full of bad attitude. She could hardly stand them some days (and was sometimes even a little afraid). The little ones, though, who had troubled older brothers and sisters in the school, were the hardest to take. They came to school with a certain amount of respect for it that she knew they would lose in time. The little ones sometimes showed up silent and withdrawn, late for school, maybe a fresh bruise or two. It always came as a surprise. And the school's hands were mostly tied. It was the law that she report it, but seldom did anything come of it. Worse,

she knew that given a few years, she wouldn't be able to stand the little ones either because by that time they would be newer versions of their bigger brothers and sisters. She'd had enough misery by the time she left and took the reins at Bastion. She'd been ready for a change, a small-town kind of change where the worst thing that happened was someone failed their exams. That hadn't been the case, of course, but it had been better. Even much better.

She almost didn't check the last exit. The last exit was used only in fire drills, it was so far back in the building, in between a maintenance closet and the room used for storing desks and equipment. That exit was down a corridor, all by itself, and it would be darker and quieter than the others. Efficiency won out.

Not expecting to find a thing, her eyes flicked up and down the hallways. The exit was two double doors with a foyer passage, like the others. It was in shadow. She decided to go all the way through so that she would feel the task was completed.

Candace walked briskly to the door, gave a hard push on the horizontal bar and barely poked her head in to give a cursory glance at the snow-covered outside doors.

That's when she saw a kid, a boy or a girl, she couldn't tell at first, sitting with knees pulled up to the chest, head down, as though sleeping, or crying. Maybe just hiding.

"Hey—"

A girl lifted her head, listlessly looking up, almost without interest.

"You get your butt—"

It was Shannon Wilson, who wasn't at school today.

The girl's eyes opened wide, and they were rimmed with red, like she'd been crying hard and was only taking a break.

"Shandy? What happened?" She didn't even seem to understand the question, because she was just looking up at Candace, blankly, with a horribly pathetic, hurt look. Candace bent down and took one of her arms, giving her a soft tug up. Shandy moved robotically, on the command. When she was standing, Candace repeated the question. "What happened?"

Shandy choked, a gagging sound came out. She shook her head.

There was a draft coming under the doors in the foyer, and Candace led the two of them out, still guiding Shandy by the arm. She followed easily, like putty. The door closed sharply behind them.

Still holding on to the girl, Candace asked if she was all right and then asked what she was doing at school. Through it all, Shandy just looked at her, her mind seemingly a million miles away. Candace thought about giving the girl a shake, just to set her thinking straight, all sorts of horrors running through her mind, the child could have been raped, beaten, hit by a car with all that snow, hypothermic, oh god—Candace ran her hands up and down the girl's arms, feeling for what, she did not know—until Shandy finally showed some animation. She started to cry again. She fell against Candace with a terrible sob.

"It's my fault! It's all my fault!" was all she could get out of the girl. Holding on to her (uncomfortably), Candace led her toward one of the rooms where they could sit down and she could calm her. She mumbled unintelligible comfort noises, as her mother would have when she was a child, and patted her on the side. The best she could do.

No, the best Candace could do is fix whatever happened. And she had a good idea what exactly happened, the obvious facts in front of her: disturbed girl, new boyfriend, too much alone time on their hands on a cozy stormy afternoon. Fixing it would begin with a report to the police. Whatever boy did this to her—and she had a pretty good idea which boy it was—is going to get it. She would see to that.

15

Marilyn shifted uncomfortably on the display bed in the department store. She was still asleep, although she didn't know this. Inside of her mind, Marilyn was forty miles away from the department store. She was just outside Bastion town limits, in the yard of her childhood home. She was dreaming, but also didn't know this.

Dream-Marilyn was standing in the back yard, which was really nothing more than a field. Although she hadn't been a child in thirty years, she was one in her dream. A child in her present, grown-up body. It was late summer, and the field still had many of the wildflowers blooming; she was picking them. All around her were the smells of fall coming, the earth smelled rich, as though gathering all of the summer life within itself, preparing for a long winter. The air carried a faint whiff of dead things, the moldering leaves that were beginning to blanket the yard; the wind was turning cooler, in spite of the sun. As she picked the flowers the blooms dried and fell off, so that all that was left in her hand was a gathering of stems, brown and stiff. She kept picking, hoping that one would stay together.

From far away, farther away than the house behind her, she heard her mother call.

She moved effortlessly, in dream-motion, to the sound of the voice. *Coming mama I'm coming.*

As though she had never been in the field, she found herself suddenly in the house of her childhood. Everything was the same. In the corner there was the giant wood stove, still giant, in spite of her grown-up body. Heat came off it, it had been lit summer and winter, making the kitchen sometimes an unbearable place to be even though her mother seldom left it. *Mama,* she said now, *don't light the stove it's too hot let's eat cold.*

But on this day, with the winter coming over the back with the wind, it felt good. Marilyn went close to the stove, and inside, through the notch where the burner plate was lifted, she could see the orange tongues of fire. Her mother called her Mary-girl, the only one to call her that in many years.

Mary-girl come over here.

Oh mama I'm so cold I want to stay by the fire.

You'll have your fill of fire soon, girl. Come by me, I have to show you . . . Except of course her mother was dead. Even though she hadn't seen her in many years, she didn't really want to get too close to her, as though going and standing near the old woman would force a commitment to whatever it was the old woman was trying to tell Marilyn. For there was something, it was in the air of the dream, a nearly palatable sense of something . . . coming. Something cold. That was thinking coming from the conscious mind of Marilyn, and the dream-Marilyn wanted to go to her mother. But it was so warm by the stove.

Her mother sat at the huge wooden table. Seven teacups were set at seven places for her and her father and brothers and sisters. Her mother sat with one cup, and it was half full of tea.

See in here Mary-girl. Tea leaves floated and sunk inside the brown tea. The warmth was on Marilyn's back now, and she wanted so badly to turn around and get to that warmth, but her mother was speaking to her and she listened.

The tea was gone, leaving only the leaves, looking exactly like the leaves covering the ground outside the window.

See in here Mary-girl.

Oh mama you don't tell fortunes.

You listen to your mother.

Her mother didn't tell fortunes, but used to tell Marilyn about the time she had her tea leaves read at the fair. The lady told her that she would have five children and lo and behold! didn't she just.

You don't tell fortunes.

I'm your mother and I'm telling you something you listen.

Mary-girl-Marilyn stared down into the teacup at the leaves. She could see no pictures there. She could only feel the heat at her back.

Her mother tapped a fingernail on the rim of the teacup, and the sound was like bells, or *was* a bell, a big brass one like the one in the church or the one . . . There was a bell another place, and her numb and fuzzy dream-brain couldn't grasp the where.

Her mother stopped tapping and pointed out the

window that looked over the back yard. The back yard was gone. In its place was a huge building of stone and steel bars, like a prison. It tickled in Marilyn's dream memory.

Her mother told her. *Go Mary-girl out there now.*

Marilyn shook her head *no,* trying to *say* it, but her mouth wouldn't open. Her mother kept pointing. She reached out to take her mother's arm, because she didn't want to go, but her mother's arm seemed elusive, not there.

Something I'm showing you now listen to me girl. And then Mary-girl, understanding that she had to go and see, stepped up on the big kitchen table. She could hear the cups rattle in the saucers. Climbing on the furniture a forbidden thing, yet the Marilyn in her grown-lady-clothes, but a child still, climbed without admonishment, and stepped through the glassless window into what used to be the back yard of her childhood home but really just a field.

She hit the ground with a thud, and the hard earth sent a jolt through her body. It was frozen, the ground hard and cold against the palms of her hands; she steadied herself and stood. She looked back over her shoulder, to get a glimpse of her mother one last time (*bye mama*), but the house was gone. A wall was in its place, a wall of solid stone, the limestone readily found around her house.

A feeling of dread overcame her, and she put her hands against the wall, hoping to push it away and see her house, see her mother again.

In her sleep, Marilyn stirred restlessly, a moan slipping through her throat, although her mouth stayed shut. She turned over in her sleep as the dream-Marilyn turned around to face a line of soldiers walking in a circle, all around the inside of the wall. As the line of them approached where she stood, she joined them. She went around and around with them, getting dizzy and feeling trapped. She tried to speak with them; they couldn't hear her over the roar of the fire? wind? It was cold. She huddled in her own arms, and it started to snow. The snow built up fast around them all, but the men marched on, regardless of the depth of the snow. Marilyn straggled, wondered at all the snow, the sky turning orange from the . . . The walls were on fire.

Marilyn screamed. When she did, hearty and loud, the men turned toward her, noticing her for the first time. Their eyes looked into her, *inside* her. They crowded around her.

Marilyn oh Marilyn, and she recognized the voices, amused, contemptuous they were *chuckling* as they said her name.

It was the voices she heard in the snow. She opened her mouth wide, to scream again, and could feel the heat of the flames in her throat, scoring it raw; she couldn't make a sound. One of the men came closer.

Mary-girl Marilyn don't be afraid stay and talk to us you must stay and talk and he reached out his hand to touch her except he didn't touch her he put his hand on her mouth, his body changing, elongating, darkening; a man no more, he turned black, solid, flat. Then it was going *inside* her to where its voice could be heard and finally she found she could scream and she did as loudly as she could and under that sound her mother, *go on now girl.*

Marilyn woke, not screaming, but with her own

hand clamped against her mouth, closing it off completely, only to hear another voice, an older one.

Mary-girl you listen to your mother.

Shandy was sitting in the science lab, all the way across the mall complex, telling Candace (Herr Bergenmeister, poor David) what had happened to her outside in the storm.

She started by telling just the bare facts, leaving out as many details (that only she could know) as possible. But the details snuck in. They snuck in slowly. And as they did, Shandy felt compelled, almost, to tell it all.

It was so freeing to tell everything: about who she was and where she came from and what she saw that no one else did. It was almost like a confession: cleansing, as though once told, she wouldn't have to be the only one to carry the heavy load.

At first everything came out garbled and unconnected, protected facts, surrounded by fences of sharp barbed wire, it seemed to her, because she was so used to *not* telling, the telling of it was hard. As it unfolded, she *had* to tell, and that somehow made it easier.

She told it all: the ladies, the "tell me something," the followers, her mother, the leftovers, her uncle, her auntie Ellen, her father gone and forgotten, auras, the constant, unrelenting knowing, the knowing the bad stuff mostly, the letters the phone calls the car the bomb the deciding to never, never tell (and what her mother would say if she knew Shandy was telling), her mother going on forever until Shandy could hardly see anymore the light not going on at her place that night in her mind; she told until she was exhausted and through it all she could hear—as she could always, she just shouldn't look—the tiny, hidden thoughts in Candace's mind that told her in turn that she would believe her.

She told her everything, what happened to David, what she *saw* happen to David; she told everything, except what she saw while she ran to the school, what she knew after she sat in the foyer, trying not to think, trying not to see what she already saw; not to see any more of it.

Finally, Shandy stopped talking. In between the two of them hung all the unbelievable words Shandy had offered up to Candace to believe. The silence after all of the words seemed very silent indeed. Too tired to look inside Candace (besides, she already knew), she just said, "You believe me, don't you." She said it as a statement, a little in awe that someone might *really* believe her. What surprised her was what Candace said.

"No."

Yes you do!

Confused beyond asking, Shandy did what she always did: she poked around inside Candace's head and saw a boy, a young man, and a car, a flash of something bad, and nothing else, because it was shut away good from her. One thing remained certain: under all the not-believing was the believing. It made Shandy angry, and just a little embarrassed, because she was only fifteen and she told a secret and now the returning secret was being denied. Like a fifteen-year-old, she argued.

"Yes, you do, I know you do," she said, mouth suddenly set, ready to pout, or hit maybe.

"Shandy, I believe that you had a terrible experience," Candace started.

Barry.

"But I think that what happened to David and your experience in the storm has made you—"

have a car accident

"—more upset than you know. I think maybe you fell asleep—"

at the wheel

"—and you dreamed . . ." She trailed off, other things on her mind; remembering the young man.

Shandy's eyes went wide. There it was. While Candace talked, Shandy poked in her head. And saw it.

"You do know. You know because you—dreamed about . . . Barry? And you *knew!* And it happened!" After letting the facts and her *knowing* of them speak for themselves, she added, more confidently, "Like me."

Candace flushed, unable just then to speak in any case, full as she suddenly was with the image of the young man, as young as herself then. They were both in school, and wildly in love. She was a dorm student, with a roommate, and her roommate was out of town. She even told him about it, because they were in love, and she told him *everything,* even the dirty dreams she'd had as a young girl, no more than five. About going fishing and swimming naked with the boy who lived down the block *oh you dirty girl* he said and laughed and they said they were going to go swimming/fishing naked and make love after she'd turned red because he hadn't seen her all the way naked yet but they never went because he . . .

Shandy heard her thoughts, not heard exactly because it was never that way, just picked up some of the pictures and all of the feelings. The feeling she got most of all was of course horrible grieving; sick sad, because it seemed to be the way it worked. The bad feelings were clearer than the good.

Candace didn't cry exactly, because it had all happened so many years before. But the fact was, she hadn't thought of it in years, either. Somewhere in her house was a T-shirt, white and never washed, probably quite yellow by now, that he had left at her house. A silly romantic thing. A long time ago, she had slept with it. A remembrance about a boy she might have married was too romantic for practical Candace. The girl who had cried then would have cried now, but that girl probably disappeared sometime between the funeral and the year after that. But now, so many years later, the grown Candace did feel like crying; that was something. Her eyes felt hot and full. If she wasn't going to let herself cry, one thing she did let herself feel is what it had been like to be twenty. She told.

"Brad. His name was Brad. He was my . . . boyfriend, I guess. But it wasn't like that. I felt like he was my . . . I'm not going to tell all of this."

"You don't have to," Shandy said simply. They looked at each other, for a telling moment.

It was just a dream.

You knew.

"If I believe you," Candace began, slowly, "then I have to believe that I could have stopped him. That I really knew, and yet I didn't make him stay, or walk."

He'd been asleep in her arms, or she in his, they were tangled with each other. But it was a dorm room and her roommate was coming back on the early bus, he had to go. They'd made love until the morning and he was so tired. She didn't wake him; he was a responsible man. He woke himself up and had to go, he said. Candace was foggy with sleep, but just before he left, seconds before she could have said stop, she thought about her dream, a twisted car, a sleeping dark head a broken—

"I'm sorry," Shandy said. She thought about David for a minute and compared the two, and found her own first love experience lacking. David seemed now, not so long after, just something that had happened to her. To Candace, her Brad was some*body* that had happened.

"No matter," Candace said. "We are, apparently, the masters of our own destiny. I could have stopped him, and I didn't. I think I've always believed that," she added quietly.

Shandy shook her head no, hoping to comfort the woman. But she too believed that to be true, that destiny could change with single acts. Because of what she saw, inside, when she waited in the foyer for everything to go away.

Again, there was the silence between them. Shandy could feel Candace changing again, getting more of the Ms. Bergen Bergenmeister; inside Candace's head she could feel her pushing aside the Brad memory and laying a cloth (shirt?) across the memory, patting it down gently, putting it away.

Finally she stood up and looked at her watch. Outside the planet was dark, maybe everywhere, but Bastion for sure. How late it was Shandy had no idea.

"Black monsters . . . I'm going to have to leave you. Actually, you should come with me and get something to eat. They've probably shut up shop by now, but I bet I could rustle you up something."

Best forgotten is the feeling Shandy found inside Candace's head; she didn't know if it was directed at her.

Shandy didn't feel hungry. But because of the one part she *didn't* tell Ms. Bergen, she thought maybe she'd better eat. Might need extra strength. It was a long way; could be a long night.

Candace walked to the door of the science lab, suddenly uncomfortable with the person she had just shared an intimate memory with, a fifteen-year-old girl. It hadn't felt good to remember, either. It felt shitty.

Shandy felt she'd broken a promise, and had actually. She had always promised her mother that she'd never tell. She couldn't stop the *knowing,* but she didn't have to tell. Still, the telling had felt good, felt like it wasn't just her fault. And knowing that sometimes other people felt responsible for terrible things gave her a perverse satisfaction. But the responsibility for later was going to be hers alone. While she walked out the door with Ms. Bergenmeister she was frightened again, feeling the way she had in the foyer: fifteen and all by herself.

16

Don went right from the meeting with the shop folks to the back of the store where the inventory was kept. He really didn't know what he'd find that would be of any help, but there were a bunch of boxes up high, way at the back (about a hundred years old, he thought) that he wanted to check into. Besides that, he wanted to be alone. To think.

He passed by Marilyn, still asleep on the bed in the furniture department, surrounded by blankets that the well-meaning girls had put over her. She was huddled underneath them, her body moving slightly. At one point, out of the corner of his eye, he thought he saw her jump, just a little. The blankets were tangled around her legs, and her hands under her head were curled into tight fists. He estimated that she'd walked a good twelve miles, most of that slogging through two-foot snow-drifts, with zero visibility. She was a lucky girl. He would check on her again when he came back out, maybe wake her up. In the meantime, he would check out whatever would constitute emergency supplies in the back of the store.

The Treasure Chest Department Store had started out as a trading post in Bastion, set up to foster the trade of animal skins between the fort and the native trappers. The skins were initially used for clothing and bedding by the soldiers and government people (although they weren't government people at first, that came later), and when it was discovered that there was an ample market for the "exotic" furs on the coast and in Europe, that trade made the Treasure Chest a corporation. The national chain of department stores started out as a sideline for the corporation, proved itself cheap and lucrative, and was now its only venture, although no longer cheap and lucrative. Don wasn't thinking about any of that when he pushed open the narrow door and stepped into the dark back room where everything smelled like the cardboard boxes it came in, a wet-paper smell that reminded Don of moving days.

The back, that mythical place where customers asked you to look when they couldn't find something up front, always looked a little bit like a grandma's attic to Don. Especially this one, which wasn't a neat, orderly place like the branch that he'd come from in the city. It wasn't neat and orderly because it was full. Things were difficult to ship in and out, and a lot of the merchandise that might have been sent to other branches just stayed in Bastion, living out its usefulness surrounded by other things gone out of style, out of date, obsolete. There were lamps, tables and chairs with the plastic wrapped still around their legs, boxes of dishes with discontinued patterns or broken pieces. (Bridal registry in Bastion was reserved for those who could ship in from the city, preferring Birks silver to Treasure Chest flatware.) There was a pile of children's swimming pools that never really caught on in Bastion since the water hardly ever got warm enough to swim in, but when it did they swam in the lakes and rivers; the Toman was almost shallow enough in some places for the kids to wade across. Somewhere in the mess there was a big box of clothing no longer good to sell, not so much because of style but because it had sat so long in front and then later in back that it was yellowed and faded. Clothes were not sold in Bastion for style, but for comfort: warmth and freedom. The company insisted on sending out the latest trends and many of those garments stayed on the sale rack for months before being relegated to the back and, ultimately, to The Box. Don had meant a long time ago to donate it to the church (or wherever things were donated in Bastion), and it had slipped his mind after being packed up. Out of sight, out of mind.

The things that sold in Bastion were practical items, and if a fancier, less than practical item sold, there was probably a wedding going on in town. About four times a year the Treasure Chest sold a tiny lace bed thing to a group of blushing girls going in on a bridal gift. They sold about four wedding gowns a year, and Don didn't know what the grooms wore, because they seldom sold any suits. The people that wore suits seemed to feel more comfortable buying them on their trips down south into the city, where the selection and quality were better and didn't include dark green polyester-cotton blends. It was a practical town.

The room was lit with a bare bulb somewhere in the middle of the shelves. He should have brought a flashlight. Every time he went into the back he swore he was going to do something about the lighting, get some long fluorescents put in, but never got around to it. But this time it was a problem. It was too dark to see enough to get to the bulb. He propped the door open with a box of cheap cutlery and hoped that enough light from the store would get him to the long string on the end of the bulb. He fumbled around the shelves, twice bumping himself on boxes strewn about the floor. In the middle of the room, he waved a hand around in the general vicinity of where the string should hang. He waved for quite a while, beginning to feel foolish, waving his awkward hello! hello everybody! to an empty room, when he felt the brush of the string across the back of his hand. He caught it, gave it a pull, and *voila!* the room did not bloom with the light that he had expected. Instead the glow was fragile and yellow, and made everything look dusty, which it was, and spooky, which it wasn't. Not much spooky about a bunch of boxes, he supposed, unless they're coffins.

No coffins at the Treasure Chest. A market study seventeen years ago proved they were a slow-moving item.

He whistled to himself, hoping the noise would ward off a little of the gloom, and gave the room a sweep with his eyes. He was looking specifically for extras: extra pillows, extra blankets, maybe a cot or mattress or two for the older folks, although the beds out front had box springs and mattresses and could be split up. He really didn't want to use those display beds for random sleeping since they were supposed to be for sale. (He also didn't want to be asking any pillars of the community if they were incontinent, but it was something in the back of his mind ever since Joe had mentioned the front beds.) It was better to find something that was adjustable for sitting, sleeping, like lawn loungers or foldaway cots. Don started looking at the boxes, checking the labels for the brand names, all of which he knew by heart.

He found a shelf with a box of Sealy blankets, which were expensive, and passed them over, pulling down instead a box of generic blankets. They weren't built to last, but they would certainly do the populace for the night. Along the same shelf he found a box of pillows, and some plastic mattress covers for the worrisomely incontinent. He also found a plastic bag packed with four sleeping blankets. They should be a last resort since the sleeping bag season was coming up and those would sell quickly. They were last year's, but this year's shipment wouldn't be in until late September, if then with the snowfall. There would probably be some delay, there usually was. Don would listen to the wild tales from head office about why this was late and that was late and he always had this mental picture of his inventory being delivered by plane, truck, dog sled, and on foot by intrepid men with beards and ratty clothing, using code words and living hard. That was how they made it sound, like they were bringing the stuff up to the high Arctic, not just to Bastion Falls.

He now turned his attention to the far back, where there might be sleeping apparatus in the forms of lawn chairs, cots and maybe a hammock or two. While he didn't think it would come to hammocks, he thought he might give one to Joe for a laugh. That guy would laugh at anything.

He stepped past the shelves, but it was much too dark to look for anything. He wished he'd thought to bring in a flashlight. He would have to go find one. He went back to the shelf where the store tools were kept (such as they were, the "tools" consisting of a wrench, too large for anything in the store unless they had to open a fire hydrant, a pair of wire clippers, a flat-head screwdriver and the flashlight. Somewhere in his office was a hammer). He picked himself up the big Eveready standup, the kind with two settings, the same kind that he and his dad used when he was a kid, to put up the tent at night on a camping trip. His dad called it "a man's flashlight," as opposed to the dainty female's, Don supposed. Armed with light, he headed for the back again on his quest for beds.

The shelves at the back went right to the ceiling—a very high ceiling—and stretched the length of the wall. Instead of being divided every few feet, these ones ran at least ten feet across. All the big merchandise was stored here. They were deep shelves, too, going six feet back to the wall. The shelves were crammed with all manner of goodies, and Don was suddenly sorry that he'd put forth the idea of cots and loungers at all. There was an awful lot of stuff to look through.

He shone the beam into the first division, stacked high with boxes of what looked like occasional tables, magazine racks and shelving units—ironic, he thought— and portable television sets. That was just a lead in to the CD equipment, blasters and radios on the other side. No cots or loungers. He moved farther toward the back of the room, where there was a mish-mash of items without any sort of theme. The beam caught upon several plastic bags, packed flat, one on top of another, and he saw the familiar blue stripes of the loungers. Bingo. He pulled them down, wondering if the likes of those would hold the very fat Mr. Leskew, or his equally fat wife. He hoped plastic didn't weaken with age.

As he was pulling down the loungers, something else caught in his beam. Covered in dust were three long packages, wrapped in brown packing paper and tied together with twine. Don frowned, trying to think what they might be. He was going to leave it—he still had to carry all that other stuff out into the mall and over to Joe—but curiosity got the better of him. The packages looked like tiny flat canoes from where he stood, and were remotely familiar. They were set in a pile, fitting snugly underneath the shelves. He had to bend down to pull them out, and then he recognized them immediately. They were snowshoes.

He pulled the wrap from one. They had been there for years, he guessed, from the dryness of the paper and the layers of dust on them so thick it felt like fur. Inside the package, though, the shoes were brand new, the traces stiff and new, folded securely in their wrapped-up position. He pushed down hard in the middle of the top one and felt the slight give of the mesh.

Then he stood up with sudden determination and took the loungers in each hand, half carrying, half dragging their awkward weight to the front of the storage room. He then carted out the blankets and pillows. He could hear behind him, through the loading doors, the wind whistling and waning.

Do I really want to do this?

Don thought distractedly about the snowshoes. He pictured the distance from the mall to his house. He imagined, but tried not to, what he would find when he got there. The pictures floated around accusingly in his head.

He thought he might think about the idea over a drink.

While Don was doing his duty to town and people, progress of a sort was being made across town.

Tully stood in the doorway staring down at her.

Similarly, her mind raced with solutions to her imminent problem because, like a trapped animal, she *knew*. It could be read on his face, in his eyes that looked blank and black. It was in the air, an energy in the space that separated them, twelve tiny feet, four of his steps, less if he reached out with his arms extended. He was going to kill her. Emma had long ago in school read about a thing that she used to call quarrel physics but was really called quantum physics. At that moment, while her mind picked and discarded what-to-dos, she remembered that whatever was going to happen had in fact already happened in the space-time continuum and that destiny had already decreed that she was either dead or nearly so.

Destiny could go to hell. She was *not* going to let him kill her.

There was no quandary in his mind, because he wasn't that deep a thinker; he knew no quantum or quarrel physics; his world was black and white, full of *do* or *do not*. He had depended before on spontaneous instinct and had suffered for it later, but that in no way would be reflected in future decisions, such as now. When he looked at Emma he heard and saw Annie/ Emma, but not nearly so clearly as he saw a way out. It was a simple formula to Tully: state the problem (Annie/ Emma); find a solution (make them stop). He didn't moralize, or rationalize, or try to think of alternatives.

Annie was out there, Emma was in here. He needed to be free of them both. Simple, really.

He listened with an ear cocked back toward the kitchen. The howl of the wind seemed louder in the house than it had before. His eyes he kept forward, on Emma. She had long ago (since Annie had shown up) stopped being a woman that Tully had sex with, had, in his way, enjoyed. She was no one specific now, just a tenuous connector to a bad memory.

He stepped forward, with a strange sigh of purpose. Twelve short feet, no need to rush.

This was it.

Her heart beat fast and she felt that previously theoretical rush of adrenaline and something else that she hadn't expected. Her life flashed before her eyes. If she had the energy that she'd had that morning she might have even laughed with anticipation.

Big moments in her life flashed by quickly, just like they always said it did: Bob Debbie being born, Bobby talking first, the time he lost a tooth, the time he fell and cut his lip, her wedding, her mother, missing the coffee this morning, Don Don Don.

Emma's jaws pushed down hard together, her face a grimace of purpose, like Tully's sigh. If he saw the determination in her face, he gave no indication. He came so slowly, and silently.

Theirs was a silent confrontation, a solemn physical debate.

Emma pulled herself up by her arms on the ties, Don's ties that he tied her with, until the back of her head was resting against the headboard. Every muscle strained, waiting. She was almost counting, one two three, as he approached her. She drew her knees up, and as she feared, he reached for her throat.

There was—finally—a sound: when his hands met her throat, Emma gave a jugular scream, anger and terror.

Her legs kicked, her head swung from side to side. He never lost his grip, and the only sound he made was a grunt when one of her feet caught him in the groin. He never lost his grip.

Tully squeezed until she was still.

He stared at her for a long time afterward, not so much looking at her as waiting for something to happen. He did not feel things were completed. He untied her hands, thinking that might be it, and when he did so, he realized that she was still warm. Annie had been cold. Colder now, under all that ice.

Emma's arms fell to the bed, bent awkwardly at her elbows. It looked like an impossible position, so Tully pulled them down so they rested at her sides.

That still wasn't it. He guessed he had to leave. That was it. He was done. He had to go home.

Tully turned his back and left Emma where she lay. He walked down the hallway toward the light in the kitchen.

He wanted to feel relieved, finished, completed, and didn't. He had done exactly what he thought was right, the thing he felt would put an end to the nagging Annie that lived still inside his head, his ears, his eyes. About halfway down the hall, he heard her.

She was laughing. It was very faint, and could have been the wind. Only Tully knew better.

The light in the kitchen should have been comforting

now. He had *planned* on feeling better. But she was still there, still out there.

A tremble rose and fell in him, followed by more very simple logic. He would have to do it again, that was all. He would have to kill Annie a second time. He would have to kill something until that sound was gone, until he didn't have to listen anymore.

He walked cautiously, on cat feet, to the kitchen door and looked in, toward the back door. Across the floormat was a drift of pure white snow, fresh and sparkling in the electric glow of the kitchen light. The whistle of the wind under the door was louder still. As were the other sounds.

He could stay in the house, hide from her. But she would keep calling and calling and sneaking up on him. He could close his eyes and put his fingers in his ears like a child, but he didn't think that would keep her away. She was inside him, outside him, she had to be stopped. He squinted up his eyes and tried to see through the window on the outside door. The sky was black. The snow had drifted about halfway, soft snow, because of the wind. The big drifts were at the back of the house. He could get out the door.

"I'm coming," he whispered to the air. He picked up his jacket, shrugging it on, never taking his eyes off the black window. He moved slowly, resolutely, with the same cat-like movements.

It took some pushing, but he got the door open wide enough to slip through, nearly sideways, free of the safety of the house. The town seemed blacker and much much colder than when he'd arrived. Wind ruffled his hair, spraying his face with fine flakes of icy snow. The snow was falling so thickly he could barely see two feet in front of him. He stood on the stoop that way, watching the snow fall, listening for the sounds.

No sounds except the wind whispering over his ears. Silent, dark and black. Almost . . . nice, almost *peaceful*. He stood that way, sinking into himself. His legs moved without command, and he stepped off the stoop, into the yard, sinking deeply into the soft snow up to his knees.

He stumbled a little but regained his balance easily, using one hand plunged up to the wrist. He didn't notice how cold he was turning. His jacket was open and the snow gathered inside, some of it falling into his shirt, open at the throat. His eyes felt as if they might close, but it was not unpleasant. He felt sleepy. Soft. Loose. *Nice.*

He forgot what he had been looking for, thinking now only of how it all felt around him. How the snow falling looked like tiny stars, how quiet the town could be late at night; everything seemed fine, right. He was as still as he'd ever been. Frozen still.

His body turned, his legs moving thickly, slowly in the drift, and took another step, deeper into the yard, toward the gate, as though leaving. He stopped again. The trail his legs made filled up quickly.

He stared ahead until he saw her.

"I'm cold, Tully," said dead Annie.

Tully's eyes fogged over and it was years before.

"Huh?"

"I'm cold," she said again.

Annie came out of the snow and walked toward Tully, her movements slow because of the years of ice caked on her body. Her limbs were swollen with the river water, her flesh a pale, dead white.

"I'm cold, Tully," she said. He saw her finally, and remembered, remembered everything. Screamed.

The life came back into his body quite suddenly and when he tried to run he found he was trapped by the snow. The snow while he stood still and pondered had traveled to his waist, and still it swirled above him. He wriggled frantically, and dug at the snow with freezing hands, trying desperately to get away.

Annie came on, raising ice hands. She was cold, she told him.

She walked to him, seeming to float on top of the snow, looming above him. She told him more.

"You can go to the bad place now," she said. Her voice didn't seem to come from her body but from inside Tully's head. "Go be dead."

When she was directly opposite his scrambling form, barely visible in the blinding whiteness, her hands came down on him, like his had on her. She brought both arms down on him.

He screamed for his life. Her hands came down and dug through his light jacket that offered no protection, the ice cutting through his skin and tearing into his chest. Blood poured out of him, flying up, drenching his face with warmth.

Long-dead Annie tore at him. It was a long time before he died.

The snow snowed on, covering Tully gently, as a mother might.

17

By eleven-thirty, people were starting to lay claim to the space that they would hold through the night. The amiable party atmosphere that had been present earlier in the adventure had been replaced with an unavoidable melancholy.

Some people lingered near the doors and looked out into the night, even after they had set up camp in some appropriate spot, laying down blankets or sleeping bags, pillows and whatever personal effects they had with them. Still they looked out into the storm, anticipating a break, even as it got later and later, and the sky showed no sign of abating its torrent of white.

The long buffet table that had formerly held cheering cups of coffee was still there, but the coffee pot was unplugged and the white table cloth bore stains from the constant spills and was littered with crumbs of doughnuts past. The adjustable lights in the cafeteria were at their lowest, and in the back Gerry and Phyllis could be heard shutting down the kitchen. Larry Talgart had two or three friends in the Variety Store with him—he was doing a big business in toothbrushes and trial-sized toothpastes—but the drinking had turned into sipping and the conversation, when there was any, was quiet.

There was an awkwardness apparent, centering on the correct way for a dignified adult to lie down on a sleeping bag in the middle of a mall; a feeling as though caught in an overaged, twisted slumber party, or a convention of the homeless. People were showing signs of wanting to go to sleep, setting up their camps, making trips to the restrooms, getting a last drink of something, yawning. They were talking barely above whispers; even the radio was cooperating: the CBC that Joe had piped into the mall earlier was softly ruminating the jazz experience, the female broadcaster's smoky voice as soothing as a lullaby. But no one was bedding down, and the uneasy feeling that had permeated the mall earlier hadn't gone away, if it had become less pervading. The radio had seemed to forget all about Bastion and its storm, and the loss had been less depressing than disinteresting.

The benches were fuller than they had been, and the people left to stand were close to the walls where they could at least lean while they spoke. It was so quiet that when someone got up to walk to the washroom, everyone turned and watched, listening to the clicking of their heels on the tiled floors. Distantly, but close enough to cause some red faces, the toilets could be heard flushing. One lady commented that she had no idea that they were so loud and wondered if they didn't get louder at night, echoing through the dark, maybe. As absurd as the observation was, no one said anything. People were getting too tired to really think, and it seemed to some that after this monstrous overnight, anything might be possible, including night toilets.

Joe was in the midst of it all, wandering from group to group, feeling responsible for their comfort. Someone asked him to turn the heat up, another told him that there was only one stall that had any paper in the ladies' washroom; he reassured, assured and ensured them all that everything would be taken care of. He repeated offers of backyard loungers for people to sleep on, but they had almost overwhelmingly been turned down. Except for one man and a young lady, no one wanted to sleep on a lawn chair unless it was on a lawn, as one gentleman put it. Three cots had finally been dug up, and by general agreement they had been gently offered to the mall's three oldest patrons. Every blanket and pillow, however, was taken with appreciation, and many folks had laid their sweaters and jackets—thin as they were—under the sleeping bags and blankets to cushion themselves from the floor. Joe tried to instill the former sense of fun and adventure into people, referring to the evening as "camping out", but most spared him little more than a wry smile.

The crowd had thinned out some, as all of the parents in the mall except one dad had gone over to the hotel in hopes of at least getting a regular bed in exchange for their chaperoning duties.

Candace was not a real smoker. She could have one every day for a month, if it was a stressful one, and then not do it any more until the next time. She simply was not a habitual person. She sympathized with her friends when they tried to quit and had a terrible time of it, but like a thin person who has never had to diet, she couldn't really empathize. Cigarettes attracted her in the most minimal way. Somewhere in her office she knew she had a pack. They were probably more than a month old. She thought that might be a bit much. She would go into the mall and buy a fresh pack. Between black snow monsters and bad dreams, whiny teachers and loud children, she was dead on her feet and in need of a little freedom.

She left the school, alerting only the unassuming Miss Loopol, the least judgmental or questioning of the teachers. She was taking a break, for sanity's sake. That wasn't what she told Loophole, though. She muttered something about "that time of the you-know" and Miss Loophole nodded gravely and knowingly and let her go off; Thurston would have looked disapprovingly at her, not suspecting a lie but for still having the dreaded curse at her age—whatever her age was.

Candace was surprised at the number of people in the mall. It looked so *populated*. It just might have been the most adults in one place that she had ever seen in Bastion, excluding the school Christmas concert. She briefly had second thoughts about having a cigarette in case there were parents still around.

There were about a dozen men in front of the only store open, and that was the Variety Store. That was also the only place, besides the Esso outside, to get a pack of cigarettes. And she wasn't going outside. She was suddenly acutely conscious of all the people in the mall, and particularly the men in the store. Everyone was so quiet. She could hear her heels, which she *really* wanted to take off, tapping out a Morse code. There were no runs in her stockings, but she was wearing a skirt and she wondered why men always had to stand so close together and stop talking when a woman approached. Even if they weren't staring, it made her feel they were. Maybe teenage girls thought that groups of men were admiring them when they approached, but Candace always felt they were judging.

She saw Larry at his usual post behind the counter, in spite of the hour.

"Larry," she said, nodding to the others, willing them away. Larry at least knew she smoked occasionally, and she wouldn't have to explain. A teacher smoking—even though most of them did—was a bad thing; a principal, it was almost intolerable. Of course, it was pretty much intolerable for everyone these days. He grabbed a pack of her brand.

"Here you go, Miss Bergen."

Somebody snickered. At the Miss? at the skirt? smoking?

She took the pack and paid him. She took a book of matches off the counter, free to the folks that bought, as Larry would tell whoever bought a pack as if it was a big premium or something.

From behind the counter Larry seemed to feel that he had to make conversation. He leaned forward. "Quite a storm out there," he said solemnly.

Later she would claim it was at that moment when all the stress of the whole day kicked in, the cumulative package of no phones, smug know-nothing secretaries, motherless children, shouting teenagers, disruptive boys, gym teachers who didn't like to give up their offices to helpless city principals, and being in heels for no less than fourteen hours, came home to roost, as her mother would have said. She laughed at his understated comment until everyone—just about—stared. The laughter dropped off.

"You're right," she said. "It's quite a storm." She walked past the group of staring, almost frightened men, feeling suddenly, lightly, refreshed.

She saw Phyllis, just come out from cleaning the kitchen, sitting with a group of women and girls, some of whom she recognized. The one girl, Betty, was on work-experience somewhere in the mall. She was a conscientious student with decent grades who was hardly ever truant without cause. Candace tended to think of everyone under twenty in terms of truancy, grades and conscientiousness. She walked over to them.

"Hello, Phyllis," she said. She wanted to add "quite a storm out there," just for fun, but didn't think she would be able to without laughing. Instead she started to unravel her cigarette package.

"Candace, hello," Phyllis said, sounding more than tired, just plain wore out. "I didn't know you smoked."

"Well, I don't, usually. Special occasion." There were murmurs of agreement, and Betty giggled a wired-up giggle.

"Betty, how was your first day on the job? Quite a day, anyhow," she said gently.

Betty nodded, adding the wired giggle again. "It was crazy in there! I did inventory with everybody else, on account of we had to pull out all the winter stuff, even though we were just supposed to be doing office stuff." Then she added in a lower voice, moving in a little closer as she told, "And Mrs. Barefoot, Marilyn, came in, frozen like a popsicle and I thought she was *dead*. She was just worn right through, coming through that snow and all, but I bet you when she takes a look she's going to find some black toes on her!"

"What's this? I feel like I haven't left the school since this morning," Candace said. Marilyn? She got a mental picture of a woman not unlike herself. She didn't really approve of gossip, but like the cigarette, it was something worth indulging in once in a while. The thought of someone outside made her think suddenly of Shandy, and Shandy's story. "She all right? What happened?"

"Her car broke down, I think," said Betty. Because she sounded like she knew it all, everyone looked at her. She blushed.

"Where is she now?"

"Still in the store, I think. On one of the beds in there," said another lady, maybe just a trace of jealousy, Candace thought, and supposed it was for the bed. Candace could have been a little jealous herself if she wasn't so tired. *I wonder what she saw.*

Candace, with the others, turned and looked toward the department store entry. The lights were down, except for something coming from high above, maybe Don Clanstar's office. Candace looked at her watch. It was nearly midnight. The witching hour.

She took the last drag off her cigarette—not really even wanting that anymore—and stubbed it out in the industrial-size ashtray provided by the mall. It was overflowing with cigarettes, and much to her disgust, she had to root around in the tray to make a space big enough to put hers out. *She thought his name was Barry, for chrissakes. What does that tell you? Close enough.*

Candace asked, "So how is she? Anybody seen her up and about? Anybody . . . talk to her?"

"I haven't," Betty said, giving up her authority.

Phyllis snorted out a contemptuous laugh then and said, "Gee, I wonder if Marilyn will have as good a tale to tell about her trip through the Great Storm of '92 as that old drunk did."

Candace felt the blood rush through her body up to her face, like a premonition. Casually, she asked, "Oh? What was that?"

Phyllis, anxious to repeat it for reasons of her own, told Candace about Lawrence and Chester and Ronnie.

Can't be, thought Candace.

18

He had dozed off. Hickory squirmed in his sleep, a light film of sweat cooling off his face; the spaces under his arms, covered by only a light T-shirt—standard phys. ed. costume—were darkening with black circles of perspiration. He mumbled something, almost unintelligible, but if someone listened close enough it would have sounded like "I'm sorry."

He was dreaming. Random pictures and images (familiar, nonetheless) went round and round on a loop inside his head. Dream pictures: *naked shapes banging into him wet flesh pressing hotly against his own wet flesh bumping into him like on a crowded bus and he was saying sorry but he wasn't really but kept saying it because it was required.*

When Mr. MacGregor woke him, shaking him by the shoulder, Hickory jumped and gave a startled—guilty, even in sleep—yell.

"Sorry, man," Mac told him. "I'm relieving you for the next watch. Hated to wake you. Go get some real sleep, they've set up some cots and things for the teachers in the science lab.''

Not quite awake, Hickory stared for a few more startled seconds before the naked people of his dream faded and he recognized the decidedly unnaked Mac. He rubbed both eyes with his hand and stood shakily.

"Yes,'' Hickory said numbly, and walked blindly toward the gym doors, outlined in light from the hallway. Behind him he heard Mac move the chair in a squelch, getting himself comfortable. The sound grated through Hickory's body, still damp and half in the dream. He had an urge to turn around and apologize.

A walk where it was cool, that was what he decided he needed. The gym was so close, so . . . sweaty. Feeling a little more awake, he pushed open one side of the gym's double doors, opening it as quietly and as minutely as possible, and slipped through into the light.

Hickory had a favorite haunt in the school, especially after a particularly warm workout in gym class, a place where it was always cool. Down in the sub-level of the school, not really a basement but lower than the rest. The pipes were there, damp with condensation, and near the back, where the emergency doors were, it was cool. A little walk downstairs would perk him up considerably, he decided. He could be alone. Think.

The hallway was empty and quiet. From somewhere he could hear steps on the tiled floor, and muted voices from one of the classrooms. It occurred to him that even though it was pitch dark outside—he could see through the windows as he passed—most of the teachers were likely awake. They were probably as nervous as the kindergarteners, away from home for the first time. It made him feel suddenly lonely, because he would be alone in his relief that he *wasn't* at home, that he wasn't where he could be reached. And with good reason, he was glad to be unreachable.

He turned down the hall toward the stairs that led to the sub-level, pushed open the door and felt immensely better already. The pipes, even just the thought of them, brought back some of the better feelings of himself, being alone, where it was quiet enough to think. He went quickly down the stairs.

So sorry.

It had only happened once. His dreams notwithstanding, it had only happened actually, really, once. That memory, in spite of the blacker parts, had been enough to sustain him for many years. Now it would all be different. He would do it, he knew, in the way he knew he was what he was without ever really admitting the truth to himself, or ever having to say the word. It would happen again.

It had been his first teaching job, at a city school. He wasn't Hickory yet, he was just plain Allen, or Mr. Tinsdale to the younger students. He had already been thinking about it before then, but had pushed it further and further back in his mind until some days it seemed as though the thoughts had never occurred to him. They became like a memory of a dream. A good dream.

Through high school, and later university, he'd simply denied any feelings at all, and pursued a "normal" set of activities, copying others. He dated girls, trying hard to get to first base, but seldom pushing beyond that; he lost interest and sometimes even became afraid if a girl showed an interest in going further, so terrified that he would be expected to go all the way he would sometimes panic, react badly, pressing the issue into a

never-articulated violence. Girls in that day and age—
thank god—would back off quickly, frightened by their
own forces as much as his. He dated lots of girls, hoping
that quantity could replace the quality of his sexuality
and no one would get wise. No one did. He even devel-
oped a bit of a reputation by dating nice girls and trying
to get them to go too far. The nice girls started to avoid
him, and whispered to each other. The whispers got
around. His reputation—if not theirs—was preserved.

He got his teaching position at one of the many
anonymous city schools where teachers start out at the
bottom. His first year he taught a regular schedule of
phys. ed. and a half-course in current events. Hickory
found he loved to teach, and for the longest time it took
over all of his mind.

Halfway through the school year the juniors peti-
tioned for a basketball team. There had been a senior
basketball team (which Hickory coached with relish),
but no junior team. Hickory appealed to the staff for a
volunteer to coach the juniors.

From the first moment he came to see Allen about
coaching, there was something; something happened.
Allen had been sitting at his desk in the cubby-hole they
called the phys. ed. teacher's office, filling out forms. A
week had gone by since he had tacked up the request for
a volunteer coach on the staff room bulletin board, and
he was beginning to think he would coach the junior
team himself, simply work things out. It would mean
much longer hours, and more dedication, and a total
focus on work, which didn't seem like such a bad idea.
It seemed like something to take his mind off the things
he thought about when he was at home, alone, *in the*

*shower in front of the TV cooking dinner lying in bed
taking the elevator going to the toilet,* alone.

He was filling out the forms, completely distracted.
In the gym—right outside the office—the girls' volleyball
coach was running drills. The noise echoed through the
big room and funneled into the small office.

"Excuse me, I'm here about coaching the juniors,"
said the voice, right at his elbow, practically in his ear.
Hickory looked up, smiling a jovial hail-fellow-well-
met, and saw Robert Chesway. He recognized him
vaguely as someone in the halls between classes carrying
books whatever, a first-year teacher, but when he looked
up, suddenly, and vulnerably, mind on something else,
he was unprepared for the click *oh* that went off inside
his head, as though pieces of a puzzle were falling into
place, a light going on, the snap of a lock being opened.

"Basketball?" Robert Chesway said, when Allen
hadn't responded.

"Basketball, yes."

That was how he met Robert Chesway, although he
didn't know it then, didn't know that he'd *met* Robert.
But it wasn't long after that.

For a long time they coached at different times, in
spite of the large gym, the two sides of which could be
separated by a retractable wall. It was as if Hickory pur-
posely scheduled their practices for different times to
avoid any contact. Except for brief exchanges in the
staff room and occasionally in the gym about how teams
were doing, they hardly spoke. But whenever there was
conversation, or even the mere physical presence, there
was also that . . . lock being snapped open.

Later, when he had ample opportunity, Hickory
would realize that the whole thing had been inevitable,

as though God, or destiny even, was stepping in and providing a chance for Allen to know who he was. Freeing him, keeping him from becoming one of those people who deny themselves all their lives and wind up crazy lonely, or just crazy. Feeding fish in a small apartment and ordering movies by mail.

In March both teams were invited to play in a tournament. It was an all-day thing, a Saturday. By the time it wrapped up, it was late. The buses took the students back to the school, and they were picked up by parents or rode bikes home, tired, excited, overwound. Allen and Robert stayed until the last kid had driven or ridden off and then faced the exhausting responsibility of being alone. That was how Allen saw it.

He went to his office to put some things away.

Robert followed him inside.

"Listen, Allen, I'm a little wound up myself. Don't feel much like going home yet, you wanna get a drink or something? Coffee?"

It seemed a long time before Allen could answer.

"A drink," he said. Destiny thrown in his way.

The first drink was talking about school. The second drink was talking about their own schools and university. The third drink things got a little quieter, and a little more personal. After that, they both got drunk in earnest.

They ended their evening at Robert's apartment, deciding to continue drinking after the bar had closed. Robert had some wine, he said, that he'd been saving. Neither of them mentioned the fact that while Allen lived within walking distance of the bar, Robert lived across town in another district.

Before he opened the door to the apartment, Robert

told him gravely, "Maid's day off." Allen, who could barely afford cable on what he was making and knew it had to be the same for Robert, thought this was enormously funny and started to laugh. They both laughed drunkenly and eventually painfully, falling into the apartment, holding stomachs full of butterflies and beer.

Allen suggested that maybe Robert should kill the maid. The place was a disaster. He lifted some clothes off the sofa to sit down. Robert disappeared to get wine and glasses.

On the sofa, alone, he decided. Later Hickory would tell himself that Bogart said it best: it was the beginning of a beautiful . . . something.

Then, it didn't happen. They passed out on the sofa, waking up with sore heads and memories of nothing. It was still there, between them, but nothing was said. Nothing. Allen went home after an awkward breakfast.

It was after track practice, basketball season over, the drunken night, the near-experience almost forgotten. Another Saturday afternoon, the team showered. The track was empty except for Allen and Robert, who came to the track after practice to work out. He was running laps, slowly, gracefully; Allen was pretending to make notes on times in the black notebook that he carried to all the practices, dragging his eyes away from the running Robert. Finally he found he had to remove himself from the field and go into the shower room where the others were shouting and throwing towels and clothes at each other. The noise and confusion helped. He yelled at the boys to shower up and get the hell out. He always said that, though, and none of the boys really listened. They did rush out. It was Saturday and there were girls to pick up and games to watch on TV and parties to be arranged. Within ten minutes the shower room was empty and silent.

Hickory picked the towels off the floor, tossed them into the laundry cart. His heart was pounding and he was sweating because it was steamy and hot in the shower room.

Behind him then he heard the sound he had been waiting for. The door snicked open quietly and swung shut. Before he turned around he could smell Robert's sweat, hot smelling and pungent in the room steamy from the showers.

It was this damp smell, that scent of man, that always came to Hickory whenever he thought of the incident. The smell of the gym after a practice often brought it back. Now as he made his way through the maze of pipes toward the back of the basement, he could smell himself, and that too made him smell Robert. He walked more slowly, gracefully in the sub-level.

Robert had smiled at him from the door. They made small talk about the track team, about school. Robert undressed unselfconsciously. As hard as he tried, Hickory couldn't help but sneak peeks at him while he picked up after the track team. When Robert was naked, he walked over to the open showers, turning one on. Hickory followed him.

He was standing under the stream of water, an unreadable smile on his face, apologetic maybe, or pleading. It was much hotter where the showers were and Hickory still tried to tell himself that was why the sweat beaded up on his forehead and the trickles ran down from underneath his arms and in the curve of his back.

Robert was sinewy and gently muscled, every curve of his body defined. He was watching Hickory, leaning now and again to put his head under the water and run a hand through his hair, pushing it wetly out of his eyes. Absolutely unable to help himself, Hickory looked down. Robert had an erection, as large as the one Hickory had, except Hickory's was straining against the confines of his sweatpants.

"Allen," he said. They joined in the shower, and that first time, Hickory didn't remember if either of them had said another word.

He had no idea how anyone found out. The thing in the shower had been an enormous mistake, but they had come through it unscathed. It wasn't until much later that they began to suspect that someone knew something. They had been careful to avoid being seen together at school but had been seeing each other frequently outside of school.

They had each been called into the office separately, and fired.

Hickory was removed unceremoniously from his post. It had been a mortifying, black experience, and he had been forced to look for another post as though looking for his first. The school would not give him a letter of recommendation. He knew he could have gone to the Human Rights Commission, or something like that, but it would have meant *telling*. He couldn't, not after years of hiding, even from himself. Being fired had a terrible effect on the already delicate relationship. Robert packed up, moved back to his home town.

The first part of the remembering clung to Hickory as he walked toward the back of the pipes, to where they paused before curling up toward the front again. The first part refused to be scared away by the last, blacker, humiliating part of the remembering. All around him, he could still smell that afternoon in the shower room. He was alone. Upon entering the restricted area he had looked surreptitiously around for the fellow whose job it was to stay in the sub-level and do whatever it was that was done down there, and hadn't seen him at all. He was alone and that made him feel safe, like the way he felt safe to think his thoughts in the shower just before he turned the cold on full force to wash it all away. So he let himself think.

It was happening again.

He had felt safe in Bastion, as though temptation was left behind when he left the city, where there were places to go if you wanted to, people like himself. He was no longer denying the truth about who he was, felt almost free about admitting it, but only to himself. No one else could know. He buried the feelings in work and thought about it all only when he was alone.

He had made a trip to the city during his summer break and had met someone there, being sure to let him know that this was only a brief thing, nothing permanent. Summer ended, and so did that. It hadn't been enough, or even what he wanted. There had been no quality there, just as there hadn't been years before during unsatisfying relationships with girls in school.

Then he'd been picking out a novel in the drugstore one afternoon when a gentleman also looking through the books had begun talking to him. As soon as he looked at the man and they sized each other up, Hickory knew. Against his better judgment, he agreed to have a cup of coffee with the man. In the cafeteria, the two of them had drawn one or two hooded glances, and Hickory realized immediately the man must be known.

After fifteen minutes or so of desultory conversation

on Hickory's part, heart-pounding terror-filled fifteen minutes, he had excused himself and almost ran home. It couldn't happen again. He didn't want it to. It was not only a risk to his job, it was too complicated. He just didn't *want* to.

Yes I do by god I do.

But he couldn't stop thinking about the man. He had been attractive, interesting, funny; he had been like Robert in a way. Older, though, and more sure.

He had finally called the man, spending twenty minutes going through the complicated many-exchanges phone book for Bastion and surrounding towns. Then he'd spent two or three hours looking at the number guiltily on the piece of paper beside the phone. He dialed and hung up no fewer than three times before going through with the call. Now, alone in the basement, he checked his watch, and realized their meeting would probably be over (or into something deeper) by this time. They would have been meeting this evening. The storm, Hickory thought, was an omen for him. The freedom to be who he was had been snatched away. Obviously, God or that higher being did not want him to go through with it. It had almost happened again, and he had been saved from himself.

He found that he had walked all the way to the back and was standing in front of the emergency door, a big solid steel door with a small windowpane. Hickory looked out into the black night. Delicate flakes of snow fluttered this way and that in front of the glass, between the black and the window.

Then he saw him.

Richard?

It couldn't be him.

Keeping our date?

It was just a face in the window, a man's face frowning with cold.

Instinctively, Hickory reached for the handle. He looked out the window again, and it wasn't there. He pressed his face to the glass, cupped his hands around the sides of his face to block out some of the light from behind.

He could see him, just barely, through the swirling snow. It was unmistakably Richard. Inconceivably dressed in only jeans and a T-shirt pulled tightly over slight muscles, disappearing into the waistband of his pants and clinging to the slim waist. Equally inconceivably, he was smiling. While Richard smiled, he put his arms around his waist and gave himself a small hug, supposedly against the cold, but to Hickory it seemed something else, something coquettish. The movement was hypnotic; Hickory watched, transfixed. He wanted in, Hickory was sure of that, and already, without knowing anything at all about this man, Hickory knew that the wishes would be real again. All he had to do was let him in. Against his will he licked his lips. He reached up to the side of the door and turned off the security alarm with one push of a button.

Hickory opened the door. Snow swirled in, dancing in the warm room, slinking around his feet in a circle, like a fallen halo. He held the door open wider and waited for Richard to rush inside. He felt himself getting big in that place. Hickory didn't stop to think about the implausibility of what was taking place, didn't stop to wonder how someone—anyone—had made it to the mall complex in this weather in clothes better suited for summer. His eyes half closed, and he didn't see the man come in so much as he smelled the achingly familiar scent of jogging clothes discarded, shower room towels, sweat. White continued its dancing march into the room. When Hickory opened his eyes, he saw Richard, who looked more beautiful than he remembered. Richard opened his arms, wide and yawning, and Hickory stepped into them, relieved at last of his long wait, the yearning, longing for someone, and all of this after nearly a lifetime; the pause all the more unbearable because of the opportunity. He groaned, opened his eyes to see all of the man.

When he did, finally, see all of the man, he screamed. The door shut slowly on its automatic hinge. Ice formed along the metal jam. The door couldn't close all of the way.

19

She was awake and drinking a cup of coffee, day-old from the taste of it. It was skunky but it was warm, and since she'd come in, Marilyn might have traded her sex organs for warm, or at least that's what she told Phyllis when she brought the coffee to her. She had gently resisted Phyllis's other kindnesses, and being the understanding—read gossipy—person that she was, Phyllis dismissed herself, off no doubt to tell everyone about the dark circles under Marilyn's eyes and that she woke up with a little scream perched on the edge of her lips. It had just barely escaped. The sweaty brow and fearful eyes hadn't escaped Phyllis, for sure. It would all be part of the tale.

She held the cup in both hands, wrapping them around the mug and resting it in her lap, against both thighs. She was sitting on a display bed, in the furniture department, if you could call it that: a display bed, a display washing machine (the display dryer had been purchased three months ago but the new shipment wasn't in), a display sofa and several boxes of cheap pressed-wood tables that could be put together by a child, if need be, that they always meant to put together to "display" but hadn't gotten around to. It was a lot like her bedroom at home.

While her eyes wandered over the stuff around her, stuff she'd seen every day for the million years that she'd worked in the store, her mind slipped over the last walk through the courtyard, over the parking lot, to the mall from the Esso to the horrible sleep she'd had, almost like being drugged or hypnotized. She didn't want it to, but her mind kept dragging it back. Bringing the mug to her lips, she wished for a toke and a shot of rye, in that order. Her hands were shaking. She remembered, against her better judgment, against her will.

It was the voices that were the worst of it. The hours before, when she'd come in, she would have sworn up and down all over her mother's grave, the Bible, the Koran, the Torah, the Shroud of fucken Turin, that they had been real, truth be known, might still be, but they weren't and that was what was frightening her. Is that what happens just before you freeze to death? That was most on her mind, that she must have been inches, almost literally, from death. The mall so close, and she almost missed it. And she still felt, when she wasn't thinking hard about it, that those voices had really been there. Using her name, not calling her exactly, but talking to her, over those hot cups of coffee they'd been holding. She could convince herself that it was the wind, her ears freezing, her mind going numb, she could convince herself through most of it, right up until the laugh. A chuckle, of amusement. The sort that you hear in light conversation following a mildly amusing bon mot, not in the middle of an empty parking lot with a ton of snow falling around your ears. That was the stumbling stone, the place she could get to but not leave. She was fine up until the laugh. And up to the dream. Mustn't forget the dream.

She didn't think she was going to mention that particular aspect of her adventure to anyone, unless she slipped out of town and into the city to see some psychiatrist, which is just what anyone that found out would suggest. That was the very hallmark of crazy. Well, Doctor, I heard voices. Yup, and easily amused voices at that; they were laughing at me. *Ant, how lung hav you hat dis problimk?*

To help drag herself away from questioning her sanity, or pondering the likelihood of her narrow escape from death, she shifted herself so that her feet were on the ground, where they belonged literally and figuratively, and sat on the edge of the bed, the slight dizziness from sitting up disappearing after a minute.

"Time to get up, Marilyn," she muttered to herself. What to do next was the problem. She was mildly embarrassed, the way any healthy person would be, at the fact of her short convalescence. Of course, she had been dragged from the edge of death, and that was sort of heroic, or at least stalwart, and she tried to take heart from that. People never saw it that way, though. She would have to endure the "are you okay's?" for at least a day or two, depending on how many people she was likely to run into before leaving this place. She wished a person could just send a memo, or put up a poster, declaring a complete and total recovery from the edge of death and not be bothered about recounting to each and every soul in town how she was fine, it was just a little

thing, it was pretty fucken cold out there, *you know?*
She sighed.

And as for the other, she was not going to think
about it, mention it or do anything about it at all, period, end of discussion. It didn't happen, didn't happen,
didn't happen.

The store was dark, the lights all off. Outside the
front window she could see a glow: the outside lights.
Ditto in the direction of the mall. Phyllis had told her
that folks were going to sleep every which way in there,
and some of them were finally settling in. In any case,
the mall was dark, just a few overhead dims were on.
She could see a couple of people wandering around. She
did not want to go there.

She looked up. The light in Don's office was on.
Yeeha. An escape route.

Don was upstairs, and lo and behold, he was having
a beer.

"It warms a girl's heart to see a man with a six
pack," she told him, smiling, so glad he was there and
no one else was. "And mine could use warming," she
added, sitting down across from him.

"Hey, pal," he said, without smiling. He stared intensely at her for a deliberating minute. "You all right?
Should I get Dr. Briggs?"

She shook her head. "I'm a little shaky, I may not get
warm until summer, but I'm not going to die." And as
she said it, a little shiver went up her back; goose walked
over her grave, her mother would have said. "Besides,
he'll probably wanna give me an enema."

Don chuckled, but he didn't laugh, even though the
sexual perversions of others were among his favorite

jokes. In fact, he didn't look as though he'd heard her at all.

"Something wrong?"

His smile fell away as quickly as it had automatically appeared. Missing his wife? She didn't think so. He almost never mentioned Emma unless forced to, and being a veteran of trouble herself, Marilyn figured there must be some at their house.

"Gimme a beer, compadre," she said.

Don reached down beside the desk and took one out, opening it for her. He passed it across the top of the desk. "It's warm," he said, apologetically.

"We getting drunk tonight?"

"I guess so. No."

"What's up? Storm getting you down? Too much caffeine?" She smiled to show she was kidding and that everything was really all right. The last time he'd looked so distracted was during what had come to be affectionately known as the "Tree Trunk Scandal," when a truck with a load of inventory had gone under the ice in the river. The driver claimed he hit a tree, but since there were no trees in the middle of the river, it was widely assumed that he had been drunk. It *was* funny. But $16,000 worth of inventory had gone under while the driver escaped, and it had been Don's hide there for a while. Everyone including him thought he would be fired because he had given a drunk the pick-up job. That had been a year ago, just after he'd started. He moped and sulked around until everyone was just about ready to scream. He could be such a serious man. "Somebody hit a tree?"

She was rewarded with a small, if wry, smile. "Something's wrong. At home, I mean. I didn't know before, but I feel *sure.* Strange about it. I'm thinking of going out there." That was when the shiver returned and danced its way up and down her back, the sound of it almost being her name.

"You can't go out there," she said firmly. Perspiration formed under her arms. She added, "What in hell makes you think something's wrong? Tell me," she said, more lightly now, "and I'll tell you you're crazy."

He did.

Shandy was supposed to be going to sleep.

She had been safely ensconced in Room 21 of the Northern Lights Hotel with four other girls, each of whom now were falling asleep. Around her, Shandy could hear the soft, fluttery breath of the other girls, the sounds of baby-breathing in contrast to their earlier raucous giggling and boastful statements. The other girls seemed like children to Shandy, who didn't think she'd ever feel fifteen again, ever.

Shandy had been given a cot, since she'd arrived in the room after the beds had been divvied up. It could have been worse. The fourth girl that had come in, having been sent out of her original room for causing mischief, was sleeping on the floor in a sleeping bag, and it had been said that all the boys were sleeping on the gym floor in sleeping bags. That would be much worse, if a person planned on sleeping the night away.

She didn't.

Shandy had better—no, worse, much worse—things to do. She had to get out of here. It suddenly occurred to her that if she had been given the sleeping bag, she could have crawled out of the room practically unnoticed. Because she was on the cot, she would not only have to be much quieter—she didn't even know if the cot springs squeaked—but she would have to somehow step around the girl on the sleeping bag.

Her poor stomach was hanging on tight to the little bit of supper that she had eaten, and was balling it and unballing it, turning it around in slow circles it seemed with every breath. Shandy recognized the feeling as the same one she got before her first date with David, the same stomach cramps she got the night before she and her mom moved to Bastion, and what happened the night before a math test; she might also recognize it later in life on the night before signing for a loan, waiting for a child to come home after a night out with the car, before a job interview. It was tension. Her mother told her she'd get an ulcer if she didn't learn to let go of things that weren't her problem, but how does a person let go of this? Her cup was full, running over, and she still hadn't done a thing except think about it.

Somewhere up around the old fort site. That was where it was coming from. Whatever it was that was happening. (Something to do with the storm, the storm and those *things*.) That was where she had to go. Shandy knew this, the same way she always *knew*.

She had heard about the old fort from many people in town; even her mother had heard about it and they talked about going to see it. The strangest thing about the fort was that no one ever went to see it: there were no field trips to study Bastion heritage, no commemorative dates to mark on the calendar, no Families of the Fort to celebrate. People around Bastion almost pretended the fort didn't exist. They never denied it was there, and it was brought up, duly, during local history classes, but there was an unspoken agreement that the history of the fort was not up for public view or scrutiny. It had seemed a town eccentricity, and before today Shandy had never questioned it, it having never been important. But it was important now.

Since the morning, Shandy was a different person. And it wasn't only because she saw David die. She thought now that she had spent her whole life—and in spite of the fifteen years it seemed much longer now—preparing for this night. She could see, hear, feel more now than she ever had in her life. She guessed it was because a part of whatever kind of skill or talent she had been given had been partly asleep inside her, because she hadn't really been using it. Now she had to use it, and it woke up. Suddenly. For instance, that sleeping part, she thought, had always known that David was going to die.

She had run away from David as he fell in the snow, his body crumpling and caving in. The snow had been deep, and she tried to fight it, believing even then that the *snow* had something to do with it all. She had only gone twenty feet or so before tumbling ass over end, face first into the snow.

The terror of being vulnerable seized her then, and she lost her sense of direction; it didn't seem as though she'd fallen up or down, like when a person gets thrown into the water and it all looks the same. It all looked the same to Shandy: the white sky, the white ground, the white icy snow covering her face, her gloves, her eyes. She'd scrambled, grabbing at the snow on her face, scraping it away with hands turned to claws, scratching until her eyes watered and it all fell away. When she could see again, she *saw*.

In front of her, where there had only been tendrils of

delicate white flakes, where there should have been—
had she really been able to see—the school, there was
another building. She got to her feet and ran, dizzy and
disoriented. She didn't recognize anything around her.
The building in front of her was stone and wood, the
stone being the limestone that seemed to grow around
Bastion and that made everyone so proud. The snow
swirled and tossed in the air around her, sometimes ebbing and letting the light through, sometimes blocking her
sight and clogging her lungs so that she seemed unable
to breathe.

She had been at least a hundred yards from the building when she started running through the deep snow—
snow that had tripped her up before—and it suddenly
yielded to her and she moved almost effortlessly, and the
space between her and the building closed up rapidly.
She thought she might be dreaming, or she'd had a
bump on the head.

She reached the building and lifted her arms to bang
on the wall, for someone, anyone, to let her in, her boyfriend was dead. She banged on stone, it felt so real. For
a long time there was no response to her banging, just
the murmur of sounds, like voices, beyond the wall that
rose and fell so rhythmically that Shandy thought she
didn't hear voices at all but the wind.

She began to walk around the building, trudging
through the snow that drifted up against the side, hoping to find the entrance. The building went in a circle, a
huge circle, and just when she thought she'd rounded it,
she came to more circle. The snow by then had begun its
merciless assault again, and it thickened around her
head, around her eyes until she couldn't see, around her
mouth until she thought she wouldn't breathe, and

ebbed, pulling back only when she shut her eyes tightly against it and wished it gone. It never entirely disappeared, but as it faded back from her, she could see that it was the building it was trying to consume, and not her necessarily. It swept its way up the sides, choking off the tiny windows, sealing the stone, squeezing it, hiding it, in a thick white blanket.

The circle went on and on; Shandy followed it. Tired, she stopped and looked up, up over the side of the circle; maybe she could climb. Above her, where she'd stopped, was a tall, narrow window, not a window, really, just a slit, just enough space to squeeze through. When she reached up, she found she could get her hand into the space. When she did that, heat soared up through her arm like an electric shock, freezing, cold, electric. But it wasn't unpleasant; it was . . . nice.

Then she knew without even deciding that this was the old fort that made Bastion a town. She'd never even seen it before, had seen a picture or two, that was true, but hadn't seen it. From the moment her hand went through the slit, Shandy closed her eyes and let herself see, see right inside the place. And as though her arm was acting as a conductor, she could hear inside. The wind moaned and wailed like agonized voices from some unearthly place. Was it the sound of the dead? or the storm?

Inside, what she saw was black. The black things, moving fast and sure, angrily, bumping through the others, soundlessly. What she heard was a random frightened and frightening series of thoughts and emotions, alternately bullying and pleading.

Lost come on in here we can let you in but we won't let you go.

And something else. The anger. The burst thrust of anger she had felt, the blast that had knocked her down onto the ground in front of David's house was there too, black, horrible anger, not like anything she'd felt. It made the insides of her hurt. Pain was there too, lost underneath the anger, but she could feel it, the anger, the horrible sadness.

Something touched the tips of her gloved fingers, and it felt like a bite. A razor blade, or a snake bite.

Come on in we won't let you go we'll eat you up Shandy dear don't listen some of us just want to kill you but all of us want to eat you.

Very quietly, under the others, she could hear a hum, something almost *electrical.*

And they laughed, chuckles that had nothing to do with amusement. Another one bit her, so hard she yanked her hand away and fell onto her bum to the snow. Snow rose around her, a swirl of blinding white. Beyond that, the voices, the moans, the rise and fall of the wind.

Her hand was bleeding, the blood welling up into droplets on the tips of her fingers, through her gloves. The drop of blood grew large and formed itself into a thing that looked a lot like the black things, with a round head and a slippery tail. It pulled itself away from the glove and darted into the palm of her hand, getting under the glove there, poking in and out. Each time it went in, she could feel it, like a pin prick. She stared at it, no longer a drop of blood but a tiny black entity. It stopped. It stood straight up in her hand, no longer moving, standing there. Slowly it changed, became featured, like a person, a man, and it changed, one face melting into another.

There was one second, one short second where a face held still and there was an expression of utter longing and misery. It burst into flame. Her hand burst into flame, and there was screaming. She didn't know if it was from the face in her hand or her own voice. The flames burned on until all that was left in her palm was a little bit of ash, about the size of a dime, or a droplet of blood.

Her hand was terribly hot, and all had gone quiet above her. She felt that whatever was beyond that wall was watching her carefully. She plunged her hand into the snow, to cool some of the burning. Her glove had burned away and the snow felt cool for a moment on her damaged hand.

She opened her eyes to find herself in the snowbank where she'd fallen after leaving the house. The next thing she remembered, she was in the foyer of the school, in a fetal position, sobbing. Not crying because she was scared, although she was that, but crying because she had to do something to stop the storm before it made its way through the whole town; crying because she didn't know how and had to anyway; crying because she should have known this before and hadn't; crying because if she had, David and other people whose faces ran in and out of her mind might still be alive. Crying because it was her fault.

But that had been earlier. It was late now. Not too late, but getting there.

She had to go up there. Before the storm stopped. If the storm stopped, those things, bred by the storm, would come. If the storm stopped, and people got out of the building, they might be hurt (or worse, like David). Those things had to be stopped. They had to be stopped and sent back, or away. With the storm. She knew what she was going to do.

Her stomach curled the supper up into a ball again and turned it over.

As quietly as she could, she slipped out of bed. She stepped artfully around the sleeping girl on the floor. Her shoes were beside the door. She picked these up and carried them.

Getting out of the hotel was going to be the hardest part. She had no doubt that some self-important duenna was sitting out there with a cattle prod maybe, ready to order young saviors back to bed this instant! but she would cover that ground in a minute.

Shandy stood at the door with her ear pressed against it. Beyond the door there was the distinct sound of a mouth-breather. Snoring.

She opened the door achingly slowly, pausing only once, to look at her watch. One-thirty. Urgency rushed through her like fire. She had to hurry. She wished for the first time for her mother.

The hotel's hallway lights had been dimmed. Mrs. Jorgensen, of the town's only Swedish family, son Jon, daughter Tina, husband Franz, had resisted the yellow light's lulling lullaby and had fallen victim instead to the humming of the boiler. She had managed to stay awake for the first hour of her two-hour supervision and had drifted off with only twenty minutes to go on her second hour. She would feel just terrible in the morning, because she had insisted on the late watch, insisting in her stilted English—some wondered about her own dimming lights, her English was still bad after having been in the country for thirty years—"*Ja*," she'd said, "I cun stay avake goot! Make of stern stuff, ve Svedes!" Because of the way she spoke, she and some of her family had been dubbed *Ja*-gensen, in good humor. Ja-gensen had been granted her wish; no one else wanted to take that watch anyhow. Everyone else wanted a chance to get settled in, find a book, grab a cuppa coffee and maybe an hour or so of sleep before ascending into the dimly lit, sleep-inducing hallways of the Northern Lights.

She was not alone on the floor, however, since most of the older girls had been assigned to the second floor of the hotel. She took up her post at Room 28, directly in the middle of the hallway between the two exit doors. At the exit on Mrs. Jorgensen's right was the formidable Mrs. Henkies. Mrs. Henkies, it can be assured, would *not* be asleep. If asked, some of the children might have said she would have been wide awake taking notes out of a book on medieval torture methods or pulling the wings off of flies; the younger children might have said that she would be making potions. Mrs. Henkies taught no-nonsense math, and was alternately feared and hated in the school. She would be awake.

In reality, Mrs. Henkies was buried deep in her favorite novel of the moment, cast out on a pirate ship, captured and detained by the handsome Captain Harness, who had already—albeit against her will—taught her the ways of love. In the book she wasn't the Mrs. Henkie of no-nonsense math, but Carmen, a raven-haired beauty with a mind of her own and a body that drove men mad. The book was conservatively covered in butcher's paper and Scotch tape, not for reasons of preserving the cover as most might have thought. (At the beginning of the school year she made all of her classes clothe their math books in the same fashion—books are our friends.) Mrs. Henkies not only read such trash, she *devoured* it, sometimes at the rate of two books a week—if they were good books. Like this one. She was perhaps one of the few people that hadn't caught even a whiff of something out of the ordinary, whether it was outside the building or inside. She'd felt very, very relieved that she'd brought her book that morning after finding out that she wouldn't be leaving that night. When she'd heard the story about what Law-rinse had said, she'd mentally been on that very boat, and had hardly commented upon it at all. Instead she'd pursed her lips in the way that made most people feel that she didn't approve of them; only then would they leave her alone, and she could get back to her book. So far she hadn't heard a word of it; if she had, she would not have believed it anyway. The teller of the tale had left her alone, wondering what on earth had possessed her to tell it in the first place to an old bat like Henkie.

When the time came, neither woman heard the soft snick of door number 21 open and ease shut.

Shandy slipped down to the department store on silent stocking, stalking feet, cradling her running shoes against her breasts that David had thought so beautiful. All she had to do now was to go through the mall and not get caught.

20

At that point, Marilyn had more on her mind than just what she might have seen or heard out in the storm that day. She was thinking about what Don had told her and was busy making connections. If someone had told her what Lawrence had been busy telling everyone who would listen, not bothering to make distinctions between those that would listen and those that believed him, Marilyn would have been very interested. And *she* would have believed him. She had thought she was crazy for hearing the things she heard, for seeing what she thought she saw. But putting two and two together was not a problem for Marilyn. She was nobody's fool, and subscribed heavily to Shakespeare's little homily about there being more things in heaven and earth.

They had laughed, that was thing number one. You might imagine the sound of the wind to be children crying or animals howling; it could even sound like a woman's scream. But this had been a laugh. Second was the faces, those eyes hollow, empty holes. She didn't think she would ever forget those eyes.

She didn't know *what* was going on out there, but she was damn glad, *damn glad,* to be inside where it was warm and safe—out of the storm.

Don, on the other hand, wasn't glad at all. She had tried in her halting way—without condemning herself too much—to tell him that it was not safe out there, for man or beast. That his woman was stuck somewhere and got that way between phone calls, and was just as worried about him as he was about her.

The thing about it was, Don was resigned. She had suspected that there had been trouble at home. He alluded to it but never really clued her in. There had maybe, Marilyn thought, been someone's infidelity somewhere along the line and she wasn't about to speculate on who, but it might have been her. Didn't she know the infidelity game? And dollars to doughnuts . . .

He seemed pretty ready to believe that Emma was stuck in some love nest, fucking her brains out while the storm raged on outside the window, and Don worried about her from mere blocks away, so close yet so far away. The only thing he had told Marilyn was that he was ready to let things take their natural course, that if his wife was somewhere stuck, that was fine. There was a *but* coming after that, but Don hadn't told her that part. All Marilyn knew was that her friend was up in his office partaking of the drink and not cheering up.

So she was going to slip down to the cafeteria and see if she could rustle him up some supper. (He had told her he hadn't felt like eating earlier.) She herself was starving. She hadn't eaten since breakfast, except for one bad cup of coffee. Besides, rustling up some grub would give her something to do and something else to think about. They could both use a little something.

She told Don she'd be back in a minute and to save her a beer, and she went down the stairs. She walked out into the mall, careful to take her shoes off first so she didn't wake the thirty or so people sleeping there on her way to the cafeteria. She wondered if Phyllis would be up, she wondered if they'd mind her stealing food; of course she would tell them that she had.

She thought her thoughts, and her stomach rumbled in anticipation of the food, contraband or otherwise. She had no idea that she was being watched.

Shandy watched as the woman slipped past on her way out of the department store, and then let go of the breath she was holding in. Shandy recognized her only as the lady who worked somewhere in the store, and as she went by she felt rather than heard the woman's stomach growl with hunger and heard the woman thinking about food.

It was uncanny, really, how precognitive she was this day, and how strong her ability to see through the walls people usually had around their thoughts. It had something to do with the night, or the necessity; she continued to marvel over it and play with it, like a child with a new toy.

She had made it through the mall, and hadn't really had to worry, most people were lying around on their makeshift beds, either deep in thought or deep in sleep. She ducked from doorway to doorway until she got into the heart of the mall, where there was nowhere to duck anymore until she got to the cafeteria. Then she walked very quietly, and very swiftly, and if someone stopped her, or asked her where she was going, she was on an errand, have to hurry, excuse me, but I have to go—she only wished she had a piece of paper in her hand that she could say was a note from Ms. Bergen. She wished she'd thought of it before she left the hotel room, where there were bound to be sheets of tacky stationery with the Northern Lights logo across the top.

As Shandy had walked through the mall, past the sleeping and thinking people, it was amazing what drifted across the air over to her. The dreams they were having, what they were thinking, that they had to go visit the little boys' room make pee . . . Bert's going to have a shit when I tell him what Clark said . . . goddamn thing'll be buried under twenty feet . . . won't see it till spring now oh well . . . rust bucket anyway have to get it . . . bikes'll be frozen the ground was pretty wet back of the house . . . if Marion got her supper.

She marveled at it as she had since Candace found her in the school foyer, which seemed like ten days ago.

Then that woman had gone past her and she knew she would have to hurry, have to get her stuff fast and get out of there before she was caught.

The only thing that bothered her was that it was stealing. And even though she knew it was for a good cause—perhaps good for the whole town, for criminy sakes—it was still *stealing*.

She headed for the ladies' wear section of the department store, to find a very very warm coat. And a scarf, and decent mittens. Then, there were other things she had to get. Fast.

There was a light on in the office that overlooked the

store. She thought probably the woman had left it on when she went out of the store, so she didn't do a mental feel for anyone's thoughts. It cast a vague glow over the shelves and display tables, and Shandy went to work, quietly.

Marilyn made up a couple of sandwiches for her and Don, with great big thick mouth-watering slabs of ham, and stuck on a couple of processed cheese slices for good measure. She grabbed a muffin and a day-old doughnut from the fridge too, figuring at least no one would miss them and they looked tasty enough to her deprived stomach. They looked so tasty, she decided to eat the doughnut while she rummaged for something else to take up, some fruit or a made-up salad or something that would be good. The doughnut was taken care of in three big bites, so Marilyn decided selfishly to eat the muffin too. She didn't even bother with the butter, just ate it. Her stomach murmured a sickly thanks.

She put the stuff in a plastic bread bag, stacking everything so it didn't spill over. She dropped a couple of green apples—not to her taste, but all she could find for fruit—on top, and added two small boxes of orange juice. If nothing else, it would be hearty and nutritious. She wished she could have something hot, but that would mean turning something on.

That's when she saw the microwave in the corner, waving her over, offering her a hot ham sandwich with melted cheese.

"You got it, mike," she whispered happily, and started toward it. She didn't want to be too long in case

Don fell asleep; she thought he better eat something if he didn't want to have a headache in the morning.

She set the machine for two minutes and pushed the button.

Shandy couldn't find squat for winter coats and didn't think she had time to keep looking. She settled instead for two sweatshirts too large for her, to go over her T-shirt, and a thick wool sweater over that. She thought it would do the trick, since she was sweating by the time she got them all on.

She couldn't find any women's gloves and decided she would have to check the boys' department. Her time, she knew, was running out. She thought that lady would be coming back pretty soon. She was only going for food.

She was not familiar at all with the boys' department and had no idea where to start looking. The good thing was that this was Bastion, and the boys' department was no bigger than any other in the small department store. It didn't take her long to find a very sad collection of mismatched mittens and garbage gloves. She chose both.

She had two very good ideas at once in the boys' department. One, she pulled a pair of boys' sweatpants over her jeans for extra warmth down there. And she grabbed a pair of longjohns, which made an excellent scarf. She would have to make do with her running shoes. It wasn't as if they hadn't seen bad weather, but the snowdrifts would be up to her knees in most places. But they would have to do.

She thought the best course of action would be to slip out the doors at the back of the store, the loading-dock doors that led in the direction of the old fort. Still carrying her runners, she slipped to the back on stocking feet, grabbing an extra pair of socks, also from the boys' department, and made it to the set of narrow double doors where hours earlier Don had found the blankets and sleeping bags. Shandy was surprised to find the door to the back room propped open with a half-empty box of cutlery, but she didn't stop to investigate. She had no idea what it was going to be like to open the huge double doors at the back. She figured they were going to be the biggest problem of all, because there might be an alarm, and there would surely be big locks to go with such big doors.

When she stepped over the box, something caught in the light that shone from the overhead office. She looked down.

Oh, thank you, thank you.

A big heavy-duty six-volt beauty, the kind her mother used to call an emergency light. It would be heavy to carry, but a definite bonus in the dark. When she touched it, she heard faintly *bingo,* he called it bingo the man who put it there. To Shandy, it felt still warm to the touch, even though that was impossible.

The moon would probably provide enough light once she was outside of town—in town there would be the mall lights and the bounce of the mall lights off the snow to guide her for a while—but it would make her feel safer to have a light of her own.

She went farther into the back room, some of the urgency leaving her now that she was out of sight. At the back of the room, she stepped around shelves stacked high with boxes. She had one more thing to get. A bag of some sort. With a mental kick to herself she realized that was something that she should have grabbed inside: a backpack, or even one of those huge lady's purses that carried everything from makeup to six novels, the kind that women carried baby stuff in.

She turned the flashlight on and quickly swung the beam in an arc, like Don had earlier in the evening. As Don did, Shandy discovered a package, lying open, like a birthday present from someone who knew what she really needed.

"Oh!" She put the light down on the floor.

Three pairs of brand-new snowshoes, just what the doctor ordered, her name written all over them, just like the ones they used in gym that time Hickory took them on their winter excursion. She remembered the sore ankles she got that time, but didn't care. She bet they would cut her time in half. She dragged the pile out.

Marilyn carried the hot sandwiches, which were getting sort of sticky and fogging up the bag because of the hot cheese, in one hand and the juice boxes in the other, so they would stay cold.

She almost missed it. If she had turned her head the other way, she never would have seen the light shining in the back room. She thought it might be Don doing something stupid, like sneaking out the back way, and she would have to put a stop to that. She marched over to the back room, prepared to make trouble for him and tell him he wasn't going anywhere. Liquor, she supposed, was making him stupid or brave.

Under that thought was another one, that maybe it was one of those things.

It was in part fifteen-year-old distraction, and the fascination with her discovery, that made Shandy careless; it was also that she felt totally alone and almost invisible.

Under the beam of the flashlight, Shandy pulled the parcels, three pairs, two pairs still wrapped, out from the shelves and took the top pair off, examining them, wondering if they would fit, knowing it wouldn't really matter. She would *make* them fit.

"Don?" the voice called in a semi-whisper from the doorway.

Shandy sucked in her breath. She didn't breathe or move. She wished she could fade back into the shadow behind the light, for surely whoever it was would come way to the back to see where the light was shining.

She stayed very still, clutching the set of snowshoes in one hand.

"Don?" came the voice again, not a whisper this time but more determined, and Shandy could hear slight fear in the woman's voice, too. Shandy closed her eyes and tried to feel the woman through the darkness. She stood quietly up, not making a sound, holding the shoes firmly so they wouldn't clack together.

The two women, one grown, one getting there, saw each other at the same time. They locked eyes. Shandy dropped the snowshoes. They fell to the floor in a hollow clatter of wood on concrete, and Marilyn winced. Through the clatter Shandy heard *thank god it's just a kid*.

"What exactly are you doing?" Marilyn asked. Feeling great relief when she saw that it was not something bad. Shandy heard it all, the way you do if you eavesdrop through a closed door.

The two stared at each other for what seemed a long time after Marilyn had spoken. Neither of them wanted to move, for fear of the other.

Shandy listened and heard what was in Marilyn's head, and again wondered abstractly at how clear everything was that day.

Confidently, no longer doubting the things she was being allowed to know, she said nothing to the woman she knew now was Marilyn divorced from Stan.

"Did you hear me?" Marilyn said, in her best authoritative voice.

"I have to go out there," Shandy said, pointing at the double doors. To show she meant it, she knelt down and picked up the snowshoes.

"What?"

"A knapsack. I still need a knapsack. Do you know where there might be one back here?" Shandy was already going to the back of the room, back to where she'd found the snowshoes to collect the flashlight that had given her away.

"Who are you," Marilyn said, "and what are you doing back here, really?" Her legs moving, following Shandy halfway to the back before thinking that she couldn't let her go because she was just a kid and going out there was how . . . the storm got you. She could hardly say that: *hey, kid, don't go out there it's storming.* She stopped dead in her tracks.

Shandy heard it, heard her thought.

"I know what it's like out there," she said pointedly. "You're the woman they were talking about in the home ec. room, aren't you? You were out there today," she said matter-of-factly. "You're—" *Mary-girl no not that* "Marilyn. You work here. I knew that." Then, because

Marilyn barely reacted to the good news, she said, "I'm not one of those things you saw." When Marilyn refused to react, Shandy continued, "Whatever it was that you saw. I think we all see something different."

She picked up the light and didn't bother to turn it off. She started emptying out the pocket in the sweatshirt that she had on under the sweater. Matches, lighter fluid, a Bic lighter and the newspaper cones tumbled out onto the floor at Shandy's feet. "I could carry it all in my pocket but it would really stretch—"

"What do you mean, you're not one of those things?" Marilyn asked her.

The two found themselves in a locked, knowing gaze again. Shandy felt around inside Marilyn's head, in a way that she hadn't been able to do successfully ever, unless she really knew a person or spent a lot of time with them. She poked into corners, saw heard lots of useless stuff that she didn't need to know, skipped over the personal stuff. What she felt in Marilyn was fear, panic, wonder, and something else.

"I'm not one of those, uh—faces?—you saw today. David saw his dad." She was weary of the telling. She didn't feel like telling about herself again and risking the sudden slamming of doors inside this woman's head that she had got from Ms. Bergen. Shandy sighed. And besides, there just wasn't time. "It has something to do with the snow, the storm. If you like, I can tell you how I know some other time. But I have to go. I have to." Her voice trailed off and her eyes narrowed into slits. Just for a moment.

"You cannot, under no condition, go out there," Marilyn told her, deciding that however it was possible, they both knew what they were talking about. She didn't know how she knew, but the dream came back to her in a flood when she saw Shandy's look. "It's dangerous out there" was what she said.

Shandy began rummaging around in the shelves with the flashlight in one hand, moving the stuff around with the other.

"I need a knapsack, or a big bag. Is there one back here?" She didn't want to go look back out front. If she did, some sort of spell would be broken, some kind of charm that had been with her so far. She thought it might have been broken when the woman—Marilyn—came back, but it hadn't been. Going to the front, where the mannequins, special sales stickers, pots and pans, makeup and cheap furniture and real life was, might mean that she wouldn't get back in. She looked some more, shining the flashlight across the tops of shelves into the shelves on the other side. She saw what might be a bunch of purses and stepped around the shelf to get a better look.

Marilyn's heart was beginning to hammer in her chest, along with the feeling that time had stopped, or that she was back in the middle of her dream.

"What is out there? Wait. Stop. I thought I was crazy or something. Now I think you're crazy. I had this dream, and I saw my . . . Never mind. I saw the place I think you're going. The old fort." She shook her head. Why was she saying anything at all? "You can't go out there, kiddo. I would be remiss in my responsibility if I let you. Also, you're stealing." She crossed her arms over her chest.

"I'll give it all back. What I can't give back, I'll pay for. And I am going," Shandy said firmly. She'd found a knapsack, and was beginning to load it up with her things when she thought of something.

She looked up at Marilyn, with wide eyes. Too afraid to look, see what could, would happen up here. "If you're so worried about me, come with me, then," she said, a half-plea.

Marilyn-Mary-girl saw all the things that she saw in her dream as real and happening. The old fort, the fire, her mother. She shuddered against the pictures, the fear, the sound of those voices, the way the wind made them sound like laughter.

Shandy continued in the same matter-of-fact way. "When I was in the home ec. room getting supper, this, um, person told me that another man saw his friend get . . . killed by one of the black things. They're angry, you see." A picture of David started to come clear in her mind, while she thought about the drunk man that had told the story. She shoved it away. "It's got something to do with how we're all trapped here, stuck. They want that. So I have to go while we're still all trapped here." The bag was full. She was ready to go. "Are you going to come with me?"

"No!" Marilyn said, incredulously. "And you're not going either! You're crazy, you're just a kid!" Her mind fumbled with what the girl was saying; how she knew who she was; especially, how she knew what she *dreamed,* not to mention what she saw in the snow. "How do you know what's up there?" she said. She'd had a dream unrelated to what she'd seen out in the storm, and still made the connection somehow. "Did you have a dream?"

Shandy nodded. "Not a dream, a *vision*. I get them

sometimes," she added, with the weariness of the very old. She knew that wouldn't would be enough.

"I had a dream," Marilyn said, and let the details of the dream ramble through her mind. "How do you know where to go?"

"I know the same way you do." She watched Marilyn's reaction carefully.

"Yes," Marilyn said.

Come with me, she pleaded again, without saying the words. "Maybe you had the dream because you're supposed to help me," she told Marilyn, her voice slow and hopeful. She shrugged, a little bit of self-pity sneaking into the gesture, but she managed to make it sound speechlike and almost noble. "I *have* to go. It's like . . ." She tried to remember the words she had used with Candace. "It's like destiny or something, fate. I think it might be why I came to Bastion in the first place." The saying of it felt right, as if acknowledging something that had been a truth for a long time—and then letting it be the truth.

"If you're going to come, come. But I *have* to go." She said, a little sadly, "If I don't stop them before all of these people get out of here, they're all going to end up like David, like that man's friends. And I don't know how many other people, but I think they got my neighbors, too. I think maybe they tried to get you.

"I think the important thing is not to let them inside. Not to *believe* that they're real, and not to let them . . . well, *get* you. David saw his dad come to him. He really misses his dad. That's how they got in him." Her eyes were filling up with tears, thinking about how much David would have liked to see his dad.

She swung the knapsack over her neck, shifting it

firmly to the middle like they were taught in phys. ed. so she didn't disturb her balance too much. She picked the snowshoes up and carried them over to the big double doors. Marilyn watched her.

They weren't locked. Shandy wasn't surprised. It seemed that, along with a lot of things, it was part of a plan. Standing so close to the outside made her heart beat faster, and she had a rush of doubt and adrenaline. But it was time. She turned to Marilyn, the older woman's face an odd combination of fear and disbelief. They stared at each other a moment, Shandy saving her energy, and not taking a peek inside the woman.

"We're like . . . fish in a barrel here." She adjusted the bag again, the weight of it already bearing down. "You better come over here and help me get these doors shut after I'm out," she said, turning to face the doors. "You don't want any of those things to get in here."

Marilyn went to the girl, grabbed her by the arm and swung her around. "You can't go out there!" She wanted to slap her. She could wrestle her to the ground; she could go and get someone to help drag her back. And yet . . .

Shandy pulled her arm gently away. "You think I can't because of those things. I don't think they'll get me, but somehow I'm tied up in this, 'cause of my brain or something." She smiled wryly. "I'm going to burn the place down. Fire is . . ." She couldn't find the right word, then wondered about the torches, an image of steam rising from the snow.

Marilyn thought it. *Cleansing.*

"Yes," Shandy said.

She gave the left-hand door a yank, using all of her strength. For a minute it seemed it wasn't going to move, and she yanked again, hearing the door break away from the ice that had formed underneath. The door groaned open slowly, and snow rushed in, hitting her face with a burst of cold. There it was.

Marilyn stared in mad panic as the night sky was revealed.

When Shandy had opened the door enough to get through, she looked out into the night. Snow covered the floor at her feet and she stood on it, hearing the crunch of it under her shoes as she looked out. She saw nothing. She had half expected to see them there, a whole slew of them waiting for her, to show her whatever she wanted to see. *Like my mom,* she thought. Instead, the night was still and black, with the dim light from the back of the store shining on the sparkling snow that still fell so gently. It was beautiful. The light reflected off the crust of snow on the ground, making it glow a deep blue.

"It's hardly snowing anymore," Marilyn said.

Shandy nodded. "And by morning it will have stopped. Then the plows are going to want to get going, and people are going to go out there and go home, probably walking. People who don't know what's out there. I'm nearly too late now," she said. Enough snow had fallen during the storm that it came up past the loading dock about a foot. She tossed the snowshoes outside. "Close these doors good when I get out," she said. Shandy looked once more behind her, at the mall, the lights dim but glowing from in the mall, inviting her back in.

She stepped up onto the snow where the shoes were, using the door for balance, and put the flashlight down beside her. It cast a sparkling beam across the snow.

Making it look sort of like sand, she thought. "Shut them good," she repeated to Marilyn, but didn't turn to look at her, because she didn't want the woman to see how scared she was.

Shandy stood precariously on the snow, sinking in slightly, but it had fallen hard for a long time and was packed nicely for her light weight. Flakes melted on her skin, like they always had, for each winter of her fifteen years. As though it was an ordinary snowfall, a regular winter day.

She started to pull the door shut from outside, because Marilyn didn't. Finally Marilyn started to help. When the door was nearly shut the woman said, "Stay here." The door closed, taking the rest of the light with it.

Marilyn stared at the closed door for a long time, listening to Shandy crunching around on the snow, putting on her snowshoes. She listened until she heard the girl move. Still, she stood there, very aware of the extra snowshoes lying on the floor, so close beside her.

"Christ, she's just a *kid,*" she said to herself, as though by saying it she could somehow make it all better.

21

Candace was forcing herself to believe things she wasn't ready to believe.

Candace was not as fortunate as the sleeping Mrs. Jorgensen she assigned to supervise the second floor of the hotel. She was lying on the sofa in her office, trying to get some sleep, maybe just to let her mind drift while her eyes rested, but instead found herself staring out the window, which had frosted over so badly it looked as though it had been painted white on the outside, like her grandmother's bathroom window when she was a girl.

She couldn't get the conversation with Shandy off her mind. In fact wondered if she'd even been the same since having it. The urge to believe it all had been tickling at her since she left the slowly calming girl in the home ec. room to get something to eat. It had followed her around while she organized teams of supervisors, assigned minor jobs to troublemakers; it had been with her while she darted off for a smoke in the mall later. And that was when it came home to roost. All of the things about the bizarre day suddenly leaped up together and connected: like the black things that Shandy said were out there, what Lawrence the drunkard said was out there, that his two friends were dead, and that Shandy knew Brad's name.

If what Phyllis had said was true, and that would mean that what Lawrence had said was true, then Shandy's story had some semblance of truth too.

Candace was, by Bastion standards, the most progressive principal the town had ever known. If she had known, for instance, about Hickory's little concern, she would not have batted an eye. But by standards formed by the rest of the liberal world, she was conservative in the highest degree. In that case, had she known about Hickory's little concern, she would have wished him well and probably fired him anyway. She would have written him a glowing letter of recommendation and trumped up a different reason, because she wanted to believe herself enlightened, but she would not likely have wanted him teaching in her school (*especially* gym). She never would have admitted it, but people like Hickory shook the book of rights and wrongs in her head, a book written by people long before she was born and taught to her stringently by the people that had given her life. There was, however, a little section in that book, at the very end, difficult to get to because you had to go through pages and pages of black marks before you found it. That section was called "notes." In the notes section was the Japanese friend she'd had at university, the premarital sex from the same era, the people she knew to be gay that didn't have horns or keep small boys in cages, the pot she'd tried after high school that didn't turn her into a raving lunatic or a heroin addict or teach her to fly. Even deeper in the back of that section was a girl she suspected of having an abortion—a girl she respected for her cool head and responsible life—and another friend she used to have who was married and had an affair. Also there were the even grayer issues: women who killed their husbands after years of abuse; that when a woman says no and a man says oh yes whether you like it or not, it's rape. These things filled the section almost overwhelmingly, as though Candace had simply reached her point of learning all she was going to about human nature. There was no section for open marriages, kinky bondage sex, or ghosts, spirits, alien abductions or things that were black and scary and poked their way into your body and took away your life, anymore than there was a section for little fifteen-year-old truants who saw your boyfriend being killed inside your head a decade after it happened.

And yet, since she'd been a teacher at an inner-city school, some other pages had been added. A neglected child isn't always neglected by a lazy welfare woman, that poverty is an incurable disease and that the women that were caught in it were as much victims as the children; that it isn't always easy for someone to leave an abusive situation, that abortion might be an answer for someone and it isn't necessarily everyone else's issue. These were new notes that she always meant to add but didn't feel ready to. That meant that maybe . . .

None of this can be true. Not possible. Barry? She said, "You dreamed about . . . Barry? And you knew!"

She had, though. She had dreamed that something that night was going to happen exactly as it did, and she dreamed it before he left. She could have stopped him and didn't.

But it was just a dream! It was a dream, but she didn't tell him about it because that section of the book in the back of her head was still more or less locked up.

It was many years later, but Candace now found herself in the dream again. In her dream, the boy/man that she had loved had left her dorm, sleepy and satisfied, his hair sticking up in a lick at the back, making him look just a little like a rooster—a very sexy, lovable rooster. He had a smile on his face that looked just like hers, a smile that they both had been smiling since they fell in love, incredibly in love, a way Candace had never dreamed it would be, putting every highschool crush to shame, making her think she was the only one who ever ever ever felt that way about anyone. The smile that people teased her about, and when they were together, that people teased *them* about and sounded just slightly annoyed and more than a little envious when they did.

Lying on the sofa, alone, some of the hardness and the just-don't-think-about-it faded from her, and she cried. Not big weeping sobs, but like the pain had never gone away, never faded, as if she was just picking up on a continuous cry that went on for days. A deep, silent, pained cry.

I knew.

She did not want to believe that she could have changed a damned thing. She couldn't have. He could not have stayed at the dorm. What would she have done? gone with him? died with him? It would be much easier to believe that Shandy had guessed. She'd guessed and that was all there was to it.

The lady from the department store had spent hours in that storm trying to crawl back to the mall from the sounds of it. What about her? Why did she get back if there were things out there just ready to snatch the life from you?

Candace sat up and wiped the tears from her face. She imagined her nose and eyes would be red and puffed. She would look a fright. She took a deep breath, hoping that would clear some of the fuzz out of her head. She was in her office, a successful, if conservative, school principal, living a life that hadn't been planned this way, but a good life, a full life. One boy/man does not a life ruin, one dream not a destiny make, one kid did not have all the answers to everything.

Just to show herself, she was going to take a walk down to the department store and if Marilyn was there and awake, Candace would make some careful conversation with her, and if she said that there were little black monsters out there, and if she said that they tried to poke their way into her body like a supernatural gynecologist, then she would rustle up Shandy and tell her she was sorry. She would rewrite pages in her book, most particularly the ones at the back of her head.

The one thing that she didn't tell herself was that she believed the girl. She didn't even really know it yet. It was still buried, under the shirt that she'd kept; that boy/man's shirt that used to smell like him. *She called him Barry*. And part of the reason she was going to go see Marilyn was to take a little walk through the mall, because she had a feeling that Shandy was hiding something. It wasn't a lot different from her dream, but Candace wasn't a lot different from Shandy that way. Just a little older, a little weaker.

Candace got a comb from her purse, thinking maybe

tidy hair might camouflage the puffy eyes and red nose. That done, she slipped quietly out of her office and headed for the mall.

Don was not a drinking man. The four beers he had managed to consume had not produced the desired euphoria that he occasionally got from tossing a few. Instead he dozed, leaning back on his chair precariously, resting his head against the wall. He did not dream, because he did not sleep; his mind wandered the gray area between sleep and slumber. Had he been fully awake, even after four beers, he would have heard the murmur of voices coming from his back room. If he hadn't heard the voices, he would have heard the scraping of wood and metal on the ice and snow that had built up under the double doors that led outside to the loading dock. Don heard neither. He dozed, waiting for Marilyn to come back with something to eat. The impatient growl and the hollowness in his stomach were two of the things that kept him from succumbing to a deeper state.

He did hear it the second time the door scraped open, and his mind registered the sound and discarded it, much in the way a person will hear and discard the sound of the refrigerator clicking into action in the middle of the night: a familiar sound of little consequence.

Don dozed and waited for his midnight snack.

Like Shandy had, Candace removed her shoes to walk through the mall, remembering the attention the clicking of her heels on tile had attracted on her first trip through. Now the people were sleeping, and she didn't want to wake them. For reasons uncharted by Candace, frown lines had appeared between her brows and held fast, from the time she left her office, all the way through the mall, to the approach of the department store.

From the mall she could see the glow of a light, coming from above, in the Treasure Chest. That was the office, she knew from trips into the store. Don Clanstar, the manager. She had met him a time or two, as is inevitable in a small town. He had two children in school, too young to have made much of an impression just yet. She did know that he and his wife had come from the city, and that made her feel an instant kinship. She wondered if he would be up there with Marilyn, or if Marilyn was still recuperating in the bed department, as the girl Betty had said earlier. If the lady was sleeping, Candace would leave. If she wasn't on one of the beds, she would work her way up to the office, pretending— what? to be shopping? a last-minute purchase? I just have to have that burgundy vinyl purse I saw—to have seen the light and thought someone besides herself was awake. Feasible enough.

She wished she could shake the strange feeling she had, the unaccountable urge to follow this through. She was spooking herself. It was foolish, and Candace hated being a fool, had left it behind, she'd thought, when she covered her guilt from so long ago with the shirt that he'd worn. The girl was just a child with an overactive imagination, maybe even a penchant for attention that had heretofore gone unnoticed. Maybe she was trying to excuse herself from trouble for skipping school.

Except none of that seemed right. The girl's near-hysteria, her earnestness and exhaustion, her total belief in her story and her inability to offer any explanations of the *why* all tempered Candace's well-developed sense for bullshit.

On stocking feet, Candace made her way to the light at the end of the mall.

The inside of the store was darker than it had seemed from the mall, and Candace found she had to feel her way to where the furniture was displayed in the center of the store. If she squinted she could just make out the line of kitchen tables (particleboard with cheap Formica—not to her taste) about twenty feet ahead of her. She wondered why she was even doing this, because if the lights were out, clearly the woman would be sleeping, or not there at all.

She juggled her way around some open boxes and hit her shin on the edge of a box full of Rubbermaid accessories. She stifled a cry, bending over to rub the offended bone. With a lower eyeline, Candace caught the outline of a bed, jumbled with blankets. It was empty.

Candace limped slightly toward the stairs that led to the lighted office.

Partway up the stairs, she put her heels back on, thus alerting the folks up there that someone was coming, and giving her the dignity that stocking feet would not allow.

She had no idea what she was going to say. *Excuse me there's this kid that*—She'd have to think on her feet.

Of course, there was always the chance that the woman was telepathic. Or maybe she'll have a black illusive shadow stuck to her face. I could say, gee what's that you have on your face? Maybe I'll just say hello and go back to the school.

———

Don had heard the feet on the stairs and his stomach growled in anticipation. He felt better about something for the first time just about all day. Emma and company temporarily forgotten, Don decided that it wasn't just his stomach that was hungry, but he was too. The beer sat inside him like an appetizer.

He was surprised to see the school principal walking through the outer office. He put a polite smile on his face, and a curl of fear started up inside him. Had something happened to the kids?

"Hello," she said as she approached his door. She stopped in the doorway, waiting to be invited in. She smiled—and he felt instantly better. "I'm Candace Bergen from the school," she added.

"Yes, I know," Don said, and stood politely.

This seemed to Candace an invitation, and she stepped into the room, still hovering around the doorway.

"I—I'm, uh, looking for your—the woman who works in the office here. Marilyn?" At a loss for what to say next, it came to her in the pause on Don's face. "I understand she had a rough time this afternoon. I came by to see if there was anything I could do." Could he know that she had never met the woman?

"She's feeling much better. As a matter of fact"— Don felt himself blushing slightly, as if about to give illicit, personal, information—"she's downstairs in the cafeteria rustling us up some grub."

"Oh," she said. *Shit now what.* "Well, I just wanted to say hello." She would just go back to the school and forget the whole thing. A woman didn't see little black men one minute and rustle up grub the next.

Candace didn't acknowledge the sudden fall in her

stomach, the disappointment that Shandy had (maybe) been pulling her chain. She felt instead a slight relief, mostly that she would not have to open her mind again, at least no wider than it was already.

Don said, "Listen, we could go get her. You hungry?" He looked at his watch, thinking that Marilyn had actually been gone quite a long time, although he had no idea how long. It seemed to be a day when time stretched around and over distance. Physics. Tricks.

"Oh, well, not really. I ate with the kids. I think I'll just get back to the school."

"I'll walk down with you. Maybe she got stuck in the microwave or something. I could use the exercise, frankly. Too much relaxing." He smiled.

As he got closer, Candace smelled the beer on his breath and knew what he meant. She could use a drink herself. Maybe a whole bunch of them. "Sure," she said, with a little snort that was a laugh she hoped he didn't notice.

Don walked ahead, down the stairs. When he got to the bottom, he looked out toward the cafeteria. He couldn't quite see into the kitchen, but he could see the light on in there. He waited for Candace to catch up, her negotiating the stairs on high-heeled shoes.

He gave the store a cursory look as he always did when he came down his stairs. His eye caught on a plastic bag on the toiletries counter, and next to the bag, two juice boxes.

"Huh?" He walked to the counter. Candace followed him.

He picked up the bag with what looked like sandwiches squashed together inside, and something fell and fluttered to the floor. Candace bent over and picked it up. It was a note.

"That's odd," said Don, frowning. "I think this might be my supper . . ." Candace handed him the paper.

Don read the note. It was from Marilyn and said she would explain later, but a girl had gone out into the storm and Marilyn went to drag her back. That was all the note said, ending in, "Don't worry."

Don't worry? Worry was just what he planned to do. He turned to Candace. "Well, it looks as if we both missed her. This is very—" He thought suddenly that she couldn't have been gone very long and that he should try to stop her. He went directly to the back room . . . had he heard something while he had been dozing? Candace grabbed him before he got too far, her hand clamping tightly on his arm. He turned to her, confused. She was white, her face almost glowing in the meager light from the office.

"A girl? Did the note say a girl?"

"Yes," he started.

Candace ran off through the department store.

"What!" he called after her, but she didn't stop. Someone in the mall sat up and looked blankly toward the store before lying back down. He watched as Candace stopped briefly to take her shoes off, barely breaking stride, and continued on in the direction of the school.

Worry he would.

A girl, he said. A girl, Marilyn had gone out after a girl. Of course. She'd taken off to do whatever it was she thought a fifteen-year-old girl with psychic abilities thought she could do against something that Candace still didn't believe. While she dashed through the mall on bare feet, she tried frantically to think who had the list of which girl was in which room. It would be posted in the staff room, where most of the teachers were sleeping and trading watch-duty. Candace headed straight there. She was crazy to have let that girl out of her sight. She should have had her sedated and watched. She should have had her committed.

Out there with those—

22

Marilyn wished she'd grabbed a flashlight before leaving the building. She wished she'd not left the building.

The moon was high enough, and full enough, to give a bit of light to the sky. She was still mostly in town, a town she hadn't seen this way for a whole season, bathed in snow, white as it could be in the morning after the first snowfall. Which was, essentially, the case. Any other time she would think it beautiful. But this was one definite case of beauty being only skin deep, she thought. The snow had lightened to a slow undulation, it had nearly stopped. Marilyn sensed the peace held something ominous; the calm before the storm.

The girl hadn't gotten much of a head start, but Marilyn had to admit she got her start on much younger legs. Never again would snowshoes be her personal choice of travel; not only were they complicated things to get on but they required muscle to operate. The tightened strings and awkward angle one had to walk in order to stay up were already wreaking havoc with her calf muscles, her ankles and her knees. Even the muscles on the bottoms of her feet seemed to be aching. It had taken Marilyn about ten minutes to get the damn things on, and that had been the kid's head start. Marilyn was following what was left of her tracks in the snow, but even in the calm they were filling up with snow. If she didn't hurry, the ones farther ahead would be all but gone.

She had been out at least twenty minutes and knew that if she looked back, she would see the faint lights of the store. She could see at least as far ahead, and she couldn't see the girl. The tracks were what held her focus.

Marilyn paused, trying to put as little weight on her calves as possible, a nearly impossible task. She breathed deeply and listened carefully, hoping to hear the swoosh of snow underneath the girl's shoes. Sound carried well on dark clear nights, like the way you could get a certain radio station at night that you never heard during the day.

The night was still and clear enough to spook her. It was the utter lack of sound or movement that unnerved. In the North, especially when the cold begins to hit, there's always a breeze coming off the lake up north, or a pocket of warm air moving in from the west, arguing with Mother Nature and warming things up for an hour or two. Tonight there was nothing: no breeze, no cats wandering around in the fresh snow looking for adventure, no dogs barking. Just silence.

But there was something, under the silence, like a hum, a radio wave, the sound of something on in the house when you're sleeping. She wondered if it was those voices she'd heard, or even the storm, speaking.

She wasn't afraid, not the way she had been. Like

when she stepped out onto the snow, tattooed with the girl's snowshoes. She'd been afraid then. She felt now as though this was something that she'd planned to do all along. Resigned and determined, at the same time.

Marilyn had rested long enough. She listened, hearing only muscles and joints protest as she stood up. Her legs were already throbbing as the blood rushed through them and if—*when*—she was through with this, her body would be a mass of aches and pains. Tomorrow or the next day, and the next day. She tried to imagine a time after this, when she would be home, warm tea, warm bed, and no dreams. When she couldn't imagine it, she stopped. No need for premonitions, she told herself.

She started off slowly, until her body found some rhythm with which to work. It did, and she loped and half-hopped her way toward the block of houses that stood on the edge of town. Beyond that would be what seemed like acres of bush that would open up into another field. That last field was the back yard to the old fort. The whole thing would probably take more than an hour, maybe more at the rate she was going. More than an hour in which to chicken out.

When she was practically across what would have been a street had the snow not buried everything up to its arsehole, she stopped and stood on the road farthest across from the mall, cleverly named Park Avenue.

She looked up one side, and then down the other. The street was as silent as it would be anywhere at that hour of the morning. There were no lights on anywhere, except for one house way down at the end of the block. The streetlights were farther apart here, supposedly because people had porch lights to light the way for weary travelers. It was too bad; it would have been comforting to at least think someone was at home in *those* houses. Marilyn didn't want to wonder why folks were sleeping with their lights all off on one of the strangest nights of the year, because it would make her think about what could happen, what might have happened, and this was not good for the mind.

In front of her was a break between two homes. Two ordinary run-of-the-mill Bastion homes, black as pitch inside, each inviting her through the dark passageway the separated them, covered in snow so high that when she walked through, she would be able to touch the branches of the tree that arched over the driveway in one yard. The tree had all its leaves still, and something could very easily hide in one of those tree branches and if someone was to walk under . . .

"Stop it," she whispered to herself. Her breath came out in a smoky gasp.

She chose the house without the tree in the driveway.

The girl had obviously not been so picky. Marilyn could just see the path of Shandy's tracks. They led through the most direct route, passing right under the tree. Marilyn thought maybe she should take the same route. But she would meet up with the girl's tracks, maybe even the girl herself, when she got through the yard.

The snow crunched and squeaked under the snow-shoes. It wasn't far, just thirty feet or so of yard. Her snowshoes scraped across something hard, and the snow gave way slightly. Lawn furniture, maybe, or some-body's bike, she thought. It occurred to her that she could fall through the snow and get buried if she wasn't careful to balance her weight across the shoes. She kept her weight a little bit forward, her center of gravity parallel with the shoes.

She made it. Marilyn climbed over the back fence and stepped out into the alley. There she rested again.

The snow was more uneven in the back lane, presumably because it had to wind its way around cars and garbage cans and bikes and lawn furniture and back sheds. The result was a beautiful, uneven landscape of sparkling white dunes, shadowed and lit by the moon and the stars, dusted with light, powdery snow. It was another world.

When she and Stan had first been married, way back when they'd been crazy for each other, they would sometimes go outside right after making love. Especially if it was really late at night, or early in the morning, depending on your perspective. They wouldn't bother getting dressed, since they lived so far from town. The breeze would skim over their flesh, drying the sweat and kisses that had been there before. It had always been the winter nights that thrilled Marilyn most, because of the readiness of nature, standing right by. You could die in the middle of winter in a place like Bastion, and many had. Marilyn and Stan wouldn't stay out long, just long enough to be invigorated. Sometimes the night air so thrilled her that she would want to make love again.

Her breath puffed out in clouds, slowing down as her heart slowed after the exertion. She squatted down on her haunches like a child.

She sat facing the back alley, in front of her a long set of dune-like snowbanks sparkling and smiling with her as though they too were remembering the times they had frolicked in the snow, or when she dumped a drink on his head.

Another time they played with food in the kitchen. They were having supper, steak and salad, and he was telling a story, his arms waving in the air, making his point. He knocked his salad right off the table and sent it plowing into Marilyn. Bits of radish and lettuce stuck to her blouse and jeans, held fast by the dressing.

Oh god I looked like a giant sandwich!

She laughed deep in her belly, hugging herself with her arms, rocking precariously on the snowshoes. His face! she remembered. *And the bowl shattered, I found dressing behind the stove long after he left, and I had to scrape it off with a knife.*

The falling snow picked up some, flakes fell softly around her, coming to rest on her hair, her shoulders, forming a neat little blanket around her squatting knees. It was nice. Almost warm.

Her eyes teared up from the cold and the remembering. The night became a piece of broken glass that she couldn't quite see through, but it didn't matter, because Marilyn wasn't looking anymore.

A gust of something whizzed past her face. The air turned colder around her head, and her laughing stopped as quickly as it had started. She sucked in a startled breath, suddenly alert, her eyes darted from side to side. She rubbed at them with her gloved hands, smearing the tears aside. Her whole body was tense, fear making her stomach contract and feel as cold as if exposed. The hairs on the back of her neck stood up. Goddamn!

Marilyn stood up on tight, hardened muscles, teetering but ready at least to make war with whatever she sensed was nearby. Around her the snow had gathered into a deep pile, pushing at her with its weight. She looked rapidly from side to side, her eyes grabbing at the shadows, thinking she could see something in each of them, actually seeing nothing. All around her there was silence. And snow falling, as though it were just waiting quietly for her to drift off in memories like she had, to begin thinking again of Stan, or Don—

Stop!

Marilyn scrambled into the hollow that would have been the road, shaking snow off of her as she went, brushing at her hair and clothes with both hands. She took the first cut through the first yard she saw, moving so fast on the shoes she stumbled again and again, almost losing her balance. She looked back once and saw the spot where she had rested now filled in with snow as though it had never been disturbed. It seemed to fall faster, harder in that one spot, drifting quickly as though driven by some wind she couldn't feel. The only sign of her having been there was a small pile, like a pyramid, on each side. Marilyn had a feeling that it wished those piles had been her.

Along the street, to her left, she caught sight of two parallel trails in the snow that might have been the girl's tracks. She ran at an angle until she was running on top of them, her breath coming in gasps, and she called out, "Hey!" and let the sound echo in the black, carrying far into the night, she hoped, to the girl, whom she hoped hadn't stopped to go over old times.

She kept moving, and at intervals gave a call for attention. She kept her mind on the present, letting the fear stay. It kept things in perspective.

She ran with the tracks, and the night opened up to her.

———

At first, the sound mingled in with the other sounds. The muffled voices of the dead, the gusts of thoughts from before, now, later even, maybe; the sounds of nature alive and living, the storm waiting. The electric hum that seemed to exist under everything else. Never before in her lifetime had Shandy felt so alive, or so in tune with her visions; for the first time it was as though the visions and herself were part of the whole, not separated. As if they could never now be separated.

She had made her way across the night on the snow-shoes. Her feet had found their rhythm quickly, and after that she forgot about them. She hadn't seen the black images that she had seen before the whole thing had started, but she felt them. Sensed them. Mostly she could hear them, a battery of electric humming, like the buzzing of bees. Every part of her mind was attuned to these feelings. This was not the tell-me-something that she associated with her visions, this was the after and before of nature itself, and the sounds that surrounded her were charged with emotion, making those emotions that she associated with people seem petulant and primitive. The anger was so fierce it could be tasted, a metallic taste; the despair had made her face wet with tears, even if she didn't notice. So lost in this world, so entranced was she with what was going on in the air around her, that she had ceased to think of her body's movements; she became an energy, her body just a vehicle, directed toward the source.

Every so often, she could see the outline of someone from this world, shadowed against the white backdrop. They were the dead, the dead as she had seen them all her life. They were a part of this too, a connector between her and the world she had a feeling she was fast approaching. The power of the night, her power, the way she could feel and see it all was overwhelming, at the same time it was *usual,* like her whole life had been directed to this moment. She was the power.

She heard the cry the first time but hadn't thought it was anything other than the sounds that she had been hearing since she got out of sight of the mall. The second time she heard it, she realized it was distinctly human.

Marilyn?

The buzzing ran constant. The echo of the human voice in her mind rang and stopped, bouncing only once or twice in the hollows made by the snow and the trees that were behind the old fort.

Shandy stopped and listened.

She couldn't have known it, but her face had changed since she'd left the mall. The look that had been Shandy's since birth, that had only changed and altered with size, was gone. The face that had replaced it was flat and emotionless, the pretty, high cheekbones and the hollows beneath her round eyes had turned shapeless, formless.

Now she stood, her head cocked to one side, listening intently. She wanted to speak, to call back, but couldn't think of the words. Words were not hers anymore, she had no control over her mouth and throat; her tongue sat still and useless. She tried to make the words come—*I'm over here.* She could think them but couldn't say them.

She had to close her eyes and drag herself away from this new white-world and find inside herself the person that was Shandy again. Her face changed. It slowly became more animated.

"Over here," she said, but was disappointed. It

sounded to her ineffectual, impotent, almost soundless in the cacophony around her.

It must have been effective, because the human sound came back to her.

"Don't move!" the voice called back. "I'm following your voice!"

Shandy had no emotion about the voice. She wasn't in need of help any longer; she wasn't the fifteen-year-old girl who had left the building earlier; she wasn't frightened. She was at one with the source, at the place where Shandy would find her destiny. The woman didn't matter.

The air changed with the woman's voice in it. Shandy looked over the expanse that would lead her to the fort and sighed. She waited as the sound got closer and closer. She waited and could hear the screech of the snow under the weight of the woman.

In the space between Shandy and the other world, something else waited too.

23

Hickory's corpse, wizened and empty, shifted and swelled on the concrete floor of the basement. Something searched for escape, provoked an undulation of tissues and flesh.

The belly enlarged unnaturally, like a pregnancy suddenly liberated, until the bulge moved upwards to the chest. The cavity filled, expanded, tearing flesh and muscle, harbored by bone. In the throat, the thing elongated, swelled again, a grim caricature of a swallow. It found its escape through the thinner tissues of the corpse's face, where the flesh split easily.

It was bigger now, stronger. It moved away from the man that had seen what he wanted to see and searched for others by tasting the air for their heat. It moved slowly through the catacombs of the basement, poking here and there, moving in and out of things stagnant and inanimate, looking, searching, discarding, moving again, without haste.

Above the thing, there was heat, which made it shrink and swell in anticipation. The others like it poked around out of doors, trying to get into the homes that offered little once there. This one sensed enormous pickings above it. It did not hasten, but it continued its search for a way to the heat. As was its way, it wanted.

24

Candace had woken up just about everyone on the second floor trying to find out what had happened to the fifteen-year-old girl who was supposed to be sleeping in Room 21. She had lots of time to regret having mentioned the whole thing. Shandy was gone, and her running shoes were gone too, so she might have gone far. Now she was tired of the questions, and sorely regretted having ever thought that Bastion or any place like it would have been sufficient to chase away a young, prematurely gray school principal's ghosts.

Mrs. Jorgensen was beside herself. "Ohh, *ja*, I em so sorry, Masses Baregen! Ohhh, dat little gerl outside? Ohhhh . . ." Masses Baregen extradited herself from the lady as quickly as possible, leaving her to be cheered and comforted by the gang of girls that had been woken up during the search.

Shandy must have been particularly quiet, and that didn't surprise Candace in the least. It wouldn't have surprised her to find that the girl had shrunk up and floated through the keyhole. She would not, however, share that information with Mrs. Jorgensen. She sent the formidable Mrs. Henkies to put everyone back into their rooms with the insistence that everything was under control. Both women were relieved of their duties, since their watch was up. This did not hearten either lady, since Mrs. Henkies was hell-bent for finding the heathen Shandy, and Mrs. Jorgensen felt that some kind of restitution was necessary. Candace heard Mrs. Henkies tell her smugly that taking another watch was not a form of restitution, given the circumstances. The Swedish woman was crying when Candace made her way down the stairs.

There was always the possibility—remote, but possible—that the girl had chickened out and not left the building. Perhaps she had gone outside but come back. Candace was going to go back to the store, because she didn't know what else to do.

Don had eaten one of the sandwiches, mostly because, like Candace, he didn't know what else to do. He left the other for Marilyn, thinking it was only right, thinking strangely that hunger might even bring her back.

He thought he shouldn't worry. She was a big girl. His mind had spent most of the day in a wandering mode, and now he was thinking again about the snowcat in the shed behind the Northern Lights. It was beginning to seem like the only possibility.

He had twice checked the phone in his office to see if it had been restored. He hadn't been the only one preoccupied with communication. After Candace had run through the mall as though something were chasing her, he had seen a few people get up off their makeshift couches and walk over to the bank of pay phones, lifting up the receiver and listening. A couple of diehards had put in a coin and jiggled the buttons.

He imagined Emma at home, as he had throughout the day. This time he imagined her alone, no one with her at all.

Nothing was wrong, he told himself. She was fine, and asleep for sure by now, maybe a little lonely, but fine. She'd had a little supper, listened to the TV while she read, and then turned in. What a surprise it would be if he managed somehow to even get to the snowcat, and then if there was enough gas in it to get anywhere, and if it would run after sitting in a shed all season long—she would be surprised to see him. She would be surprised enough to think that he was checking up on her.

Was he? *Hi, honey. Who's here?*

Don was thinking sincerely about the snowcat and damning it all to hell when Candace came back into the office, her hair flying about her face, her face flushed, eyes wide and red-rimmed, though she was obviously trying to look composed.

"Did you find her?" he asked. He knew she hadn't before Candace shook her head.

"Not much you can do about the girl, Mrs. Bergen," he said. "Not now, anyway. You can't even call her house, see if she's there. You're going to have to trust that she's a smart enough girl to get into some shelter and stay put until the roads are cleared." He spread his arms wide.

Candace smiled a very tired smile at both the assumption and the sympathy. "Can you show me where they could have gone out? It couldn't have been through the front doors, after all," she said.

He hadn't thought about it just that way, and he supposed she was right. A troop of folks through the front door would probably have sent them all out there. Mass hysteria.

Don went into the back room, where he knew they had gone. He thought about the snowshoes again. That made him think about the cat.

Candace followed him without speaking into the back room, where she assumed they had gone, too. It was dark back there, with only a small amount of light filtering through from the office above and, more dimly, from the mall.

"Just a sec," Don said. "I left a flashlight—" He rummaged around by the door. "I was sure I left a great big flashlight right here." He looked at Candace, gesturing its size with his hands, as though she may have seen it.

"She probably took it with her," Candace said. That was good, she had a light.

Don nodded. "One of them did, I guess. I've got another." He opened a cupboard beside the door and fished around, coming out with a much smaller version of the other flashlight. He switched it on. The batteries were low, and all the light that was thrown seemed only to create more shadows. He shrugged. "Good enough to find the bulb switch with," he said, walking with the flashlight farther into the room. He found the string hanging from the light above and switched it on. The room lightened up some.

Candace let go of a breath.

"Bit spooky back here," he apologized.

Candace looked around the room, then walked to the back, where the loading-dock doors were. She gave one a tap. "They left this way, right?" she asked. She wanted to take a look outside, maybe they hadn't gotten far, she wondered if maybe Shandy would be close enough to see and she could yell out for her to come back. "I'm going to open this door, see if I can see her," she said to Don, and started to push the door. Don gave her a hand.

The doors gave easily. There was a build-up of snow and ice underneath, and it cracked and crunched as the doors slid open.

"That's good enough!" Candace said too loudly, too quickly. Don stopped immediately, dropping his hands from the door as if it were on fire. "Don't want the storm to come in, do we?"

The two looked out through the narrow opening. It looked like a story-book, picture-clear night. The sky showed through above the snow, a deep indigo. It was beautiful.

"I don't think the storm's going to come through," Don said softly. "It's beautiful out there." *Good night for a drive,* he added to himself.

Candace stood hesitantly on tiptoe, not sure what to be afraid of, but afraid in any case, and peered out into the landscape. She had a clear view of the field and could see quite a way thanks to the light over the back of the store and the clear, calm night. There wasn't even a breeze. He was right, it looked beautiful and inviting. Everything Shandy had told her faded. None of it could be true. Not in a world that looked like this. From where she could see, the houses across the way were all dark. People were sleeping. *How far could she have gone?*

"What time do you suppose they left?" she asked Don.

He looked at his watch, tried to figure. "An hour ago?"

"An hour!"

"Fifty-five at the inside. I think they've had a bit of a head start. You shouldn't worry about the kid. Mare will catch up with her and drag her back, like she said. Marc's really responsible."

The image of a young boy came into her mind and she shuffled it off. She wondered how far away the old fort was. Wouldn't they be there by now? Trudging through four feet of snow?

Don moved back from the door, tiring of idleness, of standing and looking out. It had been a long night, and the picture of the snowcat ran through his mind. He backpedaled and almost tripped over the last pair of snowshoes that had been in the bundle.

"Aha!" he said theatrically. He pointed to the shoes. "They were here, Watson."

"Snowshoes. They wore snowshoes?" How far could they get on snowshoes? Farther, she thought, than on foot. They were probably wherever they were going. She had an urge to slam the doors shut. Instead she shivered, for his sake. "Let's shut these doors," she told him, already moving to do so. "I'm getting cold."

Don helped her close them. She looked suspiciously at the tiny, almost non-existent crack left between them after they were shut and latched and wondered *could something get inside?*

With the closing of the doors, Don had his own feelings. It looked beautiful out there. It was almost morning. A few hours and this whole thing would be over. He wouldn't go and wake up Ed and drag the snowcat out, Ed wanting to help him because he was such a good guy;

Ed had his own troubles tonight, Don was sure of it. The bar had probably been full. That guy talking about monsters; a whole bunch of drunks drinking on credit. Like everyone else, Don would wait out the storm.

Candace asked, "You mind if I wait here? In case they come back?"

"Not at all. I guess I'll wait with you." He went and got them a couple of chairs, and after thinking about it, ran upstairs and got the last couple of beers. He gave one to Candace and she looked up at him gratefully, and tiredly.

"I could use this," she said.

The two of them sat near the entrance doors and looked back at the double doors that their two charges had left through. Neither of them spoke.

25

Marilyn shambled across the hundred yards that separated her and the girl, following not the sound of the girl's voice any longer but the light that dangled from her hand. Once she was past the trees, she could see her clearly. Her breath came too fast through her throat, and she was breathing through her mouth with the exertion of fast travel on old legs over bad ground. She slowed to a funny hopping trot, still moving, but trying to catch her breath at the same time. The girl made no move to come closer to her, but only stared in her direction. Marilyn couldn't see the girl's face in the shadow of the moonlight.

"J-just, a-bout." She tried to shout it, but it came out in gasps of stolen breath. Regardless of the folly of the whole adventure, Marilyn felt relieved to see the girl unhurt, whole. It seemed to take too long to get to where she was standing, in the field before the old fort.

When she reached the girl she hunkered down on her snowshoes, feeling safer with the kid. She tried to catch her breath, sucking hard at the cold air, taking it into her sorry lungs. When she was sufficiently recovered, she looked up at Shandy, who hadn't said a word. The girl's face was still in shadow. She hadn't moved.

"You all right?" Marilyn asked her, suddenly aware of the silence, and of . . . something else. In the air. The humming she'd heard earlier, it was louder here. The moan of the wind again? "Do you hear that?" she whispered to Shandy.

That was when the girl moved. She half-turned toward the fort. The moon shone on her face, and Marilyn looked into it.

Her first thought was that the storm had got to Shandy, too. That she'd stayed in one spot too long and looked into the past, remembered something good, something bad, but lost herself in the blinding white.

She stood abruptly and touched the girl's arm, grabbed it, turning her around. The arm didn't seem attached to the girl, it felt lifeless and foreign. Like putty, the girl turned back to her. Marilyn was able to see full into her face.

She barely recognized her. The girl's face was flat, blank, eyes void, empty of emotion except for the tears that had fallen, dried and frozen on her cheeks. Marilyn spoke to her and her eyes fluttered, her mouth shook as though to speak, but she couldn't get the words out.

"Are you all right? What's happened?" *Jesus, I don't even know her name,* she thought.

"Shannon Marie," Shandy whispered through lips that were chapped and cracked with cold and tears. Marilyn's hand dropped in shock from Shandy's arm. The girl, Shannon to Marilyn, let tears fall. She spoke.

"It's here. At Fort Bastion," she said. Her voice was stronger as she went along, but never strayed above a whisper. If Marilyn hadn't been listening, or if she stood back a little, she might not have been able to hear her.

"I'm taking you back. That's why I followed you. I don't think you should be out here—"

"Can't go back. I have to . . . go there." She jerked her head toward the fort. The peaks of jagged rock that used to be walls peeked out over the tops of the trees that surrounded it. She turned her full face back to Marilyn, and Marilyn thought she had never in her lifetime seen such anguish on anyone's face—so clearly.

"There is much here," she said. "The storm did something. I don't understand, exactly. The power is here. Substance." She stuck her hands over her face.

Marilyn reached out and put her arm around Shandy's shoulder, as much to turn her around and start walking her away from the place as for comfort. "I don't know what you're talking about, and I really think that we should—"

Shandy yanked herself away with more strength than it looked like she had. "No!" she screamed. "I can feel the dead inside me, the way I can see the living." She moaned and wavered, clutching at her sides with her arms. She continued more quietly, "I can feel the storm taking me. Using me up.

"I wanted you to come. Because I was scared to go by myself. But now I don't know what's going to happen to you and I don't think I can help you if something bad happens to you." Her shoulders slumped. She looked tired, and for a moment she looked like the kid she was.

Shandy pointed to the peaks over the trees. "If you listen, you can hear it." She began walking in the direction of the fort.

She did hear it. She heard the storm before. It was that hum, like electricity, energy. Was that what she'd heard earlier in the day? Was that what spoke to her?

Her mother had tried to tell her. That was why she had followed this girl, Shannon Marie, out into the night to see this through. She watched the girl walk, undecided about whether to follow.

"Wait!" she called. She hobbled over to the girl on her tired, sore ankles. Her mind, too, was suffering. From fatigue. "I—I'll come with you."

Shandy pointed into the trees, still carrying their leaves from summer. On the horizon, underneath the foliage, it looked like the sun might be thinking of coming up. Marilyn stared into the trees, where the girl was pointing. Slowly, she thought she saw what the girl was pointing to.

"My god," she gasped. The snow had all but swallowed the fort. The line between earth and sky could no longer be seen. In its place was a blanket of white, glowing yellow from the center out, as though the snow itself was lit up. Drifts of white snow had climbed up the walls of the fort until only the very tops of the turrets could still be seen. Where the tiny, narrow windows had been, the drifts fell inward. The humming sound was coming from that direction. The air seemed suddenly thicker, as though there was something in it, something electric. Her hair clung to her face, stuck there, static electricity. She realized that was the glow that she could see beyond the trees; it was like a light burning. Energy.

"I'm going to burn it down," Shandy said, and began to walk again.

Marilyn followed slowly.

———

The dark, shadowed thing moved silently through the maze of plumbing pipes and shuttered rooms in the basement of the mall complex, moving itself into things, looking for an opening and moving on when it found none. The heat and energy burned above it, giving it purpose. It wanted *life;* it desired it.

Ed's gloom over the responsibility of so many souls— most of them drunk as goddamn skunks—had changed into an intense, mind-numbing tiredness. He was almost giddy, not having been quite this bone-tired since he hosted the Fourth Order of Honorable Buffaloes in his bar, a bunch of Americans that could've drunk a river dry, but only if the river had been made out of vodka martinis. Those folks had actually drunk him dry; everything in the bar. After that particular night that had turned into a day, he had sworn off hosting convention groups, hunting groups and most of all drinking groups. This night had been just as long, and even though he was on personal terms with most everyone that had been in the bar, there had been moments when he felt he'd lost control of the crowd. This was—as far as Ed was concern—the barkeep's biggest fear. Never let them get away from you. There had certainly been moments.

Just before he cut everyone off for good, a bad fight had broken out. Snakey Pete Saunders had stumbled and lost his balance right on top of Roger Morrow, not exactly Mr. Congeniality on a good day. Drunk since about seven that night, Roger had claimed Snakey did it on purpose, and decided to take him out. He busted a beer glass on top of the boy's head, and both of them ended up bleeding. Not much—Snakey it seemed had a pretty hard head and Roger's hand had seen worse—the sight of blood at that hour of the morning with everyone the worse for wear would normally be enough to set the whole place to fighting. Ed with the help of a couple of the more or less sober guys had been able to make peace. They got the pair separated and Ed bought them each a drink to shut them up—or better yet, pass them out. Then he cut everybody off.

The Northern Lights Hotel was what was keeping Ed from letting his tiredness fall into melancholy; it was making him downright giddy. If he'd been a more expressive man, he might have outright giggled and rubbed his hands together. Instead, he was trying hard to tally up numbers inside a brain that had seen better days. The hotel had thirty rooms, each and every one of them filled to capacity. He'd packed the girls in five and some cases six to a room, and that ended up with about five rooms empty for his beer-happy patrons, who had nowhere else to go. Blankets took care of the lack of actual beds, and there he was, the first time since the Buffaloes that he'd been filled up.

There were still a number of drunks left in the barroom, with nowhere else to go, but Ed had chosen wisely. He kept the folks that he knew would give him the least trouble, that were the least likely to dip into the depleted stock, the easiest ones to handle.

Left in the bar to sleep off their troubles were Cherry, the girl who had worked the whole day and night. She was asleep within minutes, over in the corner on the carpet, wrapped up in a standard-issue woolen blanket stamped "Hotel." Poor kid.

Natty was nodding off on the floor not too far away. Lawrence was twitching around over in the corner, not quite asleep. Two or three other guys, kids really, stayed where they had fallen. One of them had been asleep for hours. Hardly Knowles was still awake, sitting at the bar, sucking on a beer glass that wasn't quite empty.

"For chrissakes, Hardly, that's goddamn spit you're drinking. Backwash," Ed said, disgusted.

"Gimme another one, then," Hardly slurred.

Ed grunted. He finished up the rough tally in his head, and the figures made him smile. He had been wondering how much he'd be able to stick the school board for, and the image of all those little girls came up in his mind. Besides, it would be like taking his own money back, for chrissakes, it would be tax money that they paid him in, and he paid his fucken taxes. He'd give them some kind of groupie-type discount, he supposed. The drunks were another story. He'd be sticking some of them pretty good. 'Specially those troublemakers.

Ed took a peek inside the cash register, the sound of the bell giving Hardly a jump. The cash, cheques and IOUs bulged over, almost spilling out. Most of the IOUs would prove worthless, he knew, but at that hour he didn't care. The government money would come through.

Ed broke a cardinal rule and decided to grab himself a brew. He opened up the fridge door and looked inside. All that was left were two lite beers. The draught faucets were completely dry, although there had been enough beer spilled on the floor to fill at least a keg. The lites were it. He grimaced, but grabbed one anyway. At least it was cold.

"You damn buggers cleaned me right out of the good stuff," he told Hardly. He opened the beer and took a long swallow. Not bad for sissy beer. He thought he might just drink both of them.

"Gimme one o' them," Hardly said.

Ed laughed. "You're a case, Hardly," he said. Hardly was a case. He'd been Hardly as long as Ed had known him. His real name was Harding. But with a last name like Knowles on a man as dumb as a post, Hardly just came out of the mouth naturally. Goodnaturedly, Ed poured about a sip's worth of the sissy beer into Hardly's glass.

"Look at this fucken place," he said, half to Hardly, who was only half listening. The room was a dire mess. Sometime, it seemed like hours ago, and if Ed had looked at his watch he would find it had been, he'd told Cherry to slip in the back and drag out a big box of the potato chips that were kept back there. He thought he'd pass them around to the folks. A lot of them had been in there all day and hadn't even had anything to eat. The kids passed out early, like that one on the floor in the back, but the inveterate drinkers could go for days with no more sustenance than provided by the barley in the liquor. He had thought maybe something in their stomach might make them easier to deal with. He didn't know if it had worked, but they had certainly eaten what was put in front of them.

"Their mudders would be proud," Ed muttered.

"Huh?"

"Drink up, Hardly."

Like every bar, Ed had to serve food where he sold liquor, and he got around the law the way most small businessmen did: by doing it the least legal way. He sold food. He sold terrible microwave hot dogs and burgers that were so bad most folks wouldn't even eat them unless they were really drunk. Then they usually barfed them up. And he sold bagged potato chips, candy bars, spreadable cheese-looking things that Ed hadn't even tried and never would, and coffee and soda pop. The room was strewn with potato chip bags, candy wrappers and the shrink wrap that came on the terrible micro-waved burgers and hot dogs. The cupboards were currently bare, the crumbs were all over the room.

Cherry had accidentally—or maybe just in general fatigue and hopelessness—left open the door to the cold room, where all the boxes of food were kept, and the animals had been just going in there and helping themselves. Ed figured he lost a few bucks on the food, cheap as it was. He didn't really care.

The cold room was a mess too. Ed could see in from where he stood behind the bar. A couple of empty boxes lay on their sides on the floor, and someone had spilled open a bag of curlycue popcorn, and they were all over the floor in there, worked into the linoleum and the edge of the carpet that stopped in the doorway. The light had been left on in there, and he could see that the mess went across the floor and all the way over to the basement steps. On the top step, a lone bag of salt and vinegar chips lay, puffed up and full. Probably the last of its kind, Ed thought, an endangered species.

"Well, I ain't cleaning up tonight, I tell ya," Ed said. He took the last slug of his beer, and belched. "Bone-fucken-tired, I am, Hardly."

Hardly nodded.

Ed conscientiously put the bottle away in the case, choosing to ignore the pandemonium around him, in his bar. He figured he would just sleep on the floor; wouldn't get more'n a couple hours, anyway. It was probably nearly morning.

He stepped out from behind the bar, picking up a

couple of glasses on the way, kicking a bag of jujubes out of his way. A few spilled out. He figured he better at least turn off the light in the cold room and shut that door before one of these drunks woke up looking for the can and stumbled down the stairs. That would just be icing on the cake.

Ed walked into the cold room.

The shadow had moved all the way to the end of the mall complex. Above it was sound, vibration, movement and heat. It nearly ached with need. At the end wall, it moved upwards, as it had all along the length of the complex. Before it had met with barriers. This time it was able to rise, nothing stopped it, there were no barriers. It floated up, resolutely.

Natty had been very nearly asleep, what had promised to be a blessedly dreamless sleep, when Lawrence had startled her awake. She was not as kind in the half-state as she was when she was entirely awake. The man was making a horrible monotonous moaning sound—not all that different from the sounds Natty made when she woke up with a sick-hangover, but she didn't know that.

"Shut up!" she shouted as best she could. She was too far away to give him a kick. He didn't stop the moaning.

"Go to sleep!" she tried. Through a sleep-foggy mind, she tried to make sense of him. She struggled up, leaning her head against the back wall of the bar where she'd tried to fall asleep. Her head pounded with yesterday's hangover and a new one. She cupped her hands over her ears. His noise was making her head hurt. She gave a moan herself.

"Ohhhhh . . . come on, Law-rinse." *I got a bad head.*

Then he was saying something. Natty's stomach tightened.

"Ed! It's got Ed!" he screamed.

Natty saw.

26

The two of them had crossed the field and reached the trees that surrounded the old fort. Shandy (Shannon Marie to Marilyn) had not so much walked as stumbled, drawn by brute force to the source. The electric hymn that played through the air grew louder as they approached, and no longer did Marilyn pretend it was the wind calling around the corners of the trees but accepted it for what it was. It was the storm.

The girl hadn't said a word since she told Marilyn that she was going to burn it down. Marilyn hadn't asked. But her mind ran overtime, knowing it was impossible to burn rock and stone. She had thought several times to tell the girl this, but she knew she wouldn't listen. Besides, it might not matter, not with the way things were looking.

She didn't think that Shannon would be able to listen to, or to hear, anything. Her mind seemed entirely focused on the distance between the women and the walls. She walked in an absolute straight line, stepping onto the small dunes the snow made, slipping through them where the snow wasn't packed enough to hold even her light weight, struggling out, only to maintain the same straight line as before. Once, she'd stopped and looked back at Marilyn, and in that moment, Marilyn had thought she'd seen a ghost. The girl was as pale as the snow that still swirled around them, that fell heavier, more intensely, as they got closer to the fort.

The sound of the storm: as though she had known it all her life, she knew what she was hearing. The source of both worlds, this one and the other one. It was like déjà vu, a thing she had known and forgotten. She heard them now. She felt as though she was back in her dream.

Shandy stumbled gracelessly forward, straightening up and taking another step. Marilyn could hear her breathing, and see her breath in the cold air, short, labored breaths, spread too far apart. Every now and then, she would hear the girl moan above the wind. Marilyn had tried to catch up to her but hadn't been able to. Helping the girl seemed a moot point now; she had no idea what help she could be. Marilyn followed for reasons she didn't understand.

She didn't know why she didn't catch up and just grab the child, knock her over the head, drag her back. Except that she had a feeling she couldn't have turned around and gone home even if she had wanted to. She was now compelled to see it all through. In the back of her mind, she heard her mother's voice: *fire cleanses, girl.*

Marilyn followed the flashlight that still dangled in Shandy's hand. The light was dimming, the batteries losing their power. In a moment it wouldn't matter. The storm around the fort had lit up the night like a carnival. Marilyn kept her eyes on the smaller light for now, a familiar and calming focal point on a night gone mad, and just tried to put one foot in front of the other.

Shandy stopped at the very edge of the tree line. Marilyn had only to take a couple of steps to be beside her. Shandy put out one arm to stop her. Marilyn looked out, through trees, to the entrance of the fort.

There were thousands of them, the black things.

They weaved in and out of the snow drifted high against the walls of the fort, darting in without leaving a mark, only to ooze out again. It was crawling with them. The glow of the storm created no shadow under them, cast no reflection on the entities.

"What are they?" Marilyn whispered. She dragged her eyes away from them and looked at Shandy. Shandy held her gaze on the fort, no longer looking like a fort at all but a huge monolith.

She looked over at Marilyn briefly, her face a grimace. She shook her head. "That's what got David," she said, in a voice no longer recognizable as her own.

The entities showed no signs of dispersing. Marilyn found herself compelled to watch them, fascinated by their motions, their graceful ballet in and out of the snow. As she stared, they converged and separated again, until finally they formed a block, a mass, long and tall. They danced and shot and darted.

Within seconds, it was a group of people, standing carelessly together in a knot. Perhaps a crowd of parents at a hockey game. The black shuddered and shifted until black was indistinguishable from color. She could see (or *thought* she could see) color. Then, nearly as a group, they smiled at her, held out their hands, offering . . . a steaming mug of coffee.

Oh my god!

Then they turned their eyes toward her. The eyes were hollow. Behind them, Marilyn could see the fort.

She screamed, and reached over to grab at Shandy for confirmation that she had seen it too, but her hand waved emptily through the air. "Shandy!" she called. When she tore her eyes off the group, it dissolved, the way a snowflake does on your tongue.

Shandy was dealing with her own vision. In front of her was a large crowd, too. It was the dead. The dead that she had seen in her lifetime, as they roamed around the streets, unseen, unheard, except by people like Shandy. Rarely their loved ones, or their betrayers.

They were looking at Shandy, a thousand pairs of eyes, crying out to her. Then a silence, sudden and shocking. The electric hum was all that remained. The light was there, glowing from around.

The storm rose suddenly, without warning, and a blast of white flakes surrounded the fort, blinding the women. The black entities disappeared, swept away by the curtain of white.

Marilyn raised her hand to shield her eyes when something walked through the blanket of white.

A young man stepped through the snow, miraculously without any on his jacket, or in his hair. He was smiling. Marilyn vaguely recognized him. Shandy certainly did.

"David."

It held out its hand to Shandy. It smiled. Its eyes were hollow and empty, the way eyes in Marilyn's vision had been. Shandy's own hand began to rise, slowly, tentatively.

A screech of protest waited on Marilyn's lips.

———

Poor David, she said in her mind. The image wasn't really him. It was using poor David to get to her.

Her hand seemed to reach out to him for just seconds before it continued on and reached behind her and took the knapsack off of her back. Inside was the lighter fluid, many cans of it, and matches and lighters, all that she could carry. She dropped the flashlight to the ground. The batteries gave out. Shandy didn't even notice. The glow from the fort made the night seem like day. She was in the eye of the storm.

David faded. The last thing to disappear was his hand, still holding out to Shandy. His form melted into the blanket of snow that still swirled heavily around them. It was a whiteout, the moan and howl of the wind echoed in the ears of the women. Had they wanted to, they could not have communicated over the sound of the wind.

The energy around them was so great Shandy got a shock from the metal zipper on the knapsack. Her hair had fallen from under the scarf. It clung in clumps to her face, with static blowing off in chunks only to stick again. Her hands, trembling, didn't seem like hands, no more than Shandy felt like Shannon Marie Wilson anymore. Her mother came into her mind and was shuffled out.

Shandy tried to make her hands work, tried to get the things out of the bag. She couldn't seem to. She was all thought; she had little control over her functions. The most she could do was to feel the storm, the power. The need. She realized why the woman had come.

Marilyn held her hands over her ears to block out some of the screech of the wind. The world was white, the air was heavy with it, choking her. She sucked at the thick, heavy air, sucking in snow that was frighteningly warm. She felt trapped in a tornado of white.

"Help me," Shandy shouted, trying to make herself heard over the wail. Shandy felt herself ebbing away. Her strength slipping off. It was taking her. The storm. She was breathless. To speak took too much effort. She was a sudden invalid.

Shandy gestured weakly toward the bag, the contents now dumped into the snow, some buried already. It was sapping her strength, taking it. She was being consumed. It needed her for her own powers.

Marilyn saw Shandy gesture. Her shout—"Help me"—sounding no more than a whisper in the howling of the storm. She knelt in the snow, where Shandy had dumped the stuff in her bag, and began picking it up.

The girl said, "We have to . . . burn . . ."

"It's not going to burn! You'll never light anything in this!" she screamed, her throat aching with the work it took to get the words out over the wind.

"Fire cleanses . . ." Shandy breathed deeply, sucking at the air. She was listening to the sound of it, the power. She wondered why she had been so blind to this before. "It will burn," she whispered.

Marilyn picked up the cans of lighter fluid and stuck as many as she could into the pockets of her sweatshirt. That was what her mother had said, *fire cleanses*. Forces much larger than she could imagine were at work here, and she felt it in her chest. She would do it for her mother. For the woman that she remembered was her mother, not the visage in agony that she had seen in her vision.

She held a can in each hand. She would use the matches. You could throw a match.

"What now?" she said to Shandy.

There was a sudden drop in the wind. It slowed and felt as though it was pulling away, back toward the fort. The sound fell, the wind still roared in her ears, but the change was enough to make both women's heads shoot up in fear, looking up at where the fort would be revealed if the curtain ever dropped.

They were back. The black entities. Marilyn averted her eyes, not wanting to get caught in their visions again. Not wanting to run into the fort with torches and fire and see her mother go up in flames. There seemed to be more of them. There was no counting them, a thousand wasn't enough. There were more, many more, than that.

Shandy gasped. "More coming out," she said.

They began a swoop upwards, all of them together washed above the fort.

As Marilyn took a step toward the fort, a cloud of darkness fell over the glow. She followed their path upwards, towards the sky.

Overhead was a huge shadow, the size of the fort itself, dropping slowly, encompassing the fort.

"Now!" Shandy shouted with the last of her strength.

Marilyn popped open the spout on the can in her hand. She squeezed at the same time, and a gush of lighter fluid, strong smelling and deadly, rushed out. She did the same with the other. The stream of fluid ran right through the snow in front of her, drenching through it, melting it almost, and splashed onto the walls of the fort, running down in a fall. She squeezed the cans until they were empty, dropped them on the spot, reached into her pocket for new ones. She moved resolutely along the side of the fort, squeezing the deadly fluid onto the walls, listening for the splash as she went, concentrating on that sound in order to block out the other. She kept her eyes above, pinned on the shadow, poised to bolt if it began to drop.

She did the same again with more cans of the fluid, the stuff pouring onto her gloves until they were saturated with it. She tossed the liquid sideways, flailing with her arms, until the mercurial stuff hit the walls of the bastion, leaving great dark streaks. That seemed to be the ticket. She splashed all she could on the walls.

"Light it!" she heard. *Light it Mary*.

"Light it!" came the voice more forcefully, and stained with the same force she'd heard earlier in the day, in her vision.

Marilyn stood back and ripped off her gloves. She fished in her pocket hysterically for the matches that had been put there. She found a package, dropped it in the snow. Searched for another.

She found one, and held it. She pushed the tiny box open. Then she knelt in the snow and felt with one hand for a paper cone. All of it seemed to take so long. The shadow fell above her. A sudden breeze picked up and she heard the chuckling laugh she had heard earlier in the day. The laugh that would be with her in her darker moments for the rest of her life.

She screamed as she pulled a match out and struck it in one smooth motion, dropping it, lit, because her hands trembled.

The tiny flame hit the ground and went out in the snow. Marilyn screamed again, this time in frustration, and tried another match, trying two until one was lit. She clamped her lips together in concentration, and felt something poking in her coat. She wanted to cry, terrified. *Light it Mary.*

The match caught paper and ignited into a torch in seconds. She flung it at the wall. The flame hit the wall and it looked as though it would bounce off and drop into the snow, when it caught.

Flames, high and cleansing, burst out and upward, lighting the night, banishing the shadow as the sparkling snow lit up, reflecting a bright, glowing orange of purifying flame.

Air burst out of Marilyn's lungs in a shock. She ran to the side where she'd started and lit another match, tossing it the same way. It hit her jacket before hitting the wall—the front of her jacket went up like a candle.

"Oh god! I'm on fire!"

Automatically she reached up with her hands to put out the flames and the lighter fluid on her hands lit up too. She plunged face down into the snow, burying her hands deep under the crust.

Marilyn heard it laugh. The laugh cut itself short as the flames licked higher, up the walls of the fort, the snow melting into water impotent to the fire, they climbed higher, the smoke and tips of the flames reaching upwards, upwards, into the shadow that blocked the fort from the sky.

Her heart beat hard in her chest, the exertion made her pause by the tree line. In front of her the flames burned with a power of their own. They burned clean.

She had to get Shandy, pull her away from the trees.

Marilyn searched through the smoke for Shandy. She couldn't see her. She ran to the place where the girl had lain. She felt around on the ground, sinking into the snow where it was melting from the heat. She felt an arm and grabbed, dragging the girl through the trees, into them, the worst part, frantically struggling through the snow and branches, dragging Shandy, wearing the fucking snowshoes, trying desperately to drag her to safety.

Into the bush, she dragged them both, her own body collapsing from the strain. The two of them lay there, listening to the fire and, occasionally, almost unintelligible, the laugh. She watched the sky and saw what could have been, might have been, but what she hoped was not, a face. It faded away.

She got up and began again. Marilyn dragged the girl through the bush, and later would wonder how she'd done it; she dragged her until she got to the edge of the tree line, where she had been someone else not even an hour before.

To be safe, she took them to the middle of the field. She pulled and dragged the girl until she couldn't anymore. She was finished. She fell, spent, into the soft, yielding snow, the hated snowshoes sticking into the soft snow, sticking up. She fell backwards, her head landing hard. She breathed, sucking the smoky air and coughing it back out. The sky was still lit up with the flames, burning on their own, for their own reasons.

"Shannon?" she said. The girl didn't answer. She repeated her name, and as she did, a remarkable feeling of dread and knowing swam through her body. She turned her head sideways to look at the girl.

Shannon had fallen deeply into the snow. Marilyn pushed herself up on one elbow and edged her way, crawling, toward Shandy.

Shandy wasn't really there anymore. Her face, her pretty little young face, had sunk back into the snow. Her clothes had lost their shape, had fallen flat with the absence of body. Shandy was gone. Marilyn had dragged a dead girl to safety.

She closed her eyes and wept the day over.

Natty saw.

She had sat up in disgust, intending to go over and kick that Law-rinse's stupid silly ass and tell him to get the fuck to sleep! that there were people trying to sleep! and some people had a *headache* and wanted to go to sleep! And she stood up and she saw it all.

It was in the bar, the ghost that Lawrence had seen.

Lawrence was on his feet by this time, screaming as though it was happening to him. Hardly Knowles at the bar was staring into the cold room transfixed, his mouth hanging open, his face gone white as a ghost.

Something had Ed.

The man stood on his tiptoes, like he was hanging from a rope, and his face and neck had gone red and blustery. His eyes bulged out of his skull.

Natty screamed. She jammed her hands over her ears to cut out the screams of the others, because Lawrence and her had woken everybody up now. Cherry stood up from the table she'd been sleeping at and fell to the floor, where she stayed.

The thing that got Ed caught in his throat, you could tell by the way it stuck out.

"He's choking!" Hardly called out.

No one moved toward Ed.

Ed made choking noises, but it wasn't the kind of

choking sounds that you hear in the movies or on TV. It sounded to Natty like he was being strangled.

In a split second she just had this thought jumble into her head about all the tomato juices Ed had given her off the bill. He was a good old guy.

She ran to him, grabbing a stray beer bottle on her way. She held it way above her head, ready to hit someone with it, because it was clear to her, however how, that Ed wasn't choking on his own. Something black was hanging out his body. It was *inside* him.

She got to Ed and saw his eyes were glassing up. She didn't know what to hit. At the very least, she thought she should put him out of his misery.

She smashed the bottle against the wall and pointed the jagged edge toward the thing clinging to him, trying to get inside.

She whooped! the adrenaline pumping through her as it never had.

That was when the thing came out. It came out and made a face out of itself, a screeching, horrible face. Ed fell to the ground, red faced and gasping for breath.

Natty was afraid. The thing hovered above.

She covered her head with her hands and hunched down beside Ed, still clutching his throat and making terrible choking sounds. She was too afraid to look, but from above her she heard a horrible moan, a scream of outrage, almost, although she would never be able to articulate the fact of it. And then nothing. Silence.

For a half an hour, everyone stayed where they were, and the only sounds were the occasional sobs. Lawrence said over and over, "That's the thing what got Chester," but nobody cared to listen.

For everyone else, it was over.

Aftermath

Emma opened her eyes to light sneaking in through the bedroom window. There was no focus, no thought, at first. Her eyes felt swollen and sore, from crying or from *having the life choked out of you* or maybe being hit.

One of the first things she wondered was how she looked. Then she wondered where *he* was. She listened around her house, a place that felt distinctly odd and empty to her, and couldn't hear him.

He left me for dead, she thought.

She wasn't dead. It was over. She tried to sit up, but the breath that rasped through her throat kept her down. She put hands that were hot with fever up against her throat. She needed water.

She thought of little else. Water, and not much more. *He* was gone. Maybe he died in the storm. She turned her head only slightly toward the window to see the storm that did all this to her.

The snow had reached nearly to the top of the screen. It had to have been pretty high in order to be seen at all outside that window, which was at the top of the room. Above the snow was blue sky.

That the snow had stopped seemed good.

Emma was far past the point of crying or feeling remorse even for what she had brought on herself. She wanted, at this point, only comfort. She wanted Don.

The phone was on the other side of the bed. She remembered vaguely it ringing the day before, and Tully telling her that the lines had been cut, that he'd cut the line or maybe that the phone was dead, storm-dead. She remembered that much, and was happy for it. Maybe it was working again.

Emma's body was a mass of bruises and cracks. She didn't know it yet, but she had a broken rib, and that hurt her badly when she moved. There was a giant bruise across one thigh where he had let his weight rest on her while he raped her. He had sat there afterwards, full weight, enjoying her pain. Both wrists were bruised, and one was scraped so badly it had bled because of the way he had tied her. Her face was indeed swollen from being hit; one lip was split and blood was crusted on her chin from the injury.

She tried to move her body in the direction of the other side of the bed. The room, she saw in a glance, was a wreck. She supposed and then remembered that they had fought; she had fought hard. The table was overturned, and the phone would probably be on its side, maybe even under the bed.

Emma avoided thinking beyond reaching Don on the telephone. The rest would have to be dealt with slowly. She wasn't going to remember much of it for a while.

The phone had spilled over, and the receiver was lying on its side, beside the turned-over table. She would have to reach for it. She would have to turn over onto her stomach.

With great difficulty, she did. A funny thought went through her mind, that turning over was nothing compared to what telling Don everything was going to be like.

The hand that she reached with was numb. There was a circle of blue around the wrist, and Emma came dangerously close to remembering how she got that circle there, before cutting it off in mid-thought and thinking only of what number she would have to dial to get Don.

She settled on 0.

"Please, I have to talk to Don, the Treasure Chest, please" was what she told the woman who came on the line. The operator.

"What town?"

Emma didn't understand the question, and said nothing, her mind a complete blank. Town? *Town?*

"I'm sorry, ma'am, what town?"

Emma breathed into the phone.

"We have the Treasure Chest listed in Springhill, Altman, Bastion Falls—"

"Yes . . . yes," Emma breathed into the phone. Bastion. Falls. She listened to the operator dial the call. Listened to the familiar clicking and whizzing of the phone.

She leaned over the bed and felt nausea rising inside her. Soup. That was what she'd last eaten, she let herself remember that, but nothing else.

The line on the other end rang.

She sobbed into the phone. A tired voice answered

after many rings. She recognized his voice. She cried into the phone. He said her name.

"Don," she answered back.

No one knew anything out of the ordinary had occurred when they woke up on the Tuesday morning following the day of the storm. Folks in the mall woke up and stretched, some rising as early as the sun, ready to get on with it, to get out of the goddamn mall. More than one person was heard boasting that they would never again spend more than an hour in one place, unless they were in the hospital, and they'd have to be pretty damn sick if anyone was going to get them there. Folks joked that morning goodnaturedly that Bastion weather had a mind of its own.

People woke up from their enforced slumber party, much the worse for wear, not very well slept, and most of them were wishing for a toothbrush. The ones that hadn't thought to get one the night before gave the grocery and the variety store a booming business in folks covering their mouths with one hand while paying for their brushes, to avoid offending.

Lynn Lake, from the sewing and notions store in the mall, went over to the Treasure Chest to find a toothbrush after Larry and the grocery had run out of everything but kids' brushes. She looked around the store for a clerk, or someone, for a long time, and when no one came she pinched a toothbrush, promising herself she'd tell later. She never did.

Joe and the mall sponsored everyone half-price for breakfast, signing another note at the cafeteria. Gerry and Phyllis didn't mind, they were anxious themselves to get the day going again. Everyone just wanted to get outside, go home and get the goddamn storm behind them.

Around eight-thirty more than a few prayers were answered. The plows could be heard not far from the mall. It wouldn't be long.

Later, it would turn out to be another three hours before everyone got out, but that was because of finding Hickory's body and all.

People started wearing a dazed expression after that, and a few of the ladies were afraid to leave the building that had been sanctuary overnight at least. Some folks speculated on what got Hickory, who was referred to as Allen by Bastion folks, only after he was dead. They didn't wonder long. Lawrence did a business in believing after Hickory was found.

It was after the next body turned up, right outside the crushed double doors of the Northern Lights, right next to the snowplow, that really set the morning to edge. That one, unidentified until much later in the week, was a horrible sight, face fallen in, skin black from . . . maybe frostbite, maybe *something else*. It was the something else that effectively closed the people up. The chatter, the speculation, the possibilities stopped flowing and folks walked about with their mouths tightly sealed, an expression of dark confusion taking the place of talk. *What could have happened?* was the thought most prominent in most people's minds, and under that, a darker thought yet, not articulated for fear of an answer. *And could it happen again?*

There were a difficult few hours of transition when people didn't want to leave the mall, not after what they'd seen. There was a general feeling that the longer they stayed indoors, the longer they wouldn't know. *Could it happen again?*

The silence about the bodies lasted longest among the mall people. The bar people had had more time, it seemed, to assimilate. Long after most people had heard the story of what had happened to Ed, the story continued its rounds. If Ed himself hadn't told most of it, including the part about Natty running up to save his life with a broken beer bottle, most folks wouldn't have given it a second thought, not for real. But Ed, he was a credible man, a businessman, even if the business was liquor. He never, ever speculated on what it was she tried to save him from, but promised her *one* on-the-house rip-roaring goddamn drunk when everything was back to normal.

Just after lunchtime (chits signed by individuals this time, the mall and Joe having done their part), people began to venture out. Not alone, but in twos and threes. In the case of some of the older ladies, in small groups led by a sympathetic and brave fellow. No one wanted to find a body when they were alone. Not one like the one outside the bar.

So they found the bodies in groups. Phones that had rung and rung and had gone mysteriously unanswered, *I know she's there I called her this morning for goodness sakes she's just not answering the phone,* had their mysteries revealed. To some extent. No one really believed what the government told them had happened to the people of Bastion Falls.

The gentle Mr. Hawkins and his wife, Shandy's grownup neighbors, were the last to be found. Their children were down in the city and had spent the weekend at the charity Keno, winning and losing four hundred dollars while their father and mother slowly smothered in their own tissues, the air, the oxygen, their very lives drained and forced from their bodies. No one would ever realize that Mrs. Hawkins had stood frozen and watched her husband die, shouting his name impotently over and over again, only to have whatever it was inside him exit and begin after her. Her expression of horror could be seen, had someone known to look, but no one was looking too hard at the bodies, not anyone who had seen one before.

It was a very long time before people forgot. Most never did.

Some good came out of the situation. It was widely agreed that Joe Nashkawa should stand in the spring elections for mayor. He had kept the folks together, warm and safe, while the standing mayor sat in the Northern Lights and got himself a red nose, and not for the first time, either. The police unit in Altman got their come-uppance from the big cheeses in the capital. There was a lot of explaining to do, and theirs was sorely inadequate. Joe, sensing a certain kind of mood among the populace, began suggesting that if the right person was in office, maybe Bastion would have its own proper police force. Privately, he asked his sister what she thought of her brother running for mayor, and she just smiled and said that would be just fine. Marilyn rarely said much more after what was being referred to already as "the storm."

Marilyn had much on her mind. Pictures she wished she hadn't seen, sounds she swore she could still hear. Shandy's body was never found, even though she was lumped in with the others, a victim of the tragedy, unexplained. Only Marilyn knew what had happened.

Later, after the government people left their convo-
luted report on causes of death being some such virus or
another, people called it case closed. They'd seen the
smoke.

A lot of people would move away.

Things were getting back to normal as best they could
when Candace visited an unfamiliar house to take care
of some final business.

She walked in snowboots, even though most of the
snow that had fallen that night had disappeared into the
ground, leaving only its ghost behind. The mud was frozen for the most part, because winter, real winter, was
coming soon. The day that she'd chosen for what she
was beginning to consider a "duty" was a gray one,
fitting for her mood. Fitting for her mood for a long
time to come, she would think.

The house she approached had an old-fashioned
black wreath hung out. She stepped up on the stoop,
paused to collect herself and wonder if Shandy was
there.

She knocked.

A tiny, gray-haired lady answered. Candace recalled
that she had spoken to her on the phone before, but
couldn't remember what about. She hadn't seen her in
person before the funeral, and hadn't spoken to her that
day. She searched the woman's face for signs of Shandy,
and saw some. Around the eyes. They both had sad eyes.

"Mrs. Wilson," she said gently. "I'm Candace Bergen. I'm—I was Shandy's principal. At the school," she
added, stupidly.

The lady nodded. The tears Candace had expected

from the woman, hearing the girl's name, didn't come. Stern stuff.

She invited Candace in, opening the door and standing aside.

Candace realized when she stepped inside that she didn't know what she was supposed to say. Why had she even come?

"I just wanted to tell you how sorry I am that—"

"It's all right," Lydia said. "Do you want some coffee, or tea? Maybe a drink? I think I have something around. People brought a lot of food and drink after . . . I'm pretty sure there's something around." Lydia moved her arms in a wave, encompassing all the packages of food, some wrapped, some not. Candace guessed they had sat around for days.

She sat on the sofa, and Lydia followed suit, as if pleased to have someone show her what to do.

"I lost someone close once," Candace started, and thought how lame and contrived it sounded. She tried again. "Shandy, your girl, was a lovely young woman. We—she and I . . . Well, I think I learned a lot from her." That, at least, was the truth.

"She was like that. A lot of things people didn't know, she knew. I don't know if she told you her secrets . . . I wish I had known what to do . . . We had a promise between us that we wouldn't tell. I guess . . ." She gestured again with her hands, this time throwing them up in dismay. "You can't protect them from everything."

Lydia and Candace sat together awhile, quietly listening to the sounds in the empty room. Then Candace got up to leave.

At the door Lydia said, "She'll be around, I think,"

and that was when Candace saw the woman's tears. It seemed a wish, and not what the woman really believed.

Candace, though, believed it.

Don found Marilyn just where he thought he would.

He walked up behind her, making noise so that she wouldn't be spooked. The slightest thing spooked her lately, and he couldn't really blame her. People were spooked in general these days. She didn't turn around, but he could tell she heard him coming, because she twisted her body gently in his direction, in acknowledgment.

"Hi," she said, without turning to him.

He stood beside her, and together they looked through the trees at the old fort. She was the only one who had come up here; her and now Don.

The stones were black with soot, and more of the limestone bricks that had held such misery had fallen over. The acrid smell of smoke was still there, and under it the smell of the lighter fluid. It truly looked like ruins now. Marilyn thought it looked harmless. She knew it *felt* harmless. Her amazement at the place was mostly because she didn't feel much changed from that night. She felt no ghosts at her side; her mother didn't come to her in dreams. She was herself again. The aches were gone. There were no echoes in her head. There seemed no aftermath, except that some people had died; many that she knew, one that she felt responsibility for, even if she'd tried.

The two of them stared in silence. Don looked at Marilyn's face. It was a face of such emotion: wonder, fatigue, sorrow, fear. She shook her head. After a few minutes, she turned to him.

A breeze came up and splashed her black hair around her face, like a veil. He felt an urge to reach out and smooth it back down.

"How's Emma?" she asked, as though sensing what he had wanted to do.

Don's posture changed. So much still there that had to be worked out. "Better" was all he said. He didn't want to talk about it; he was there with her so that he wouldn't have to think about himself. He would think about Marilyn instead, being here. "You spend too much time here. When're you coming back to work?" he said, more jovially.

"That can? Never," she joked.

Together they started back to where Don had the car parked. Marilyn had walked from town.

"You know, I keep expecting to feel different. To *be* more, somehow. To know things . . . that I hadn't known before. I don't. It seems like a waste." She felt heat rising in her cheeks. Such odd things she said these days. "It just seems like maybe that poor kid died for nothing, or they all did, like she was used." She stressed the word, slapping her hand against her thigh to keep from crying. "It just . . . *took* her," she said.

She and Don walked closely together. He draped an arm companionably around her shoulders. The breeze that blew over them blew cool. He felt her shiver, but didn't know if it was from the cold. He drew her closer in, in case it was.

Her closeness, the comfort from it, made him suddenly terribly sad. A sigh came from him, and it was Marilyn's turn to put an arm up, around her friend.

"What a pair," he said. They laughed.

They walked together to the car, where they'd each

shared their stories, about that night, and about other terrible nights since.

"You know," he said, as he opened his door, "under different circumstances, you and I might . . ." Their eyes met and it was there. He was right. Under different circumstances, maybe. But not these ones. They needed something deeper than that now. A healer. Friend.

"Don't flatter yourself," she told him, and got in the car.

As they drove away, Marilyn couldn't help but look behind her, at the shrinking walls of the fort. The fort got smaller and smaller as the car traveled farther away.

She looked up into the sky and wondered where it was now.